ANGRY GHOSTS

ANGRY GHOSTS

F. Allen Farnham

To order additional copies of *Angry Ghosts*:
www.CadreOnePublishing.com
www.BN.com
www.Amazon.com

For wholesale orders of 20 or more:
fafarnham@gmail.com
Attn: Bulk Orders

CONTENTS

To Steve, Crispy, Emily, Patty, and Brett
for pointing out the weeds in the garden

PROLOGUE

The last person on Earth died suffering and alone.

Her dignity tattered and sullied as her torn silk dress, the woman shivered in the dry heat, clutching the body of her child. Like a zombie, she shuffled out of the shelter's crooked doorway. A harsh gust tossed the matted locks of her once fair hair and pelted her gaunt cheeks with the sandy dust of shattered concrete.

Roaring crackles above drew her blotchy red eyes, and she followed the strange aircraft as they climbed out of sight through hazy, darkened skies.

Her stomach heaved unexpectedly, triggering a fit of hacking coughs. Fresh blood renewed the ruddy crust on her lips and chin. Too exhausted to cry anymore, she slumped to her knees and collapsed into the thousands of bodies littering the street.

There was no warning of an attack. Power, communications, data, monetary transactions, every strand in the dense web interconnecting humanity simply disappeared at once. The night sky gleamed with the stars' dazzling luminance, unseen since times before electricity, further enhanced by the glowing trails of plummeting satellites.

Before anyone could fully comprehend the scale of the failures, the first detonations bloomed in brilliant indigo over the largest metropolitan centers.

ANGRY GHOSTS

Whole coastlines shuddered under the savage blasts, launching towering tsunamis from Greenland to Antarctica. Rampant fires and surging volcanism blotted the sky with sooty ash, reducing the sun to a pale disk. Rioting was barbaric, and in those frenzied weeks, people brutally fought one another for any resource they could scavenge.

For weeks, the detonations continued, methodically reducing the largest areas of man's endeavors to glassy, charred craters. When the indigo blasts finally ceased, small bands of confused and emaciated survivors crawled from their shelters. They struggled to comprehend the nightmare surrounding them and wondered if it was over or if the lull was prelude to something worse.

Days later, waves of heavy vessels descended through the smothered atmosphere, expelling row after row of armored soldiers. The soldiers sped through the ruined landscapes, their saffron-yellow eyes never leaving the sights of their short weapons. Like hounds, they sniffed out their prey, flushing whole groups of survivors to the streets where hovering gun ships cut them down.

The flood of soldiers cascaded into the surrounding neighborhoods, igniting panic wherever it ran. Long, slender tails gave the invaders superior balance over the piles of rubble, and their pitched-forward, loping gait was too swift for any to outrun. Shrieks, screams, and weapons' fire were continuous, and all the while, more troop carriers descended from above. The meager human resistance was annihilated, the global infrastructures were smashed.

But then, the terror was over.

As suddenly as they came, the invaders packed into their carriers and ascended. Formations of special planes replaced them, flying low and slow in wide patterns, atomizing a sweet smelling, sweet tasting mist into the air. The few still alive—desperate, starving, dying of radiation and thirst—could not stop themselves from lapping the dew off any surface it touched. In so doing, they ingested a virus tailor-made for the Human genome. Thriving amid the squalor, the pestilence ravenously devoured the last pockets of tired, ragged survivors, liquefying their internal organs.

No ambassadors were received or sent. No attempt at communication earned reply, not even the unconditional surrender.

The invasion was never about conquest. It was about extermination.

Forty thousand years of Human development were eliminated in less than two months. And so, with a hacking cough, Earth's great civilizations died.

PART ONE

AN ORDINARY DAY

The obese, azure-skinned captain reclines in his chair, boredom consuming him. A broad holoscreen floats before him, relaying various news updates while his crew performs their mundane duties, guiding the ore-stuffed freighter along its lengthy voyage.

Everything is proceeding normally.

Producing a small, spouted container from a chest pocket, the captain twists the cap and raises it to his elongated face. Throwing his head back, he takes a hearty slug, not caring that it's spilling all over his greasy gray coveralls. His saffron eyes close as the draught flows into his system, easing the tedium with pleasant sensation. He smiles as it works, drawing a thin purple tongue across the pale blue skin of his lips. Muscles relax, and he allows his mind to wander.

Bright red characters appear on screen, shaking him from relaxation. A serious looking newscaster dominates the broadcast, and the captain shifts in his seat to better focus on the well-dressed reporter.

"Another vessel is feared lost amid the Tobarentian Expanses," the newscaster exclaims. "The passenger liner *Gro El Tokai* was last seen taking fuel and passengers at Eben Station. She is now far overdue at her destination, and no transponder signal is detected along her charted course. The military has dispatched its fastest warships to investigate, but it is feared this is number eleven in a terrifying string of mysterious disappearances. When reached for comment, Eben Station governor, Met Do Teron, urged calm and assured the families of the missing that he was working non-stop to find their loved ones and that a rational answer would be found for these strange disappearances." The newscaster turns in his seat to face another camera for dramatic effect.

"Maybe they collided with something uncharted. Maybe their navigator piloted them through a star… or could it be something entirely different? On the home worlds, suspicions are growing that these disappearances are a form of supernatural revenge. Our Venerated Pontiff had this to say…"

The screen changes to a close up video of an elderly creature with scaly graying blue skin and long wisps of white hair dangling from his chin. Taupe fabric drapes liberally over his long head, sheltering his faded yellow eyes from the bright sunlight. Remorse and guilt live deep within the lines of his face.

"We have long discussed our elimination of the Humans," the elderly being states, "and thirty generations later, our culture is *still* divided over it. At what point will we understand it doesn't matter if we were correct in our strategy, or if we were acute in our foresight? We committed an *atrocity*, and it is a terrible sin looped around our necks. Now, *Da'oma Kachi'in* have returned from death, and they are claiming their just revenge."

The captain closes his eyes in thought. He was never an overly pious or superstitious person, and the old Pontiff's assertion holds little weight with him.

What he feels more than anything is relief.

There are always large spans of time from one disappearance to the next, and the Liner's disappearance means there will be ample time to pull into port before the next one.

He caps the container and slips it back into his chest pocket, no longer needing its sunny effects.

Statistically, with over twenty thousand space flights in progress and with the long interval between disappearances, a catastrophic engine failure is many times more likely. But *those* odds he can live with because a catastrophic engine failure has reasons. It can be prepared for and dealt with, not like these awful disappearances where nothing is ever found, *no trace at all.*

His relief triggers a small amount of guilt over his selfishness, and the heavy captain reflexively pities the thousands lost aboard the passenger liner. More important, though, he and his crew will make it home okay.

"Sir?"

The captain opens his eyes, looking his ensign over. She is young with spotless gray coveralls, and her whip tail undulates eagerly.

He remembers when he was that age, proud at graduating with honors from the flight officer's academy, longing to travel the stars. The excitement wore off pretty fast once he understood he was just moving rocks from one place to another. The mediocrity gives him a bitter twinge.

"Yes?"

"I have the plasma inter-flow data you asked for." She offers a tablet to him. He takes it lazily, furrowing his brow.

"This wasn't due for another twenty cycles..."

She looks straight ahead, smiling broadly.

"I know, sir."

The captain grins fondly and gives the tablet a cursory glance, no doubt in his mind that it is flawless.

"Excellent work," he praises, and hands the tablet back to her. When she reaches for it, he notices her delicate hand, her manicured claws, her soft light blue scales. They remind him there is someone waiting for him at home.

"That'll be all."

The ensign bows. "Thank you, Si-..."

A tremendous vibration rocks the bridge, knocking the ensign flat, and nearly bouncing the captain out of his chair. Alarm Klaxons wail, and the illumination shifts to an urgent hue. The captain hauls himself upright while the ensign pushes herself up with her tail. She hurries to her station.

"Navigator!" growls the captain, "What happened?"

The navigator rapidly draws information from his terminal. "Something hit us, Sir!"

"Why didn't we detect it?"

The navigator shrugs. "Sensors are blank..."

The captain's posture shifts angrily. "I want an explanation!"

Behind him, the ensign calls up ship diagnostics on her console. "Confirmed, Captain, ship's mass has increased. Whatever it is, it's sticking to us."

"Where?"

"Just ahead of the main cargo hold. Air pressure seems stable, though… no leaks."

The captain turns to his first officer. "Check it out, and make sure everyone's alright."

The commander leaps out of his seat, pausing only to grab emergency gear, and dashes out between the thick blast doors.

"Captain!" the navigator yelps, "it's cutting through!"

"*What*? Visual!"

The news holowindow closes and a much larger window opens at the front of the bridge, displaying an interior corridor of the freighter. There, a fountain of sparks jets from the leading edge of a circular cut in the hull.

Mouth agape, the captain swings to his communications officer. "Get out a distress call *right now*!" Tapping the intercom, he adds, "Commander, get our people out of there and seal that compartment!"

"Right away," the commander replies.

The captain watches the screen in terror as the spark fountain carves through the reinforced alloys. Crew members filter into view, gathering around the curiosity, trying to make sense of it. When the commander runs in, he waves his arms and shouts, ushering the crew away as fast as he can.

"This is Ore Freighter, *Ken-talsu-u*, declaring emergency!" the communications officer pleads in the background, "all vessels, please respond!"

Furious whistles and buzzes overwhelm his headset, and he throws it from his elongated head, swearing. "Massive interference, Captain! I can't transmit!"

The captain's eyes go wide, panic tugging at him. In the holoscreen, he watches the spark fountain complete its circular slice; and the metal disc explodes away. Dense smoke billows into the corridor, washing over the startled crewmen. Flashes of light strobe within the haze, and the captain hears familiar voices screaming in agony.

"We're under attack…?" he mutters, unable to believe what he is seeing. "Give me a visual of all compartments!"

Working quickly, the communications officer divides the large holoscreen into smaller sections, each section showing one of the freighter's various corridors or compartments.

The captain's pupils shrink to pinpoints as he scours the screens for attackers, but thick, roiling smoke hides their relentless advance. One by one, the divided windows of the large holoscreen are obscured, and the shrieks of dying crewmen amplify the panic in his heart.

"Commander…? Chief…? *Anyone…?*"

Terrified yelps and gunfire are his only reply.

"Seal the bridge!"

Heavy blast doors grind together, dreadfully slow.

The captain peers through the closing gap, clutching a short pendant around his broad neck. Just before the doors meet, a darkened, titanic figure runs into the far end of the corridor.

Slamming together, the heavy doors seal and the sturdy mechanical locks rotate shut.

Footfalls reverberate from the corridor and jog to a halt just outside the doors. First a pause, then a resounding clang of something metallic rams the far side. It rams three more times, but the doors do not yield, and the heavy footfalls retreat as rapidly as they came.

Recovering some of his composure, the captain stands from his crouched position behind his chair and turns to the communications officer. "You *have* to get that comm array functioning! I don't know how much time we have, so you'll have to…"

The bridge doors erupt with a deafening roar. White-hot shards of metal streak into consoles and crew, scattering the bridge officers like leaves.

The captain lies on his back, dazed, staring at the ceiling. All sounds are gone, and his tongue lolls at the edge of his mouth. The smoky air flashes all around him, and he struggles with disorientation, unaware that his organs are spilled out beside him. Trying to sit up, he finds himself looking into the barrel of a large caliber rifle, his brain just registering the muzzle flash.

Seeking Answers

Two medium-sized ships decelerate from their faster-than-light travel. The helmsman of the lead vessel taps his console with a polished talon.

"Arriving at destination, all systems normal, and... No contacts."

The muscular captain stands, smoothing his crisp black uniform. Bright metal decorations hang around his broad neck as well as above each eye.

"Record and send the following message: 'Command, Response Vessels *Seyun-gee* and *Korom* have arrived at last known location of missing freighter, *Ken-talsu-u*. Beginning search of surrounding vicinities. *Seyun-gee* out.'"

"Message sent, sir." The ensign pauses, and swivels his chair to face his captain. "Sir, do you have any idea what's causing these disappearances?"

"We're not here to speculate, Ensign, we're here to learn the truth."

He watches the young officer spin forward and sneers. Ensigns are the most useless things in the entire service, he thinks. Insecure, inexperienced, easily panicked, they are living failure machines, and the thought of having one on his ship is excruciating. This is a vessel of action, not training. Let some *other* captain play nursemaid.

"Open a channel to *Korom*."

A large holoscreen opens at the front of the bridge. In it, a younger black-uniformed officer stands from his comfortable looking chair. He, too, wears the metallic decorations, though in smaller clusters.

"Yes, *Seyun-gee?*" he asks with a slight bow.

The elder captain nods in acknowledgement. "Are you receiving any interference?"

"No, *Seyun-gee*. All channels are clear."

"Alright, begin your sweeps. Anything you find, I want to know about it."

"Understood. Korom out."

The Holoscreen closes and the senior captain leans over his science officer's shoulder.

"What do you see out there?"

"A whole lot of nothing, sir."

"Well, let's start with the obvious."

The science officer nods, and pulls up data on his console. "We have a local binary of young super-giant stars, hottest spectral class, no planetary system. The region is populated with numerous globules of dense gas, collapsing within the surrounding nebula. Stellar winds from the binary are strong enough to sweep this area clear." Leaning back in his chair, he adds, "I don't think we're going to find much here."

The captain grips the end of his chin. "Why is that?"

"A freighter's engines leave a trail of charged particles. Usually, that lets us see where it's been, but these stars would blow that delicate trail away almost instantly. Might as well track a boast in a windstorm."

The captain scans across the images of the dark globules, concentrating on the close pair of bluish stars gleaming in their midst.

"Makes it a good spot for a hi-jacking, doesn't it?"

The officer looks up at his captain in surprise. "Yes, it would... Does command believe our ships are being *captured?*"

"That's the working hypothesis. The dissident factions have used terrorism before... They may've become even *more* despicable in their methods."

Standing straight, the captain turns to his tactical officer. "Get the weapon systems primed and on-line. The instant we find anything, I want to be ready."

"Aye, sir," she replies, powering up the defenses with experienced key strokes. The captain strolls leisurely back to his chair and seats himself, opening an intercom to another part of his ship.

"Team leader," he calls, "are your troops ready?"

"Momentarily, captain. We're suiting up now. Just tell us when and where."

The black uniformed captain closes the intercom, and sits silently, considering his options.

"Let's look at our archives on the disappearances again," he announces suddenly. "Start by plotting the last locations of all vessels that have disappeared and been completely unaccounted for. Put the data on screen."

The science officer sighs quietly, having looked at little else for the entire voyage. The broad holoscreen opens with a virtual representation of large expanses of space, and one by one, twelve points appear, captioned with ship information, cargo, and date of disappearance. The dots seem totally random.

"What do we know?" the captain demands.

"Well," the science officer begins, swiveling away from his console and gesturing toward the screen, "we know that all of these vessels were on course until they disappeared. We know that a large flare of broadcasted noise directly preceded their disappearance, and we know that with the exception of two passenger liners, the disappeared ships have been heavy cargo class, most filled with raw ores and minerals."

The captain strokes a patch of hair beneath his chin as the science officer continues.

"We know that no evidence of crew or ship has yet been recovered, and we know the early disappearances had long, regular intervals, but the last two occurrences have been within a very short span of one another."

"*Da'oma Kachi'in,*" someone whispers.

The captain spins on his boot, his hard eyes drilling holes into each of his crew, seeking the one who uttered such reprehensible nonsense.

"The idea that *angry ghosts* are swallowing our ships is childish and moronic," the old officer declares, "and has *no place* in the military service." The veins in his strong neck throb perceptibly as he swivels his head, looking every crewman in the eye. "Moreover, it is an *insult* to the families of the missing to say it is anything other than *criminals* bent on disturbing our peace with violence and terrorism. *Do you understand?*"

All heads bow as one and with somber tone reply, "We do."

"Good. Let's focus on our duties." The captain restores his more typical demeanor, tucking his hands behind his back and gripping the end of his tail. "Tactical, transfer all fire control to your console. What ever we find, if it isn't one of ours, shoot it down. Helm, program a circular search and rescue pattern, and coordinate with *Korom* to maximize the area covered. Communication, listen for any potential signal that could be an enemy, and use the mainframe to assist in isolating any embedded codes if you find them. Science, let's pick up where we left off."

Before the science officer can begin however, the holowindow is overridden by the captain of *Korom*. He is on his feet and frantic.

"*Seyun-gee*, three objects have landed on our hull and are boring thr…"

The transmission bursts into bright static distortion, and *Seyun-gee's* communication officer throws off his headphones as they screech and buzz.

"This is it!" the captain shouts to his crew, setting himself down on the edge of his chair. "Science, start recording all data you can. Communication, what's happening?"

"Massive interference, sir."

"Source?"

"Three point sources, sir… attached to *Korom's* hull!"

"Visual!" shouts the Captain.

Korom's long, shining outline fills the screen. Three black bulges protrude from its midsection like cancerous moles.

"Re-establish contact with *Korom*, and magnify those black objects!" Pointing to his tactical officer, he adds, "Target those objects and wait for my command!"

In the holoscreen, the picture zooms in to one of the objects. It is a streamlined blob, like a teardrop cut in half with the flat side pressed against *Korom's* hull. Perfectly black, it is held in place by four spidery legs. The captain squints at it, unsure of what he is looking at.

"Are you... *alive?*" he wonders aloud.

"Sir!" calls out the communications officer, "I have a patch to *Korom*, very faint."

"Put it on!"

The holoscreen switches back to the bridge of *Korom*, barely intelligible from interference. The junior captain is frenetically issuing commands, and his crew rushes to comply. When he notices the holoscreen, he steps into its view.

"*Seyun-gee*," the image crackles, "we've been boarded! We need assistance!"

"I have the objects targeted, ready to fire," explains the senior captain.

"No! They've cut through the hull, and if you shoot them off, you'll depressurize the whole midsection of my ship." He looks off screen giving more orders, and turns back. "We need your boarding teams to…"

A great shudder shakes *Korom's* bridge, swaying the captain off his feet. Alarm Klaxons sound stridently.

The *Seyun-gee* captain mashes his intercom. "Team Leader, we need your troops on *Korom*. She's under attack."

"Understood, sir. Standing by for clearance."

The seasoned captain leans forward in his seat. "Communication, send a message to Command via coded laser: 'Have engaged unknown enemy.' Helm, get us close enough to *Korom* for boarding. Keep *Korom* between us and those stars so our teams have some shade to cross through."

"Aye, sir!" The helmsman guides the sleek frigate alongside the assaulted *Korom*.

In the holoscreen, *Korom's* captain is more frantic, sounds of combat and explosions filtering through the garbled audio. Bellowing orders, he grabs a side-arm from his chair.

"Seal the bridge! Don't let them up…" A bright flash washes out the holoscreen, and it drops entirely into static.

Seyun-gee's captain clenches his fists, his claws digging into his palms. "Get them back, Ensign!"

The communications officer wrestles with his console, but to no avail. "Sir, the patch is still functional, there just isn't any response."

"Can you get me a visual of the bridge?"

"Aye, sir."

The ensign makes the appropriate key taps, and a noisy window opens showing *Korom's* bridge. There is dense haze from smoke, but a seated figure can just be made out at the tactical console. It wears oversized headgear, linked by numerous wires into the consoles around it, and large goggles that flash with light. When the seated figure notices the holoscreen, it calls out to a hulking, armored biped that marches forward and shoots into the screen with a bulky weapon.

"Hardware over-loaded at the source, sir," informs the communications officer. The captain can only stare blankly.

"It couldn't be…" he mutters.

"Couldn't be what, sir?"

"Nothing," the captain says, unaware he had spoken aloud. The image deeply troubles him.

There is a quick series of pulses, and the tactical officer announces, "Grappling clamps to *Korom* are secure."

Taking his cue, the captain triggers his intercom. "Team Leader, you are clear for transport."

One by one, the troopers hook on to the grapple lines, jetting over to their companion vessel. While they file across the stout cables, the Team Leader addresses them as a group.

"We don't know who we're fighting, and it doesn't matter. We anticipated an attack, and this is what we trained for. Go in through the personnel hatches just below the bridge, and push back from there. We're not trying to capture anything here, so if you see an enemy, kill it! The medical teams are right behind us to patch up anyone that gets hit. Now get fierce!"

On *Seyun-gee's* bridge, the captain paces anxiously. The communications officer looks over his shoulder at him, asking, "Sir, what did you mean when you said, `it couldn't be'."

"Ancient history, Ensign, *never mind*. Is the boarding team there yet?"

"Nearly, sir."

"What about the interference? Any luck cutting through it?"

"Negative. It's washing out our positional fixes. I can't align the antenna, not without…"

"Without *what*, Ensign?"

"Not without destroying the sources of interference first."

The captain continues pacing, debating if he should risk depressurizing his sister ship to contain the threat. It could kill everyone aboard, even jeopardize his teams jetting across, but he could sift through the remains and, at last, find some answers to this mystery, possibly ending the disappearances. His fists open and close reflexively, a visual analogue to the raging discourse in his mind.

"Sir, boarding teams have reached the personnel hatches," announces the communications officer, just as a searing energy bolt streaks by *Seyun-gee's* bridge.

"Tactical!" roars the captain. "Where did that come from?"

The tactical officer looks out in shock. "From *Korom*, sir!"

The captain whirls in frenzy. "*Lock all weapon batteries on* Korom's *bridge and fire!*"

"But, sir," protests the tactical officer, "the boarding teams!"

The captain leaps at the tactical officer, ripping her out of her chair. He scrambles to program the target, but too late. Energy blasts shred through *Seyun-gee's* bridge, exploding the compartment and venting all into space.

From the outer hull of *Korom*, the Boarding Team Leader watches the energy blasts continue, sweeping along *Seyun-gee's* full length, tearing her inside out. Secondary explosions incinerate troops still jetting over on the cables, rocketing their singed bodies through comrades farther ahead. Large chunks of metal scatter in all directions, tearing through anyone unable to move in time. Gritting his teeth, the Team Leader curses.

"How did they get control?" asks one of his troopers.

Ignoring the query, the Leader bellows, "*Get that hatch open!*"

Seyun-gee glows with damage, venting long plumes of flame and plasma. The venting strains the grappling lines, stretching them taut.

Looking over his shoulder, the Team Leader sees his troops getting clipped, slashed, and crushed. All the while, fresh explosions aboard *Seyun-gee* renew the metallic hail, peppering the surviving troopers with still more lethal fragments. The Leader turns away, only to watch *Korom's* weapon batteries re-orient toward the taut grappling lines. With precision shots, the cables are sliced; and *Korom* lurches, swaying them in their magnetic boots.

Like snakes striking prey, the cables whip at the teams, slicing some at the waist, sweeping others off the hull. Their voices flow into the Leader's headset, turning from desperate pleas for rescue into screams of searing agony when they drift into the nearby stars' full radiance.

Fury grips the Leader, squeezing his heart in a vice, and he pushes past his troopers to get a view of the locked personnel hatch.

"What is taking so long?"

A soldier is hunched over the lock control with a small electronic device. "They must have changed all the codes. I can't get in!"

Hauling out a small torch, the Leader shoves the soldier aside and kneels down to cut the lock itself.

Korom lurches again with thrust, building distance from its burning twin and putting an end to the rain of deadly debris. The troopers breathe a grateful sigh of relief, until they see *Korom's* weapon batteries swing back toward *Seyun-gee* and loose a coordinated barrage. The shots rip through *Seyun-gee's* engines, igniting a spherical blast that consumes the tortured ship like a swelling sun. The sphere grows faster than the departing ship is traveling, and the moment of relief yields to an all new tide of panic.

"Get it open!" someone yells, starting a riot of frenzied shouting. While the Leader continues to cut, the troopers hack into the lock with their rifle butts. Some spin their weapons around and shoot into the lock, careless of the ricocheting shots plunging into their comrades.

At last, the bar severs. The surviving troopers crowd around their Leader and shove the door aside as the blast wave of superheated plasma rakes the full length of *Korom*. The Leader's team chars around him, the sudden vaporization of their flesh blowing him through the door. He gets to his feet and shoulders the door shut. More tired than he should be, he slumps down exhausted and gasps for breath. Perplexed, he looks down at the radiation gauge on his suit. It glows vividly.

Looking around the small airlock, what he knows will soon become his tomb, his eyelids get heavy. Before they close completely, a shadow steps into the window of the interior door.

Fear energizes him in his final moments as he searches for a weapon, but he finds none. Once the air pressure equalizes, the interior airlock slides open, and the gasping Team Leader looks his foe over from head to toe, accepting what he sees with great difficulty.

"*Da'oma Kachi'in…*" he whispers with his last breath.

The figure strides in, clad in stout dark armor, a heavy rifle trained squarely on the Team Leader's body. It closes the interior door and depressurizes the airlock. Keeping the rifle aimed, it steps over and jabs the slumped creature with the barrel.

A light on the outer door shifts color, and the figure slides it aside one handed. With the swift shove of a boot, the Team Leader's body is sent unceremoniously into space.

Resealing the airlock, the metal clad figure pressurizes the compartment and lifts his face plate, revealing a sweaty young man with thick stubble, already going gray. Scars cross his eyes and lips like topographical features on a map.

"Maiella, this is Thompson, over."

Via radio a female voice replies, "Go ahead, Thompson."

"We're clear. Let's get under way."

"Roger, that. Coordinates set."

BITTER HARVEST

The man slings his rifle and walks slowly to the bridge, looking carefully at the ship around him. Along the way, he stops to investigate a curious panel here and there. Soon, he strides through the twisted and wrecked doors of the bridge where a gargantuan man in bulky armor steps into his path and salutes briskly. His great round face is also stubbly, but is more weathered with lines and old burns.

"At ease."

Thompson looks the huge man over, taking in the numerous new blast and burn marks his dark metal skin wears.

"Good to see you're all right, Argo." Thompson claps Argo warmly on the arm.

The big man smiles back wryly. "They'll have to build bigger guns."

Thompson grins, then becomes stern. "Was anyone injured?"

"There are some laser wounds and contusions, but nothing serious."

Thompson raises his hand to Argo's shoulder. "I want you, Brick Brahe, and Brick Talu to set up a medical facility. Treat every wound, no matter how slight, understood?"

Argo stands straight and salutes again.

"Aye, sir."

The huge man picks up his massive weapon and jogs down the corridor, his hefty footfalls reverberating solidly.

Thompson looks around the bridge at the damage his teams caused as he kicks the lifeless blue bodies aside. There is still a thin layer of smoke, just enough to scent the air, and scorch marks streak the walls and panels.

Seated in the midst of the disarray is a slim woman in armor, wearing large goggles that flash with data. Various cables extend from her headgear to the consoles like a web. Walking carefully between them, Thompson makes his way over.

The flashing of the goggles ceases, and she lifts them to get a better look at her superior. Like the others, she bears her share of scars.

"Maiella, how much of the ship's systems have you interpreted?"

"Sixty-seven percent, including navigation, main drive, and weapons."

"So what do you think we have here?"

Maiella looks forward again, lowering her goggles. "She's fast and light, but with very good weapons—probably designed as a first responder."

Thompson kneels beside her. "How fast?"

"Well, the freighter departed over a month ago, but we'll catch up in about two days."

Thompson's brow rises in pleasant surprise. "Two days? What kind of drive system is it using?"

"I'll let you know when I find out. It's definitely new."

"Two days, eh?" He stands and activates his radio. "Gun Setee, Gun Drusus, respond."

"Drusus, here."

"Setee, here."

"Is your sweep complete?"

"Yes, sir," replies Setee. "All crew confirmed dead."

"Is there a place we can store the bodies?"

"Affirmative," answers Drusus. "We can disable the heaters in one of the compartments near the hull. It won't take long to get very cold in there."

"Good. We have two days until we meet up with the freighter. Go see Brick Argo and have your wounds tended, then police up the bodies and store them. Do it quickly because after that, we'll inventory the ship. I want a full list of everything she's carrying and everything she's capable of. Acknowledge."

"Understood, sir," answers Drusus.

"Acknowledged, sir," answers Setee.

Thompson switches off his radio and looks down at Maiella, resting his hand on the back of her chair. "Excellent work, getting control so quickly… It saved us."

Her goggles halt their flashing again so she can look at him. "How many blueskins were aboard do you think?"

Thompson thinks for a moment. "Standing crew of twenty plus fifty soldiers. If you count the soldiers from the other ship, it would have been fifty more."

"A hundred and twenty versus nine of us... pretty tall odds."

"You evened them nicely."

Maiella blushes proudly, taking great pleasure in her success. She breathes deeply and gets back to work, her goggles resuming their flashing pulses of code. Thompson looks for the nearest body to haul away, and grabs a violently torn corpse wearing the tatters of a black uniform.

"Approaching captured freighter now," announces Maiella.

Thompson looks up from the console he is studying. "Can you give me a visual?"

Maiella hesitates. "I could have," she says, pointing to the blackened scorch marks at the front of the bridge, "but it, uh, was disabled."

"Is there a backup?"

"Possibly... hang on..." Her goggles flash with data and instruction. "There!"

A small window opens in front of her and displays the bridge of the freighter. Another slim human in armor and goggles, covered in a reddish brown dust, almost leaps out of his seat in surprise. Once he realizes who is hailing him, he calms down, telling someone off screen to reset the auto-destruct safeties.

"Geek Maiella! It's good to see you alive! We didn't know if the plan would work…"

Maiella smiles demurely. "Geek Lukas, good to see you too. The plan was perfect. No problem at all."

"Were there any casualties?" the freighter pilot asks fearfully.

"No," she answers, "we're all okay."

The freighter pilot sighs in relief.

"How about *your* team?" Maiella queries. "Anyone hurt?"

"No, we're in good shape. Resistance was meager. Small crew. Easy."

Thompson slides over beside Maiella to look through the holowindow. "What's that on you? You've been doing some digging?"

The freighter pilot stiffens noticeably and salutes.

"Yes, sir, Gun Thompson! We've inventoried the ship cargoes; and she's carrying raw ores of tungsten, vanadium, iron, germanium, and silicon, plus two very high-quality ore excavators. The diamonds on the augers are bigger than Argo's fist!"

"Is that why you're covered in ore dust, Sergeant?"

The pilot looks down sheepishly. "We were waiting a long time for you, and, uh… and..."

"You tried them out."

The slim pilot looks up, jutting his lip, contemplating whether he should try to explain, but decides against it. "Yup," he replies, "we did."

Maiella brings a hand up to her face to hide her chuckling. Thompson buries his amusement. "Get yourselves ready to return."

"But, sir, it'll take us eight more months to pilot this freighter to the planned position."

"You and your team will be returning with us. We can get home sooner, which means we can all be on another rotation sooner. Program the freighter for a circuitous route—full-fail safes—if any ship approaches and doesn't transmit the access code..." Thompson begins.

"…overload power plant, induce feedback harmonics to propulsion, maximum output," finishes the pilot. He is about to sign off, but looks up hopefully. "One more thing, sir. Does your ship have any food synthesis machines?"

Thompson looks back with falling crest. "Yes, but it only spits out that cellulose stuff we can't eat."

The pilot looks down sadly and raises his head. "Maybe one of the other teams has found something, yeah?"

"Let's hope so, Lukas. Gun Thompson out."

Maiella switches off the holowindow, sorry to end on such a somber note. The richness of their cargoes is impressive, but thus far, they have been missing the one component they need most: edible compounds for their food synthesizers. It means, yet again, they will have to liquefy the bodies of the dead for nourishment.

"I guess we should be grateful this ship was so well staffed," Thompson says bitterly. Maiella closes her eyes, being forced to contemplate the grim source of their sustenance.

"I'm going down to the personnel hatch to receive the freighter team," Thompson says heavily. "After that, I'll be helping repair any damaged bulkheads. Call me if something comes up."

Maiella nods silently, resuming her duties as the tall soldier walks out of the bridge. When the freighter team is safely aboard, she sets the course home and engages the engines at high speed.

Coming Home

Maiella takes the main engines off-line, decelerating into a vast solar system. At its center, a bluish white star shines intensely, and the ship streaks by enormous gaseous planets on its way to a rocky ring still billions of kilometers away.

The distance closes swiftly, and the vessel glides to a halt several hundred thousand kilometers from a massive, but ordinary-looking asteroid. Aligning the vessel's antenna, Maiella transmits a coded message.

"Cadre One, this is Team Spectre returning from gathering rotation. Mission successful. Awaiting acknowledgement, over."

There is a considerable time delay before the clipped and staccato reply comes. "Team Spectre, transmit identification protocols, over."

Maiella conjures the code sequences mentally, sending all of the data through her headgear without lifting a finger. Her goggles flash, indicating a hugely complex series of alphanumeric sequences intermingled with patterns and shapes. "Transmission complete. Awaiting further instructions, over."

Again, there is a long delay.

"Identification protocols verified." The voice warms considerably, adding, "We're glad you're back. Proceed to 4-1-8. A shuttle will be waiting for you. Inform Gun Thompson that the Leadership Council is convening and that he is expected for debrief." There is a slight pause. "Can't wait to see you all! Cadre One out."

Maiella thrusts the ship forward and looks at Thompson beside her. "Did you get that?"

"I did," he replies. When he turns to face her, she is looking at him with big brown hopeful eyes. He stares at her, unable to keep a straight face.

"Yes, you and Argo can join me for debrief."

Maiella hops in her seat, grinning broadly. She resumes her navigational duties and peeks at Thompson, who is looking back with mild fatherly disapproval. Immediately, she straightens her posture, suppressing the giddy child within. She arches an eyebrow. "Approaching synchronous orbit, sir."

Thompson nods wordlessly, the look of disapproval faded. "Argo," he calls into his headset.

"Sir?" comes the soldier's reply via radio.

"We'll be disembarking momentarily. Get a technical detail together regarding the onboard systems. I want your assistance at debrief."

"Understood. Brick Argo out."

Maiella guides the ship closer toward the planetoid, every square kilometer of it pocked with deep craters. As she glides the ship around the great rock, two monumental parabolic reflectors appear on the horizon.

"We're home," she announces.

Slowing drastically, she maneuvers toward the reflectors which stand sentry beside a wide and shallow crater. Eleven ships of radically different design hover in the general vicinity, long tethers attaching them to the facility built into the crater walls below. As promised, a shuttle is waiting, and she halts her vessel beside it.

"Cadre shuttle, this is Geek Maiella. You are cleared for docking. Proceed to forward personnel hatch for loading. Team Spectre out." Her goggles flash a rapid sequence of shutdown commands, and the background hum from the ship's drive systems gradually fades away. She unhooks the many lanyards and filaments connecting her to the consoles, which automatically retract into her headgear. Liberated from the consoles, she leans over each arm of her chair to pick up her machine pistols. She gets to her feet and gives each weapon a quick flip around her finger before clipping them onto the small of her back. Thompson is beside her, heavy rifle slung over his right shoulder.

"Ready?" he asks.

Maiella nods quickly.

"Let's go." The two of them head off to the shuttle.

As quick a walk as it is, Argo is already there, listening as Geek Lukas explains a small device he holds. The Geek wraps up his explanation and puts the device in Argo's big hands.

Thompson can see Lukas's armor is much cleaner than before. He grips Lukas's arm, rotating it at the shoulder and inspecting underneath the overlapping plates. It is just as clean.

"Much better," says Thompson. "Any grit in the joints?"

"No, sir! I thoroughly stripped and cleaned it of ore dust. One hundred percent operational."

"Good. These suits have to last us a long time." Thompson shifts to a less-commanding stance. "What have you got there?"

Lukas looks over at Argo for assurance, and Argo gives him the nod.

"Sir, I was explaining the results from our efforts to reengineer the food machines on board. We made some progress, just recently."

Thompson raises his eyebrows thoughtfully. "Good! Positive results are always welcome to the Leadership Council." Turning to Argo, he asks, "Are you ready to present your findings?"

Argo nods affirmatively. "We'll need to research much further before we present any *conclusive* findings, but I can let the council know what we've learned so far."

"Very well," Thompson acknowledges. A quick clanking jolt beside them tells them the shuttle has arrived, and the air lock doors slide aside. Thompson pats Lukas on the back.

"Go ahead."

Lukas smiles and hurriedly steps into the shuttle, shouting a joyful greeting to the pilots within. Down the corridor, heavy steps of the other cadre teams echo in rapid pace. As they pass Thompson, Argo, and Maiella, they salute and, like Lukas, whoop with joy to see the shuttle pilots. Thompson looks at Argo and Maiella, tossing his head toward the shuttle. They nod and file in. Taking a quick head count, Thompson finds all aboard.

"All right, that's all of us. Let's go!"

"Yes, sir!" the pilots reply and spin forward in their seats. Another jolting clank and the shuttle is free of the ship, descending swiftly toward the crater below. Already, a large hangar door is opening in the crater wall ahead. With practiced precision, the pilots guide the shuttle in, setting it down perfectly in the docking station. Rugged clamps attach to the craft, drawing it back against the inner wall and locking it in tight.

The shuttle door slides aside, and the soldiers look into a crowd of elated people amassed before them. With wild shouts and cheers, the two groups throw themselves together, mingling in loud welcomes and bear hug embraces. The soldiers wrap their arms around all of their scarred and crippled brethren as desperately relieved to be home as their cadre brothers and sisters are desperately relieved to have them home. Above the noisy hoots and shouts, a team of MedTechs can just be heard forcing their way through the mass, searching for any signs of injury among the teams.

Thompson takes a deep breath, his extra bit of height allowing him to look over the crowd. For a moment, his teams' successful return has let them forget the grinding agony of their work-filled lives and the impairment of their bodies, broken by injury and twisted from genetic defect. Before it swells too large, he checks his pride, mindful of his duty, and looks down to the MedTech in front of him.

"Are you injured in *any* way?" the MedTech demands.

"No, I'm well."

The MedTech smiles, cupping the tall man's arm before moving on to the next soldier with an identical query.

Thompson looks over the crowd of ecstatic faces rejoicing in reunion and catching up on the long months apart. It swells his heart all the more to know he has been able to protect and provide for them all, even at the ultimate risk to himself and those under his command.

Reluctantly, he peels himself away, tapping Maiella and Argo. Immediately, their demeanor returns to the austere; and they march through the cadre hallways, preparing to report.

The doors to the council chamber slide at their approach, and the trio steps into a room five meters square. A semicircular table sits at the opposite end from them, flat side facing them. Filling out the round side are the five council members who stand as the team enters. They are all tall and strong like the soldiers and similar in appearance, only modestly different with the amount of decoration on their chests, the gray in their hair, and the greater number of visible scars. Their charcoal gray uniforms are spotless, though faded and threadbare in the tight-fitting shoulders and neck.

Thompson, Argo, and Maiella halt their march with a stomp, rigidly standing at attention and snapping the crispest of salutes in unison. The general, who stands at the middle of the table, returns the respectful salute and allows a smile to crack his marble face.

"It's good to have you home. At ease!"

With clocklike precision, the three unlock their helmets and lift them off, tucking them in the crook of their left arms. Thompson's short hair is salt-and-pepper gray, belying his young face. Argo's is also going gray, but retains more of the black. Maiella's hair is little more than long stubble between the gold computer contact terminals on her head.

As the general sits, the other council members do likewise.

"Any casualties?" he asks with concern.

"No, sir," replies Thompson. "All teams one hundred percent."

The council exhales at once, relaxing in their seats.

"Good, good," says the general, folding his strong hands together and leaning on his elbows. "Tell us how it went, Captain."

"Team Shade successfully acquired a big ore carrier, dispatched its crew, and departed for the rendezvous point. We monitored from a secure distance."

"Did the ore carrier get out a distress signal?"

"It tried, sir, but the interference generators Colonel Thorskild designed functioned perfectly."

Colonel Thorskild leans forward on his thick, powerful arms. "Were you able to surround the vessel before it tried to broadcast?"

"Yes, sir," Thompson replies. "From our vantage points, we confirmed any transmissions from the ore carrier were overwhelmed by our interference."

The colonel, satisfied, sits back in his seat.

"So what happened next?" asks the general.

"We waited in stasis near the location the ore carrier was collected. It was only a matter of weeks this time before the blueskins came to investigate. Two fast-moving ships arrived, alike in every way. We successfully boarded one, liquidated her crew and complement. The sister ship grappled and attempted to repel our teams, but," he looks appreciatively at his female comrade, "Geek Maiella efficiently interpreted the alien weapon systems and destroyed the sister ship. Our vessel was collected completely intact."

"Did either of *these* ships get out a distress call?" asks Thorskild.

"No, sir. Before we attacked, we monitored some ship-to-ship communication, noting the transmissions were sent and received by an antenna array on the vessels' spines. The vessels were traveling parallel, so we clustered our virus ships around one, knowing the proximity would be sufficient to overwhelm the other one's array as well. Even if the companion vessel was able to send a signal, its effective range would be less than two hundred thousand kilometers at best, and we did not detect any vessels even remotely close to that distance."

"That *is* a relief." Thorskild relaxes, becoming more comfortable. "Where is the ore carrier now?"

"Because of her slow acceleration, I ordered Geek Lukas to program her to a location we can monitor from safety. If she is intercepted by the blueskins, she will detonate. After a sufficient observation period, if no alien ships have successfully tracked the freighter, we can send out a team to bring her home. It allowed Team Shade to return with us so we can all be reassigned to another collection rotation."

General Dryden tents his hands. "That's good thinking, Captain, but you need to rest and regenerate before reassignment. Now, tell us about the vessel you piloted home."

Thompson gestures to Maiella who takes over. "She seems to be a 'first response' military vessel, requiring only a small crew to operate, but could accommodate many more in transport. Much more advanced than anything I've seen before. The propulsion is extraordinary both in speed and efficiency. She is also well armed for her size though lightly armored. I was able to completely incapacitate the sister ship with a few shots."

Major Eris moves to the edge of her chair, the gold contacts on her head richly accenting her short silver hair. "Were you able to interpret *all* of the ship's functions?"

"Almost, Major," she continues. "Several systems on board are fully automated, requiring no input. Like life support, for example, and food systems."

"What do you mean?"

"Well, since the blueskins seem to prefer a temperature of thirty-three degrees centigrade and a relative humidity of ninety percent, it was a challenge to stay hydrated."

"So that wasn't something you could take care of in flight?"

"Not without disassembling the main air processors. We decided it was wiser to endure the elevated temperature and rig a moisture condenser rather than risk a life-support failure in flight."

The general recognizes the wisdom in that, looking down the table to the heavily burn scarred man on his right. "Major Grissom, can you build a team to reengineer the life-support system?"

"Yes, General," answers Grissom. "I have a team waiting to go aboard as we speak."

The woman to Dryden's left, her longer gray hair tied tightly into a bun, lifts her broad shoulders and clasps her hands on the table. "Were you able to research the food systems on board?"

"Yes, Colonel Enyo," Argo answers, "and I'm pleased to report we were able to assemble small batches of amino acids and proteins. With additional experimentation, we may be able to coax enough out of it to support a standing crew."

The council members smile at the good news, murmuring lightly among themselves.

"Excellent!" commends the general. "Brick Argo, brief Major Grissom and his team on your findings, then you are dismissed for twenty-four hours' rest and regeneration. Geek Maiella, upload the ship data-and-system control software you interpreted into the catalogue. Then brief Colonel Thorskild on the broader points of the ship's function, after which you are dismissed for twenty-four hours' rest and regeneration."

He pauses as he looks Thompson over. "Gun Thompson, your skillful planning and good judgment have enhanced our survival, and you have again brought all of your teams home safe. Your continued efforts bring distinction and honor to yourself as well as those who serve with you. You are dismissed for twenty-four hours' rest and regeneration. We have dispatched two drones to the rec room to attend your needs."

In perfect synchronization, the Council stands and salutes respectfully.

"Thank you, General." The three operators come to attention and return the crisp salute. Looking left and right at his teammates, Thompson grins.

"Let's go."

The three spin on their heels and march out of the chamber. Once they pass the chamber doors, Thorskild leans over to General Dryden, whispering.

"Shouldn't we tell them?"

General Dryden furrows his brow. "Not yet, Thorskild. They've earned a rest, and I want them to be able to enjoy it."

Thompson puts his arms around Argo and Maiella, hauling them in close.

"I'd like to thank both of you for making me look so good in front of the council again."

Argo guffaws, "Nothin' new, Thompson."

Maiella punches Thompson in the side playfully. "Yeah, you two are lucky to have me. I don't know *where* you'd be without me saving your *asses* all the time."

Thompson looks at Argo and winks. "You know you're right, Maiella ... NOW!"

Argo and Thompson ambush Maiella, lifting her up off her feet. She squeals in protest as Argo throws her over his broad shoulder and Thompson slaps her backside over and over. "We'd be a couple of assless operators, right? Huh? *Isn't that right, Maiella?*"

Argo spins her around, and Thompson continues his paddling while she shrieks in between the howls of her own laughter. All three come to an immediate halt, however, when they look down the corridor and see they are being watched.

"Ahem," begins Thompson, retracting his arms behind his back. "As you were."

Argo sets Maiella on her feet, and she puckers her mouth to contain the remnants of her laughter.

Making sure the people viewing them can hear, Thompson adds, "I won't have this kind of behavior on *my* watch." For an extra zing, he nudges both with his elbows.

Argo purses his lips and looks at Thompson with good-natured vengeance. Maiella replies to Thompson in an equally amplified voice, "Yes, of course, sir," then mouths silently, "*I'm going to get you ...*"

The three adopt a more military posture and resume their path down the corridor, nodding soberly at the technicians who spied them as they pass.

"I'm going to get clean," announces Thompson. "How about you two?"

"I'll be in after I brief Major Grissom," answers Argo.

"The download will only take a few minutes," says Maiella, "so I'll be right behind you."

Thompson nods. "All right. See you soon." The three split up and head off to their destinations.

Thompson strides into the Cadre Operator's rest and regeneration facility. Before him are several shower stalls, various rows of metal cabinets, and flat stainless steel tables with raised edges and a drain at one end.

Standing statue-like against the far wall are two humans, male and female. They are tall and appear physically fit, but they are shaved completely bald, their scalps ending at metal domes covering their craniums from the mid-forehead up. Dark lenses hide their eyes and are attached with wires which retreat beneath the metal caps. Both are dressed in white jackets, emblazoned with large numbers, and white slacks, immaculate and well pressed. Their arms hang rigidly to the side, save their right forearms which stick straight out, supporting a thick white towel.

Thompson halts before a deep and wide metal cabinet, unlocking the plates of his armor. The rush of fresh air immediately cools his sweaty skin and unleashes a hefty waft of perspiration. He turns his head from the noxious onslaught.

Working the close-fitting plates off one at a time, he sets them inside the cabinet. His undershirt, ordinarily light gray, is streaked with yellow. Finally, he works off the last of his plating, standing in his skintight under suit. The shirt he raises over his head, nearly gagging from olfactory overload.

"Gah!" he grimaces. Wadding it up, he searches for the laundry bin and shoots the shirt at it, easily hitting the mark. He does the same with his pants and strides to one of the shower stalls. His brawny physique is deeply cut with thick muscles, scarcely any trace of fat at all, and, like his face, bears myriad scars from slices, tears, perforations, and burns.

Closing the door to the stall, he punches the button and hot jets of water with detergent scrub him head to foot. He raises his arms, allowing the jets to work, enjoying the relaxing massage of water. Moments later, the jets cease and a great rush of warm air sweeps through the chamber, vacuuming the water down through the drain in the floor, whisking it off to the recycling system. Thompson stands in the stall, disappointed by the shower's brevity.

"Drone 316, towel."

The female drone steps stoically away from the wall and stands beside Thompson's stall. When he opens the stall door, she is waiting there, arm fully extended with the towel on the end of it. Thompson takes the towel and drags it all over himself, securing it at his waist. Drone 316 returns automatically, resuming her position at the wall.

Thompson stands in the cool air for a moment, steam rising off him, and chooses a table. He loosens the towel, draping it across himself as he lay facedown. Like someone would instruct a computer, Thompson calls out, "Drone 316, activate program: massage back and shoulders."

The female drone obediently steps away from the wall again, grabbing a small container along the way. Applying some of the container's contents to her hands, she begins kneading Thompson's back and shoulders. Tension dissipates as the rough knots and lumps from the mission are smoothed away.

The door to the facility whisks aside, and Thompson looks up to see who is joining him. Maiella smiles back, waving a hand. She hurriedly unlatches the plates of her armor, tossing them piece by piece into another cabinet. She, too, seems offended by her own odor and strips quickly.

Thompson peeks up at her as she strolls to her stall, taking in her lithe shape, strong limbs, deep striation, and numerous scars. He pays particular attention to the gold contact terminals on her head, studying them with interest. The shower jets blast again, followed by the familiar rush of air, and Maiella strolls out, no towel at all. Thompson watches her, resting his head on his broad arms.

"Wow ..." he says.

She smiles in appreciation, giving him a once-over as well. "Wow, yourself ..." She hops up on the table next to him and lies prone.

"Drone 317," she calls. "Activate program: massage back and shoulders, please." The male Drone steps away from the wall, grabbing a container of oil like the first and applies it. The drone works the oil into her aching muscles, and she groans with relief as her sinews unknot.

"Why do you always say *please* to the drones?" Thompson poses. "They're not sentient, you know."

Maiella shrugs. "I don't know. I guess I feel sorry for them."

Letting it go, he shakes his head, lying on the side of his face so he can look at her. He studies her gold contacts curiously. Maiella opens her eyes and sees him looking. She closes her eyes again. "What's on your mind?"

"I was looking at your HDI terminals ... Did they hurt going in?"

Maiella shrugs. "I don't remember. I was very small when I was inducted to systems ops ... I think I went to sleep and woke up this way, actually."

"I like the way they look ..." he starts. "They make you different from the others."

"Why, because all the newer Geeks get silver contact terminals instead of gold?"

"Mm, hmm."

She looks off into space. "I'd like to be able to grow my hair out more, but if I do, it gets in the way. I have to keep it pretty close."

"Well, I think it looks great."

"Yeah, you mentioned that," she smirks. Looking at the drone massaging Thompson, she asks, "How's your massage?"

"Not bad. Yours?"

"Okay." She frowns. "I think the program is incomplete."

"Oh?"

"Yeah." Maiella rolls on her side, facing Thompson. "They just don't have any *feel*. Drone 316, Drone 317, halt program!"

The drones take a step back and wait patiently. Maiella slips off the table, taking one of the drone's containers in hand. With the other hand, she zips Thompson's towel away.

"Hey!" he protests.

"Uh, uh," she counters. "I have a point to make. Now lie down."

Warily, Thompson complies.

"The massage program is pretty good, but it leaves out a very important part of the anatomy." Coating her hands with a liberal portion of oil, she slaps them hard on Thompson's rear. "The ass should *not* be overlooked."

"What are you doing?"

Maiella shushes him. "I'm giving you a *proper* massage." She uses a similar massage technique on his backside, and he wrinkles his face confusedly.

"There, isn't that better?" she coos.

"Yeah, I guess so ... ahh! HEY!"

Maiella's teeth are clamped securely into his cheek. He whirls over, making her lose her grip.

"I told you I'd get you back ..." she leers.

"Oh, I get it," he laughs. "You *save* my ass so you can sink your *teeth* into it?"

She looks impishly at him.

Thompson grins while shaking his head. "Once again, Maiella, you're right! The ass is very important ..." he begins and lunges for her. She tries to stiff-arm his assault, but her oily hands slide right across his chest. He gets her in his grip, wrestling her across his knee, finishing, "And should not be overlooked!"

Maiella cackles like a child, pleading with him to stop in between her tears of laughter. Just when he is about to give her another paddling, her thrashing upsets the container of oil on the table, and they both slip off the table to the floor, landing with a heavy thunk. The two rub their bruised parts ruefully and, catching sight of each other tangled in a heap, burst out into a whole new round of cackling.

The door to the facility slides open, and Argo steps into the room. His square jaw drops when he sees them piled on each other, looking up at him like mischievous kids that have been caught by a parent. He folds his huge arms in front of himself and smirks, just shaking his head.

Hard Times

Thompson's eyes flick open a second before his bunk-side alarm panel goes off. It only gets a couple of beeps out before he ends it with the edge of his hand. Sitting up in his bunk, he wipes the sleep from his eyes. The panel begins beeping again, and he looks at it curiously, large red letters flashing the word ORDERS.

After entering his identification number, an image of Colonel Thorskild appears.

"Captain Thompson, belay usual duty routine and report to my office by 0600."

As abruptly as it begins, it is done, and the panel flashes the word END in the same large red letters. Thompson contemplates the message and looks at the corner of the panel where the time reads 0530. Emerging from his bunk, he stands, stretches thoroughly, and performs a rigorous calisthenics routine, including one-handed push-ups in a handstand position, intricate yoga forms, and several rounds of shadow kickboxing.

When finished, he towels off the tiny amount of sweat and applies a fine powder to his body after which he dons his spotless charcoal gray uniform. From the choker collar bearing his rank to the blue-piped trousers to his polished black boots, he is immaculately dressed. Checking the bunk-side panel, he reads the time as 0555 and departs for the colonel's office.

He reaches his destination at the stroke of 0600 and buzzes for entry. From a small speaker beside the heavy door, the colonel's deep voice says, "Come."

The door slides aside, and Thompson steps through. Upon sight of the colonel, he stands at attention and salutes.

"As you were," Thorskild declares. He lifts his massive frame from behind his desk, walking around it to sit on the front edge. "Captain, I've got some bad news. Teams Strike, Thrust, Blade, Soar, Focus, and Talon have all been lost." Thorskild swings the monitor on his desk to face him. "Here is the video..."

The colonel gestures toward the screen, but Thompson does not respond—Thorskild's words have sunk like daggers into his chest. Thompson recalls everyone in those teams, all of whom he served with. The grim look of hard times descends over his face.

He tries to speak, but falters. Embarrassed by his emotion, he steels himself and says clearly, "Sir, that's exactly half of our Operator Corps."

The colonel looks Thompson over, noticing his emotion and how he choked it down. "Yes, they were... Their loss has injured us terribly."

"What about their DNA stored in the MedLabs?"

Thorskild shakes his head. "Cloning efforts seldom made it past initial meiosis. The embryos that did form were terribly mutated. Our genetics are so heavily modified now that cloning was a long shot anyway, and they didn't take. They are truly gone, son, and we can't bring them back."

Chagrinned, Thompson looks at his feet, wondering what to do. As hard as it was, resources were collected just at the rate they were needed; but now, how could they keep up? Out of the entire cadre of four hundred, there were only thirty-six who were free enough of incurable defects to enter the Operator Corps. The rest suffered from some combination of disability or deformity, and they could never survive the demands of collection rotations.

Now the number of able operators is cut in half. How will they maintain the flow of resources? Who will be available to properly train new operators? How will they recover from this? All these questions rise in his mind at once, but one question attains supremacy.

"How did it happen?"

The colonel looks down at the monitor on his desk. "Here is our best set of images. These two energy sources were our targets, large cargo vessels." He advances the video several frames. "Here, our teams intercepted as we can detect our signature interference patterns from all six virus ships in that vicinity." He advances the video further. "You can see the virus ships intercepting, three per vessel." Letting the video roll, the colonel points to the screen. "Now watch here, here, and here..."

To Thompson's astonishment, three more large energy sources appear, seemingly from nowhere. The colonel pauses the video.

"Moments after intercept," Thorskild continues, "these vessels, presumably military, appeared in formation. We have reviewed this data extensively and found no evidence of a space-time distortion or gravitational anomaly in the area, which means..."

"Those ships were already there..." Thompson finishes.

"That's right," acknowledges the colonel, appreciating Thompson's acumen. "We believe these new ships possess a means of concealing themselves, even while under way."

"So this was a trap?" guesses Thompson.

"We're sure of it." Thorskild sets the video back in motion. "Immediately after the new ships appeared, we detected six high-output explosions, which we recognize as our auto-destruct devices."

The view screen is washed nearly white from the tandem detonations, slowly fading in intensity.

"That blast triggered secondary explosions as you can see, and only two stable energy sources remain."

"Was our secrecy compromised?" asks Thompson apprehensively.

"We're confident it was not. The virus ships are designed to vaporize completely as well as incinerate anything in their proximity. Because the blast occurred so soon after intercept, we don't believe it's possible any of our operators or equipment were captured." The colonel pauses, becoming eerily bleak. "That must've been a difficult call for Zaius to make..."

Thompson can't help but remember how Zaius trained him, helped him, guided him. Thompson rose through the ranks quickly, mostly due to Zaius's expert direction. Eventually, they split the Operator Corps down the middle, each taking charge of six teams, enjoying the competition with each other to provide the most for the Cadre. Zaius regularly edged him out in that competition, his extra years of experience making him that much wiser. Knowing the man very well, Thompson gets a vivid mental picture of Zaius watching the trap close around him and sealing all eighteen fates with the order, "Self-terminate." The thought shakes him.

"Zaius was my instructor."

"Yes," responds Thorskild, "and he taught you well. Now you must take his place. Effective immediately, you are promoted to the rank of major and will assume command of the corps—responsible for all aspects of collection, training, and candidate selection. You will continue to report to me. Understood?"

"Yes, sir!" Thompson shifts his stance. "Colonel, if I am to be the sole administrator of operator affairs, I request two assistants."

Thorskild puts a hand to his chin pensively. "Very well," he concludes. "Review your operators and notify me of your selections."

"Sir, I choose Brick Argo and Geek Maiella."

The colonel looks up in surprise at the swift response. "Are you certain? There are other fine operators as well..."

"Positive, Colonel. Their strength amplifies my own, and mine, theirs."

Thorskild looks away, contemplating Thompson's quick choices. "Argo has a solid record... dependable, stalwart, effective. On him, I place no hesitance, but Maiella..." The colonel looks directly into Thompson's eyes. "She has shown emotionality that is... *inappropriate* for a cadre operator."

Thompson does not flinch. "I have served with Geek Maiella from my earliest days, and I have never seen her equaled in systems operation. I am aware of her difficulty managing emotion at times, but she has never allowed it to interfere with her performance or her duties. She is the best, sir, and my conscience can permit me no other choice."

Thorskild weighs Thompson's words carefully, searching Thompson's eyes for any trace of uncertainty and finding none. Though he never would have considered Maiella for a leadership position, Thompson's faith in her carries great influence with him.

"Done. Effective immediately, Brick Argo and Geek Maiella are both promoted to first lieutenant and will be your aides. These duties are, of course, in addition to their regular duties. I'll leave it to you to inform them."

"Thank you, sir."

"Now then," Thorskild relates as he stands and walks behind his desk, "the leadership council is going to convene at 1900 hours today to discuss our future strategy. Clearly, we cannot suffer another loss, so we must devise a plan quickly. Worry has permeated our people, and we need to restore their confidence. We would like your input at that meeting, Major."

Thompson nods, pleased to be involved. "Yes, sir! I'd be honored."

The colonel looks down into his seat then sets himself in it. He slides up to his desk, resting his sizeable elbows upon it. "The last piece of business I have for you is to bear this news to your teams. So that all of you could enjoy your R & R, we waited to inform you of our loss. When you inform your teams, do not reprimand any minor shows of emotion—none of us have ever been through such a tragedy, so allowances will be made this time. Let your strength be an example, son. Dismissed!"

Thompson salutes sternly, spins on his heel and departs, trying to comprehend and sort out everything racing through his mind. Just as he is about to feel overwhelmed, he inhales deeply and clears his mind, forcing himself to accept that his eighteen brothers and sisters in the corps are truly gone. Surges of grief assault him wave after wave, but his conditioning holds fast, the waves coming with less and less intensity each time. Then they appear before him: all eighteen faces form a revolving circle around him in his mind, mute and staring.

He rubs his throat, trying to smooth out the lump growing there. Now, each deep breath makes him feel more and more *out* of control as the memories spill through the emotional dams of his conditioning.

"They are gone," he says aloud, forcing himself to hear it in his own voice, forcing the realization home so he can get past it. His strides become longer, more purposeful. "*They are gone!*" he echoes fiercely, driving down the weight in his chest. Rubbing his face briskly with both hands, he feels the grief changing inside him. It is becoming something else.

"*They are* GONE!" he curses, his voice a growl, adrenaline flowing.

Fire ignites inside him, and his hands curl into fists. Rage makes his whole body shake, turning his face bright red. He shuts his eyes, and his mouth falls open into a silent scream. Halting in his tracks, he turns to the wall and throws himself against it, battering it with all of his might. The metal-clad wall thuds dimly, caving under his onslaught, absorbing the brunt of his anger as his calloused hands pound again and again. At last, the rage fades.

He props himself against the wall, staring at the dent he made in metal plating four centimeters thick, and he relaxes his aching fists. He straightens his posture and uniform, stepping to the closest communication panel. After a deep inhale and slow exhale, he is ready.

"Attention!" he calls through the intercom, a drop of blood seeping from one of his knuckles. "Brick Argo and Geek Maiella report to Gun Thompson's quarters immediately." Releasing the intercom button, he marches off to meet his teammates.

Thompson sits quietly at the edge of his bunk, watching the effect the news is having on his team. Argo kneels on the floor, hands on hips, head bent in sorrow. Maiella sits across a chair, leaning sideways against its back, and stares off into space. To the distance, she mumbles, "They just weren't good enough, is all…"

Argo and Thompson look over at her in shock, scarcely believing what she said. To emphasize her point, she stands and departs, leaving the two men staring confusedly at one another.

The door seals behind her, and Maiella looks up and down the corridor. No one is there. Still wearing the stony expression, she strides away. For a while, she maintains her stoicism, but the corners of her mouth won't maintain the façade. A lone tear forms in the corner of her eye. She wipes it away angrily.

Sniffing hard, she tries to regain her composure then loses the fight. Her face shatters and her legs buckle, dropping her to the floor. Tears pour, and it takes all of her strength not to wail. Panic grips her suddenly. She scans the hallways to make sure no one is watching. When she sees it is clear, another avalanche of anguish descends over her, her shoulders bouncing with muffled sobs.

A doorway opens behind her, and she jumps to her feet, walking quickly away. Thompson and Argo step into the corridor, calling after her.

"Maiella."

She blinks hard and lowers her head, squeezing out any remaining tears. Discretely wiping them away, she thinks, *They can't see me like this.*

"Maiella!"

She pretends not to hear, squelching any show of emotion well. By the time Argo and Thompson catch up to her, she has rebuilt her stone-faced expression. Thompson spins her around to look into her cold face.

"Maiella?"

"What is it?" she demands icily. "I have duties to attend."

Her performance is convincing, but Thompson sees right through it. He reaches out to put his arms around her.

"No!" she shouts and pushes off hard. Despite her strength she can not break his grip. He draws her in close, and Argo encircles them both. Maiella struggles to free herself, then gives up. Helpless in their strong arms, she bursts, letting it all go. The three stand in the hallway, unmoving, heads together, while Maiella sobs longingly for those she will never see again.

Securing a Future

Thompson takes a seat at the flat side of a large semicircular table. Filling out the rounded side is the Leadership Council. All the same faces are present, but the joviality is gone, replaced by grave determination. General Dryden opens the meeting.

"Major Thompson, thank you for joining us. The purpose of this meeting is to analyze the new threat to our operator crews and devise a strategy to counter that threat. Before we begin, have your teams been informed of our loss?"

"Yes, sir," Thompson answers.

"How did they take it?"

"Hard, General, but they are strong."

Dryden looks deeper. "Any decrease in productivity?"

"Initially, yes," Thompson begins, "but all understand it cannot be changed and are prepared for accelerated rotation."

"So soon?"

"They are strong, sir."

Dryden nods approvingly. "Good. We need them to be." He looks to his right. "Colonel Enyo?"

Enyo, her longer silver hair tied back from her angular face, leans forward in her seat and taps the console set into the table. A three-dimensional hologram projects up from the table's center, displaying some very hazily resolved ships in space. "Here is the reconnaissance from the event…"

With another tap, she sets the image into motion, playing the same video Thompson watched hours earlier. The distinct patterns of interference appear from the cadre virus ships, followed quickly by the appearance of three hazy oblong figures. Enyo freezes the image.

"This is our best resolution of these new vessels. They are roughly fifty percent larger than the vessel Major Thompson and his teams recently collected. After analyzing their energy outputs, configuration, and offensive posture, we have determined them to be warships. Major Thompson, have you ever encountered a vessel that could conceal itself in such a way?"

"No, ma'am, I have not," he replies.

Major Grissom looks over from the left edge of the table. "Is this a new technology, or could it be another species entirely?"

"Evidence points to your first suggestion, Major, that it is a new technology. The energy signatures and the basic form are very similar to vessels we have regularly monitored. Most likely, this is a new tactic to counter our assaults on them over the years. Unless we can overcome it, we will need to find a new source to gather from."

"But the only other traffic we have seen is what we *think* was a ship over three hundred times farther away, *in another direction*!" counters Grissom.

"And there is no evidence of another species to gather from out there," adds Thorskild. "With our reduced operator corps, not only would we be stretching out our collection rotations too much just going out and returning, they might not find anything when they get there."

The council breaks into murmuring among itself.

"What if we were able to capture such a ship?"

The leaders halt their buzzing, riveting their eyes on Thompson. General Dryden looks sternly at the new major, intrigued. Colonel Thorskild speaks first however.

"Major Thompson, we admire your ferocity; but as you saw, this ambush destroyed *half* of our operator teams. We *cannot* allow the loss of any others. The most vital resources on this rock were depleted centuries ago—we *must* protect our gathering ability!"

The council members all nod in agreement, except the general who puts a hand to his chin.

Thompson considers the Thorskild's words carefully.

"There is no question that you are correct, Colonel Thorskild. Our teams must endure and be rebuilt if we are to survive." Gesturing to the video, he continues, "The reason our teams were lost is because they were ambushed. They could not have anticipated this threat. We can, and we understand its potential."

General Dryden rubs his chin as he listens. "What's on your mind, Thompson?"

Thompson breathes in and out purposefully. "What if *we* set an ambush?"

The murmuring begins again, but more thoughtfully this time. Dryden silences them by leaning forward and asking, "You have a plan?"

"Do we have a ship of little use, say, one of the earliest freighters we collected? We could attach our virus ships to its hull and deploy to deep space. Once sufficiently distant from our home, we could activate its transponder beacon. The virus ships would detach and wait nearby."

"What we've seen of the blueskins proves they are highly intelligent," argues Grissom. "No doubt, they'd be suspicious of one of their missing ships appearing out of nowhere after hundreds of years. They'd assume a trap."

"I agree, Major," states Thompson, "and that's what I am counting on. First, I don't believe they could resist the opportunity to investigate a ship they believed was lost or destroyed so long ago. Second, assuming a trap, they are likely to send their best weapons to be ready." Thompson scans the faces in front of him. "Until recently, our methods have been sufficient to capture nonmilitary vessels. Now these vessels are being escorted, and we should risk capturing more military targets if we are going to continue collecting successfully."

From the far right edge of the table, Major Eris chimes in, "I see where you're going with this. It's an opportunity to counter this new threat to our operator teams and gain a heavier punch when we encounter something unexpected. The enemy is getting seasoned by our attacks, and if we don't adapt, it won't matter how many operators we have. They won't be coming home again."

"I see your point, Major Eris," concedes Grissom, "and I think you and Thompson are right. But if they are invisible, how would we detect them to attack?"

"The video shows the ships demasking before engaging our operator teams," explains Enyo. "It is likely, therefore, that any such vessel would demask before interacting with our bait ship..."

Grissom finishes the statement for her, "At which point, our teams could engage and capture." The murmuring resumes.

General Dryden tents his hands. "That's very creative, Thompson, but suppose they use the same tactic as before—suppose they send in nonmilitary vessels to process the bait freighter while the stealth ships remain masked. If your teams attacked the nonmilitary vessels, the stealth ships could ambush just as before. If no attack is made, we lose the freighter and have wasted precious gathering time."

The heightened energy in the room ebbs, and Thompson looks down in thought; then his head springs up suddenly. "We'll use a double decoy!"

The council members look at each other with skepticism as Thompson explains.

"We'll need a decoy virus ship as well. We can program it to attach to any vessel that approaches within a certain distance. If a masked ship is present, it should reveal itself to combat the dummy attack. Then our teams can move in and capture."

General Dryden smiles. "So how many operators will you need, Major?"

"For best chance of success? All of us."

Council members launch into heated "no's!" and "out of the question's!" rejecting the thought outright, save Dryden, who silently considers it. Thompson watches him, shifting his view occasionally to the others still arguing among themselves, but focusing on the general, waiting to see what his decision will be. Before long, the arguments at the table end; and like Thompson, the council members look to Dryden, curious what he will decide. Once all is quiet, the general looks up from his contemplation.

"We have set a dangerous precedent: the attacks on our ancient enemy escalate in cost for both sides. Our only advantage lies in our anonymity—they must continue to believe they were successful in their genocide nine hundred years ago. If they were to discover that humans still live, and how few we number, we could not last long.

"I knew our successful collection rotations would not go on forever without setback. The enemy has adapted, and unless we learn about their new capability, every operator we send out faces unacceptable odds. We must act quickly to counter their new advantage. Thompson's plan is bold and shrewd, but if the enemy arrives in force, we do not have enough teams to engage more than three such vessels. To try would be a level of risk I will not accept. The choice I make now is unsettling, but we are in a corner, and waiting can only harm us. We will proceed with Major Thompson's plan."

Dryden scans his peers, taking in the damage his words have caused. Dismay is emblazoned on several faces. To their credit, none of them argue, and they set their resolve to implement his decision. When he is sure he has their complete attention again, he continues.

"A contingency will be added to this plan, however, should more than three stealth ships appear. We will make the bait ship a bomb. If there are too many enemy ships to engage, we can detonate, disabling or destroying as many of the enemy ships as possible. The confusion will allow us the initiative, and resistance will be uncoordinated. Worst case, if there are still too many active ships to engage, the teams will be ordered to slip away quietly and return to base. Because they will ride out on the bait ship, they will be fully fueled and can make the return voyage.

"Now I agree that the best chance comes with the most teams attending, so all teams will go *except yours*, Thompson. Under *no* circumstance will I risk *all* of our gathering capability, and I choose to retain the best for future training of initiates. *That is not negotiable, Major, so drop that look of protest you're putting on.* You, Brick Argo, and Geek Maiella will resume rotations in a new sector away from the blueskins. With any luck, you'll find something we can use."

Turning to his right, Dryden asks, "Colonel Enyo, how long would you need to produce a decoy virus ship?"

Enyo shrugs. "It wouldn't be hard to strip out the major components and rig it with a simple program. Four continuous four-man shifts... 320 man-hours... four days roughly."

Turning to his left, the general asks, "Colonel Thorskild, how long would you need to prep that old ore hauler we mothballed and rig it for large-scale detonation?"

Thorskild raises his eyebrows. "She's pretty far from space worthy, General. The only system I know is still functional is the main reactor, and that's supplementing power to genetics and incubation."

Dryden nods in understanding. "The only other systems we'll need will be propulsion and navigation."

"And for the loss in power to genetics and incubation?" wonders Grissom.

The general cranes his head to face the major at the end of the table. "We'll have to skim from ore processing. If Thompson is right, the freighter his teams captured is loaded with ore to the hilt. So hopefully, it won't impact us too severely over the long run." Turning back to face Colonel Thorskild, Dryden continues, "Now then, we patch up the old freighter's engines and navigation. What would we need to build a blast radius big enough for Thompson's plan to work?"

Thorskild looks at Enyo for confirmation. "I'd say, roughly, a nine-gigaton yield to provide an adequate assurance of success." Enyo nods in accordance.

"Whew," Eris whistles. "We'd have to yank cores from just about every ship we've collected and fuse them together!"

The whole council looks at Eris, silently endorsing her idea. The look of astonishment on her face fades as she realizes her argument *against* the idea is now on the table as a likely plan of action. "Wait, wait." She backpedals. "I wasn't suggesting we do that! The reactor cores on some of those ships have chewed through their shielding, and it's only the radioactive corrosion that's holding them together. Just *looking* at them could make them unstable!"

Thompson brings a hand to his chin, considering the dilemma. "The oldest ships are the smallest ones," he reasons, "because that's all we could effectively capture in the earliest days. So what if we park them inside the freighter? With careful piloting, we wouldn't disturb the reactor cores."

Thorskild smiles at the idea. "Yes," he ruminates. "Those ships aren't much good to us anyway because of their contamination, and the freighter is spacious—they should fit easily enough."

"It's going to leave us with serious power shortages however," adds Enyo. "Most of those ships are linked to the cadre grid. Take them away, and we lose a quarter of our energy."

"Understood," acknowledges Dryden. "I will determine which facilities require priority and delegate to each accordingly. Colonel Enyo, begin outfitting Major Thompson's virus ship for an extended long-range flight. It will require some unique power storage solutions, and the cryogenic systems will need some enhancement. Select whoever you need from the technical caste to work on this project, and I will authorize their transfer of duties.

"Colonel Thorskild, Major Grissom, and Major Eris, begin restoration of the old freighter for flight, and coordinate the piloting of the old ships plus core removal and transfer from the other vessels. Do you have an estimate on time required?"

Colonel Thorskild thinks for a moment. "Providing everything goes well, I estimate that with sixty workers, twelve continuous shifts, 14,400 man-hours... roughly ten days under the best circumstances."

The general frets at the requirement of personnel, wondering if he can afford to pull so many from their regular tasks. Cadre One is old, he realizes, requiring huge amounts of maintenance just to hold together. Relaxing the amount of attention it gets, even over ten days, carries its own risks.

"It must be so. Select your people, and I will authorize their transfer of duties." Dryden looks front to address Thompson.

"Your input at this meeting was invaluable, Major. Over the next four days, you will run new simulations with Brick Argo and Geek Maiella to anticipate problems you may encounter with extended cryo-sleep. Be ready to depart as soon as Colonel Enyo's team has finished modifying your virus ship. You are dismissed."

Thompson stands and snaps a crisp salute. With a half step back, he about-faces and marches out of the chamber, trying hard to suppress the disappointment of being excluded from his own plan.

THE BECKONING ABYSS

Thompson, Maiella, and Argo march purposefully toward the engineering bay. Clad in heavy armor and bulging with equipment, they sound as if a whole platoon is on parade. Their helmets are cradled in their left arms; their right arms swing in unison. The gravest determination rides on their brows, setting their expressions with fearsome intent.

At their approach, the bay doors slide aside, unleashing a cacophony of welding, grinding, and drilling. The trio marches through without missing a step.

Inside, the air is thick with the scent of industry, hot with electricity, dry from smoke. At the center of it all is a perfectly black craft, like a two-dimensional hole in existence. Roughly fifteen meters long, the blackness tapers to a point in front; and slopes up to a rounded tail with four spidery legs suspending it from the deck. At the stern, a large metal brace holds the silhouette open as technicians load a new piece of machinery. Kneeling atop the craft, more technicians weld bulbous plates into place, and the sparks cascade down the invisible contours, raining off the virus ship's light absorbing edges.

Colonel Enyo, supervising the technicians from a distance, notices the three entering and shouts above the din to them.

"Team Spectre! Over here!"

Gun, Brick, and Geek halt and look left to address their superior officer as she approaches, saluting respectfully. Enyo looks them over, scrutinizing the appearance of their charcoal armor, the condition of their weapons, and the fit of their attached gear. Satisfied, she briefs them.

"The modifications to your virus ship will be complete within the next ten minutes. I summoned you now because it will take that long to prep your flight. First, I'll explain the enhancements." Enyo turns on her booted heel, walking toward the blackened ship, and the three follow obediently. Patting the craft with her palm, she continues, "The first thing you should notice are these bulges here, here, and here. Since we are sending you out into unexplored space, we needed to upgrade your sensing ability. We don't know what you might run into, so we wanted to give the nav computer plenty of warning of any hazards in the flight path." The colonel strides toward the tapered end of the craft.

"Because your mission will be unlike attacking the well-established commerce routes of the blueskins, you'll need to be able to monitor a large volume of empty space, or something could slip by. That is why we had to flare this section of the hull to accommodate the upgraded sensor apparatus and processors."

"Sir," asks Maiella, "will these hull modifications affect the reflectivity of the craft to sensor sweeps?"

"No," answers Enyo. "The invisibility of the craft is maintained." She stoops to walk beneath the craft, crossing to the other side, and again the team follows.

"Over here," she points out, "is additional hardware to supplement your cryogenic systems. We anticipate your rotation could be up to twenty times longer than normal, and therefore, you will require more adequate preservation."

"How long can these systems maintain our frozen state before breakdown occurs?" asks Argo.

"Theoretically? Indefinitely," the colonel replies. "Additionally, the metabolic support and wake-up times are greatly improved, allowing you to react faster to threats or potential targets."

"Has the effect of extended cryo-sleep been studied by the medical caste?" Argo queries.

"It has, and the projections show a high probability of survival despite the stresses."

"How high?" asks Thompson.

Enyo looks directly into their faces. "Within an operator's tolerances."

The three tighten their jaws, understanding the painful misery they will undoubtedly face, awakening from such a long freeze.

Enyo walks toward the back of the craft, sidestepping a descending stream of sparks and gestures toward the machinery being shoehorned into the craft's stern. "We have modified the propulsion using some of the technology from your most recent capture. It is more efficient and sixty percent faster, which will permit you to pursue targets if they take evasive action." The colonel continues her path around the ship.

"The next modification was the skin of the craft itself. Because a non-reflective surface quickly builds up heat, we were forced to ambush from the edges of solar systems. We have greatly enhanced this craft's ability to convert that absorbed energy into usable or storable energy, expanding your theater of operations to within two astronomical units of a class-A star or smaller."

"Excellent," remarks Thompson. With his freehand, he reaches up to feel the edge of his craft, appreciating its new versatilities. Like his rifle, this ship is a trusted companion, serving faithfully through every difficult mission. It has been frequently modified, though never so radically. He pushes against the dark surface, wondering how all of the new additions will integrate, already preparing for the possibility of their breakdown.

He looks away from the ship and scans the bay, watching his cadre brothers and sisters toiling despite their handicaps. Never once has he questioned how hard they work to support him and his teams; the quality of their efforts and the durability of their designs have made the difference in many decisive moments in his past. His doubt shames him, and faith restores his confidence. He retracts his hand, satisfied.

Enyo moves beneath the craft again, stooping below the main hatch.

"In anticipation of thicker, armor-plated hulls, we have enhanced the cutting depth and power of the laser drills." She pulls out a small remote and taps it. Three small plates around the hatch shift aside, and the barrels of the laser drills drop to cutting position. She taps another sequence, and the drills shift, lowering themselves to the deck. Condensed vapor rolls off them, partially obscuring the rugged construction and wiring.

"We used some of the weapon technology from the military ship you captured in these drills. Energy output is tripled. The superconducting elements are more reliable over elevated temperatures, and beam focusing is far better than before. Even with such a short focal length, optimum beam width is maintained at a distance of several thousand kilometers. If necessary, you can use these as a weapon battery to attack although it would likely be more useful to assist you in escape."

Argo nods approvingly.

Enyo taps the remote, and the drills recede into the belly of the craft. With another keystroke, the main hatch opens like a camera iris.

"It's time," the colonel says.

Thompson nods in acknowledgement. "Maiella! You're up."

Donning her helmet, she duck walks over and stands up into the hatch, easily hauling herself up. From inside, there is a fair amount of clanking from her hurried storage of gear and weapons. After a minute, she calls out. "All gear stowed. I'm in position. Load next operator."

Thompson slaps Argo on the shoulder. Argo throws his helmet over his big head and shuffles to the hatch. Crouching low, he raises his arms and leaps up into the hole, disappearing entirely. More clanking ensues, and the craft sways under his bulk. Thompson starts to move into position, but Enyo grabs his arm. He looks back questioningly, and she is staring at the floor. Looking up suddenly, her eyes are pleading. "Bring them home safe, son."

Thompson looks back silently, taking her plea as his foremost command. Calling up into the craft, he orders, "Maiella, begin preflight, all systems."

"Aye, sir," Maiella replies.

Thompson turns back to face Enyo, regarding her solemnly. "There's no other option."

Enyo extends her right hand toward him, the way an arm wrestler would present a challenge to an opponent. Thompson clasps it firmly in his armored grip; and the two pull each other close together, putting their left hands gently behind the other's neck, touching their foreheads together. After a moment of silence, they pull apart, left hands sliding from the neck down to the shoulder.

From inside the craft comes Argo's deep voice. "All gear stowed. I'm in place. Load next operator."

With difficulty, Enyo and Thompson release each other, and he duck walks to the hatch. Throwing his helmet on, he takes a last look at Enyo. "We'll see you soon," he says and leaps inside.

Maiella is in her recliner on the starboard side, already hardwired into the ship's consoles. Her goggles flash with various diagnostic commands and start-up sequences. Argo is delicately maneuvering himself in the restricted space, settling into his own recliner on the port side, punching up data on his console. Thompson unslings his rifle and snaps it into its cradle on the close ceiling. His gear he removes piece by piece, snapping it all into place above his recliner. Once stripped to his armor, he slides into his recliner between them, pulling a console across his lap. Tapping rapidly, Thompson pulls up a basic diagram of the ship's functions.

"Geek, status of navigation and propulsion," he calls out.

"Start-up nearing completion, deep space drive sixty-five percent to operating temperature. Sensors online... navigation systems online... calibrating..." she answers.

"Brick, status of metabolic support and cryogenic systems?"

"Performing full-system diagnostics..." Argo answers. "Gun, lean back in your recliner, please... there... full monitoring and metabolic interface achieved. Verifying life support and fail-safes..."

"Testing interference generators, communications, and laser drill functionality," Thompson announces. His console shows multiple bars, all full and green. Activating his helmet microphone, he hails the base. "Cadre One, this is Team Spectre proving comm link prior to departure. Respond, over."

"Team Spectre, this is Cadre One," the radio buzzes. "Read you loud and clear. What is status of vessel, over?"

"Completing preflight start-ups and diagnostics," Thompson replies. "Team secure in recliners, fully interfaced." Behind him, a whirring sound rises in pitch.

"Main engine has reached operating temperature," advises Maiella. "Navigation fully calibrated and updated."

"Life-support systems fully operational, metabolic management and cryogenic systems one hundred percent," states Argo.

Thompson finishes his diagnostics. "Cadre One, all green bars, ready for stars, over."

"Received, Team Spectre. Clearing bay of personnel. Proceed toward external bay doors and await launch command, over."

Thompson taps his console, bringing up a small holoscreen in front of him showing the forward view from the ship. Smaller screens open beside the large one, displaying side and rear views. In the screens, Thompson watches the technicians finish their last welds and scramble for the exits. Throughout the bay, red lights flash in warning.

"Take us to the door, Geek," he instructs.

"With pleasure." Maiella's goggles flash, and the vessel smoothly walks forward on its limbs toward the large bay doors. Once there, Maiella halts the ship. "Cadre One, we are in position. Request permission to depart, over."

"Team Spectre, bay air pressure is equalizing. Stand by."

The three operators sit calmly in their recliners. Nothing feels any different about this mission—it's simply out into an unexplored region of space, no more or less important than any of the rotations they have been through. If anything, they feel a slight amount of boredom.

Thompson double-checks the ship while he waits, ensuring everything is as it should be. Nothing is out of line, all systems seem to be integrating seamlessly.

"Team Spectre, pressure is equalized, opening bay doors. Stand by."

In Thompson's view screen, the large metal doors slide apart, causing a tiny puff of dust to rise from the crater floor outside.

"Team Spectre, you are cleared for departure, over."

"Cadre One," Maiella replies, "Team Spectre is departing engineering bay, en route to collection rotation." She engages the mechanical legs again, walking the ship out into the crater. The ship crouches low to the ground, then with full extension, leaps high into the infinite sky. With skillful coordination, she ignites thrusters and retracts the legs into the body of the ship. The thrusters carry them above the crater rim, and the view whites out momentarily from the massive blue-white star nearby. As the screen adjusts, they find themselves near the old mothballed freighter, now a hive of activity.

Numerous ships cluster in various stages of assembly and disassembly around the ancient freighter, dulled and tarnished by centuries of solar radiation. Shuttles buzz to and fro, ferrying parts and laborers.

Muting his helmet microphone, Thompson scowls.

"That's where we ought to be..."

Argo and Maiella look over at him, nodding wordlessly in agreement.

Continuing their ascent, Thompson catches sight of the gleaming warship he and his teams recently collected. It stands a lonely guard over the huge operation at a significant distance. Seeing it further vexes him that after all the good he has done for the cadre, he should be excluded from the most important mission the cadre has ever undertaken. *Any operator would be qualified to take this mission out to deep space*, he reasons. Yet brooding will change nothing. General Dryden has given his orders, and they must be obeyed. Period.

"We have achieved minimum safe distance to engage deep space drive," alerts Maiella.

"Very well. Lock in navigational coordinates." Reactivating his helmet microphone, Thompson hails base. "Cadre One, we are ready to depart. Note date and time of mission start, over."

"Team Spectre, time and date noted in mission log..." The voice becomes more personal. "Bring us something good, okay? Cadre One out."

"We always do. Team Spectre out." Thompson kills his helmet microphone and looks over at Maiella. "Let's do it."

Her goggles flash with calculations and engine controls. "Three...

two... one... Mark."

The ship's drive surges, and the craft leaps forward into the abyss.

THE ARMS OF SOMNUS

Something is beeping.

Thompson is barely aware of it, yet an urgent, repeating tone draws him through the murky folds of slumber, carving through his blunted senses to find consciousness within.

The sound is a beacon, a singularity in the distance, summoning him, reeling him toward it. It gets closer, stronger, clearer. He cracks open one eye.

The smeared red glare of a flashing diode assaults his vision and blinks in synch with the tone, its color conveying the same urgency as the sound. He strains to focus, and the thick fog of his eyes recedes to a haze, giving the light a halo with each flash.

As his sight clears, he squints at a cramped cockpit, every centimeter covered in frost. The red light continues to flash in unwavering tempo, its light refracted by the crystals of ice around it. He can feel the iris of his eye dilating and constricting as his eyes adjust, and he notices more lights around the cockpit in random locations, all red or deep orange.

The dim light softly bathes the area, and he takes in his mysterious surroundings.

What is this place?

Disorientation swallows him whole. He searches for clues around him, noticing first his legs extending away from him. He cannot feel them. With tremendous effort, he turns his stiff neck to each side, finding two other people in the space with him, frost still covering their bodies.

Who are they?

At once, the numbness yields to biting cold, sending spasms down his length. He sits amid the twitches and jerks of his own sinews, now hearing something loudly clacking together. He discovers it is his teeth.

Thompson tries to focus on the flashing red diode on the console before him.

"Gith-ththhts—tgh geh..." His own voice is unrecognizable as he slurs through syllables, attempting to voice-command the console. Rather, he gropes dumbly with his right hand, flopping his armored fist into various buttons. Grazing the bright flashing one, a small holoscreen opens in front of him.

PROXIMITY ALERT. PROXIMITY ALERT, it reads over and over.

Thompson recoils from the bright white letters, shrinking back in his recliner. His head sways loosely on his shoulders, and he blinks to recover equilibrium. Once steady, he peers at the holowindow, making out the letters for the first time, understanding their meaning. In a rush, his mission returns to him. He remembers where he is and who the others are. Adrenaline mixes with the antifreeze in his bloodstream, propelling him from stupor. The clacking of his teeth subsides as do the violent shivers, being replaced by a sensation of warmth blooming along his spine. The blissful warmth is short-lived, however, as millions of chilled nerve endings awaken simultaneously, igniting an inferno beneath his skin.

He throws his head back, unable to contain a long bellow of agony as pain builds upon searing pain until he is sure every neuron in his body is on fire. His muscles clench involuntarily, his eyes squeezing tears through their corners, his brain disbelieving the quantity of pain. Like a slow tide, the intensity ebbs, his whole body aching and throbbing.

Fighting through the haze and disorientation, he forces himself to look at the holowindow in front of him with watery eyes. Feeling more in control, he reaches out to the console and taps some keys, highlighting the distant object on screen. Further magnifying the image, he finds a ship larger than he could ever have imagined. Thompson studies the details of its hull, looking for clues to its origin, guessing if it could be a blueskin vessel or some other species entirely. From his vantage, he can see no external markings, just multitudes of scorches and dents. The ship looks poorly maintained, almost shoddy, and ancient.

Thompson reaches to the panel again, but his left arm will not move. He casts an annoyed glance at it and discovers it is still covered in a layer of frost. Taking a deep breath, he returns to the console, entering in the commands to pursue the giant vessel with one hand. When he strikes the execute key, the entire cockpit goes black.

Thompson's eyes stretch wide in shock, searching the darkness. The silence is complete. He realizes he is holding his breath, and he lets it out, the sound of his elevated heartbeat thumping in his ears. In another moment, a panel of lights switches on, then another, eventually resuming the dim red illumination; and a low hum rises in pitch when the engines, at last, come online. Thompson's relief is immediate, but in its wake is a serious concern: with triple redundancy built into every system, there should never have been a power failure.

"Ar-r-rgo," Thompson begins, "have a l-l-look at the power systems, and... Argo?"

The Brick's still-frosted body offers no response. Thompson looks over at Maiella, and he finds her encased in frost as well. He blinks hard, not daring to ask what else could go wrong.

With his one thawed arm, he reaches to the console, calling up schematics and diagnostics of his modified craft; and he is immediately aware of a considerable lag in the computer's operation. Several seconds pass from when he enters a command to when he sees it enacted on-screen. It seemed the system was running fine before the power failure... or was it that *he* was working just as slowly as he thawed? Waving off the irrelevant dilemma, he impatiently waits for the screen to load diagrams of the main power systems on board. Every part of it displays critical failures: primary and auxiliary power, the passive collectors, even the batteries.

His face curled with confusion, he tries to lift his left arm, already forgetting it is still frozen. A powerful twinge in his shoulder where the thawed and chilled sections meet reminds him. He grips his shoulder protectively and reaches for the console to bring up a diagnostic of the three recliners. After many long seconds, the three diagrams appear side by side on-screen. Maiella's and Argo's diagrams read, WITHIN TOLERANCES, despite the abnormally low levels of power flowing to their recliners. In his own diagram, the recliner indicates a problem in his left arm. He wrinkles his brow at the information and enlarges the image of the main inflow/outflow tubes. At the outflow nozzle on his left wrist, the computer has detected a blockage, stopping the flow of antifreeze.

Thompson looks from the screen down to the corresponding outflow tube. With his right hand, he reaches over to it and twists it off easily. Like the computer diagnosed, nothing flows out. He looks back to the console, tapping some keys, increasing the flow pressure. Immediately, a cloudy, gelatinous clog is booted out, and clear fluid seeps across his frosted armor. He replaces the outflow tube and watches the frost on his arm sublimate. In a minute, his arm is loose; and he lifts it from the cradle, flexing it gingerly. First comes the warmth, then the fiery burning, and finally it moves normally.

With the use of both hands, he types much faster, poring over diagnostics of his companions' sleep recliners. His breakfast seeps in through the many connected tubes and hoses in his armor, feeding him nutrients and the neurochemical equivalent of a hyper-caffeinated espresso. His foggy mind clears, permitting him better thought, and he digs through the craft's systems attempting to troubleshoot the power problem. Try as he might, however, he finds no answer. The solar collectors are supplying only a trickle of power, the main energy source is not functioning, and the batteries are nearly drained.

Thompson glances at the distant ship he is pursuing and pressure builds. He can't cut the engines. If he loses this target, another may never present itself. He can't cut life support. To do so would doom his teammates to the gory death of an improper thaw.

In a snap decision, he starts flipping off circuit breakers: navigation, communication, interference generation and countermeasures, grappling arms, computer-assisted maneuvering— every system not immediately tied in to pushing the ship toward their quarry or unfreezing his crew. The lighted panels in the cabin go dark as each system is switched off, and the remaining lights glow brighter. With the reduced draw of the additional systems, the power bars for Argo's and Maiella's recliners climb out of red to amber.

"Initiate awakening, recliner 1 and recliner 3," he commands in a steady voice, and the whirring of pumping fluids resounds in the quiet cabin.

The lines of frost retreat from their faces, tracing down over their torsos, then out to their extremities. Monitoring the process closely, he watches the power draw; and just when it looks as if it is going to bottom out, he diverts power from his own recliner to see the process through.

Maiella sputters and coughs violently with harsh neural stimulation, then gasps with breath. Thompson anticipates her disorientation.

"You are aboard a virus ship on a collection rotation. I am Gun Thompson."

Maiella peels herself up from her recliner. Her back arches, arms back, and her mouth falls open in a silent scream, too painful to vocalize.

On the opposite side, Argo lifts his thick head and stiffly cranes it around, trying to cope with the unfamiliar surroundings. Then, he grips the rails beside him like a vice, shaking with the intensity of his burning nerves. He tucks his chin into his chest, tears streaming from his tightly shut eyes, a fierce growl his only utterance.

Thompson busies himself with the ship ahead, monitoring his craft's engines, and making minor course corrections manually. Beside him, Argo sits up in his recliner, holding his head in his hands. He heaves several times and coughs again then settles. He squints at Thompson, seeking answers.

"Wha-huppond?" he slurs.

"Power loss," Thompson replies. "I've diverted power from other systems to revive and sustain us."

"Kun-tact?" he asks, shivering.

"Affirmative," answers Thompson, "contact dead ahead, unidentified vessel, 1,200 meters long, 600 meter beam."

Argo blinks sluggishly. "Big-un."

Thompson nods in agreement. "Lie back, Brick. Let the metabolic support bring you up to speed." The huge man leans back into his recliner sleepily.

Not hearing anything from Maiella, Thompson looks over to see how she is doing. She is lying back, both hands up at the sides of her face, and her goggles pulse intermittently as she tries to reboot.

"Geek... ?" Thompson calls.

She persistently tries again and again, but no matter which method she uses, it brings the same result. Maiella drops her hands to her side, staring at the message repeatedly displayed on the inside of her goggles: NEURAL INTERFACE FAILURE.

"I'm damaged..." she announces despondently.

Argo, already more animated, pulls up his console and selects Maiella's recliner in his holowindow. "Stay hooked in a minute, Maiella, I'm going to check you out."

"Two minutes thirty to intercept," announces Thompson.

While Maiella lies patiently, Argo sifts through her implanted hardware from his console, zeroing in quickly on the trouble spots. What he finds is that almost all of her contact neurons have receded or atrophied away from their connections. With all of his medical expertise, he is still puzzled.

"Your synaptic bridges have retreated... You won't be able to interface any systems at all."

Maiella stares straight up, exhaling with exasperation. "Perfect. I was worried this rotation would be easy."

Argo looks over Thompson's physical diagnostic and notices his arm is still a few degrees cooler than the rest of him.

"How's your arm, Gun?"

Thompson swings his arm in a narrow circle at the shoulder. "A little stiff, but I'm fine. Two minutes to intercept. Geek, take over manual piloting."

"Sir!" she responds and accesses her console.

Once his two comrades have had their intravenous cocktail of nourishment and stimulants, Thompson shuts down all life support on board. "Switch to rebreathers," he orders, and they pull their helmet masks down over their faces. With a hiss, they lock tight.

"Argo, ready the laser drills and grappling limbs."

"What about interference generators?" he asks via helmet radio.

"No. Not enough power." Pushing away his console, Thompson disconnects the multiple inflow/outflow hoses connected to his armor and grabs his rifle from its cradle above. With automated precision, he checks it, loads it, and powers it up.

"Argo, are those systems ready?"

"Laser drills coming online... capacitors filling... grappling limbs standing by..."

"Gear up!" Thompson demands.

Argo quickly clears the tubes from his armor and grabs his heavy weapon from its storage cradle. Thompson reaches over to Maiella and clears her tubes for her as she guides the craft closer to their target. "Sound off equipment check... power armor?"

"Check."

"Check."

"Rebreather?"

"Check."

"Check."

"Helmet infrared displays?"

"Check."

"Check."

"Mission hardware?"

"Complete," states Argo.

"Compromised," states Maiella.

"Weapons?"

"Locked and loaded."

"Locked and loaded."

Thompson clears his lungs and fills them again. "We have never seen these creatures before, and they have never seen us. We will have the advantages of initiative and surprise, but because we can't jam their transmissions, we'll have to move *very* fast. That means risks. Geek, can you determine where the control center of that ship is located?"

"I can make a good guess and put us right next to it," she replies confidently.

"Good. Brick and I will assist you in locking down the ship computer systems. If we can't lock them down, we may have to destroy them to keep radio silence." Maiella and Argo nod in understanding, leading into an uneasy stillness. Thompson breaks it abruptly. "I'm not losing *either* of you today. *Is that clear?*"

Argo nods. "That was my understanding, sir."

"I'm with you both," Maiella adds. "Nothing touches us today."

The craft's engines fire again, and it decelerates starkly. With a resounding jolt, the craft lands on the target's hull, and the whine of cutting lasers shrieks to life.

"Clear restraints!" shouts Thompson above the noise, and all three debelt at once. Thompson presses his rifle butt into his shoulder, gritting his teeth. Adrenaline surges through him as his features form into the hard look of murder.

Maiella leans forward on her recliner and snatches her pistols from their cradles, flicking the safeties off with her thumbs. Rows of caseless ammunition clips stand like thick bristles on her armored thighs, ready to be slapped into an empty pistol with a simple wrist snap. Her eyes lock on to the exit hatch, and her boots scrape against the cold metal deck like a racehorse in a stall. She takes great gulps of air, limbering up reflexively, and pushes her consciousness to the back of her mind. Her lips curl away from her teeth in a sneer, the blackness of her eyes more demonic than human.

Argo hauls his weapon into his lap and drops his chin to his chest. His eyes narrow to slits and he stares through his eyebrows at the hatch before him, ready to charge like a bull. His respiration escalates, every breath carrying a growl. His cheeks flare with the rush of air past them, and his brow furrows with menace.

All three have left humanity behind. The cadre conditioning and genetic modifications have perfected in them the essence of anima and violence without conscience, producing living machines of the narrowest purpose. There is no thought at all, only training and instinct. Nothing of who they are is recognizable. What once was Argo, Maiella, and Thompson is now Brick, Geek, and Gun.

The whining of drills abates, and the hatch explodes open. Gun leaps into the smoke, followed closely by Brick and Geek. Glowing infrared images appear before them, swiftly folding and lurching as they are cut down by expert shots. A mottled cluster of creatures runs behind a heavy door and seals it, but Brick levels his cannon and triggers. The door shatters in its middle, blasting inward, shredding all who had taken refuge behind it.

Geek sprints up the corridor through the billowing smoke; her machine pistols echoing along the way—*brrrrrrak-ak, brrrak-kak.*

Gun runs up behind her and takes the lead, sniping every moving heat source he sees, his rifle loudly panging with every shot.

Brick keeps pace with them running backward, blasting anything behind them. With no time to clear every corridor, the trio bolts flat out for the control center, guided by Geek's one-word directions. To their surprise, they don't see any other creatures about.

The race ends when Gun jogs to a halt before a large round blast door. Geek and Brick lope up behind, fluids splattered all over them. Brick steps past Gun, immediately setting to work on the door. He punches it savagely three times, and it bends a bit, but doesn't yield.

"Find cover," he instructs. Geek and Gun scramble around a corner and lie prone. Brick pulls a block from his belt and slaps it on the blast door. With a precursory turn of a dial, he sets the timer and runs past Geek and Gun, diving to the deck just as the device detonates.

With a deep roar, the blast sweeps the team in flame and debris, shuddering the corridor violently. The three leap to their feet and run to the door, seeing a large split down its middle. Gun aims through the split while Brick grabs on to the glowing hot metal, peeling it apart with hands and feet. When too hot to keep his grip, he kicks and punches the split apart. Gun arcs through the gap, somersaulting to the floor and rolls on to his feet. The room is filled with smoke and hot shrapnel, but Thompson's sharp ears hear coughing coming from the far side of the room. With supreme agility, he sails over consoles and upset furniture to bring his weapon down on his prey.

"*No, don't!*"

Gun stares dumbstruck, his head rocking back like someone just smashed him with an iron bar. Through the smoke, the simple outline of a hand with a thumb and four fingers is outstretched defensively in front of him. He can't take his eyes off the familiar shape.

Hot on his heels, Geek storms up, leveling her pistols at the group. Gun knocks her aim off just in time, and her shots ricochet around the well-built room. Her first instinct is to shove Gun aside, but then she sees what he is staring at and her arms flop to her sides, her pistols clattering to the deck.

"We surrender!" the small voice sobs, *"just please don't kill us."*

A torrent of bewildering emotions seizes the two operators, and they don't hear Brick's hammering behind them anymore. Thompson slides his face mask up to look on his victims clearly.

The small humans look up in wonderment at his appearance, blinking with confusion and disbelief. Gun lets his weapon drop to the floor, and he sinks to one knee. The huddled group recoils at his approach.

Once Argo squeezes through the gap he hammered out, he sees Thompson and Maiella looking solemnly toward the floor, unmoving. He checks the corridor behind him to make sure no enemy is advancing on them and stands guard just in case. *It is odd for them to just sit there,* he thinks, and he risks a look to see what's going on. Peering through the haze, he can make out Geek and Gun beside a large console, but little else. He strains to hear more.

"I... I am Major Gun Thompson. I..." Thompson looks around, not knowing how to continue. The charge inside him is evaporated; his singularity of purpose is confused, unable to be reconciled with what he sees. He looks over at Maiella for reassurance and sees the red blood spattered all over her. He drops his head with the sickening realization he has done something unspeakable and unforgivable. Self-loathing drapes him like a wet blanket.

"I will accept full responsibility for your harm," he utters.

Maiella sways on her feet and leans into the console beside her with her hip. Her eyes glaze over, and she disappears to some distant place. The huddle of people scoots away in fear while Thompson looks on, mortified. He can feel how terrified these people are of him, and it shames him to his essence. Not knowing what else to do, he resumes his downward stare.

When the huddle scoots past the console's edge, Argo's eyes

bulge with disbelief. Realizing that he, too, is a player in the atrocity, Argo looks down at his mailed arms. Drying blood is sprayed all over him. Not knowing how to handle it, he wipes his hands over himself, vainly trying to clean it away.

The huddled group spends long minutes contemplating their attackers—these monsters of speed, agility, and ferocity that look so strangely familiar. They study their build, size, features, equipment, and dreary countenance.

Thompson and Maiella remain perfectly still, permitting the long uninterrupted looks. The small humans see the soldiers are not moving, nor does it seem they are likely to move anytime soon. Small whispers begin in the huddle, shushed by the more terrified. Forcing himself through his own confusion and fear, one of the small humans stops cringing, and rises up to his knees. The aged, weathered man straightens his back, looking directly at Thompson who remains statuesque in his downward gaze. The others shake their heads and murmur, all begging him not to bring attention to himself, but he reassures them with a silent wave of his hand.

A question has formed in this man's settling mind. He thinks he knows the answer, but despite the visible commonalities they seem to share, there is much that is unfamiliar in this awful greeting.

Thompson hears the murmur and raises his eyes to see the man who was moments ago begging for his comrades' lives. The fear is receding as the man studies him intently.

"Are you human?" the older man asks.

Thompson nods gravely in reply, "Yes..."

"*Then, what are you doing?*"

Thompson answers heavily, "We have standing orders to capture any vessel we encounter and return with it and its contents."

The man squints skeptically, squaring his broad shoulders and getting his feet beneath him. "Why did you stop?"

Thompson hesitates, taking a moment to look him in the eye. "Because the only meaning our lives have is in the protection and support of human life. We have failed in our most urgent duty."

The man cocks his bald head in disbelief. "Are you serious?"

"Completely." Thompson cannot maintain the eye contact, resuming his downward gaze. "I must insist we return at once."

"Let's not get ahead of ourselves," the man counters, scrunching his bushy gray eyebrows together. Rising to his feet, he says, "You said your name is Major Thompson? I am Captain Braemar Keller of the colony ship *Europa*, and these are my senior officers."

Thompson rises quickly to his feet and salutes respectfully. "It is good we encountered you, Captain Keller."

"Do any of you require medical attention?" Argo asks.

A dozen eyes turn to see the gargantuan soldier who somehow approached without them noticing.

Keller looks over his officers, gently reassuring those on the verge of panic. "No, we're fine..." He trails off once he sees the blood spatters on the Brick's armor, his expression changing to dread. "But my crew..."

Thompson whirls to face his large comrade. "Argo, retrace our steps. Check for survivors and administer aid. I will join you shortly."

Argo straightens his slumping posture and snaps a salute before spinning on his heel.

Turning back to Keller, Thompson asks, "Who handles navigation?"

A hand goes up behind Keller, and a middle-aged woman in uniform gets to her feet. "I'm the navigator."

"Maiella," Thompson commands briskly, "work together with this woman to plot our course home. I am going to assist Argo. Call me when calculations are complete."

Maiella straightens up as well, saluting sharply. Thompson grabs his rifle, slinging it over his shoulder, and marches off through the twisted blast doors. Maiella collects her pistols, tucks them into the clips on her back, and seats herself at the navigation terminal.

As Keller looks on warily, his First Officer whispers with Spanish accent. "What's going on here, Captain? This *feels* like a hijack, but... I thought *we* were the only survivors."

Keller nods subtly. "I know what you mean. They look regimented and specialized... maybe remnants of some military outpost. I could only guess what made them so *big* though..."

"What are we going to do?" the officer asks.

"We're going to survive, Ortega, as always. These three could probably kill all of us if they wanted, so they get their way for now."

Another man in the huddle, much younger than the others, climbs anxiously to his feet. "Captain, request permission to find my wife and make sure she's okay."

"Not yet, Gregor. Sit tight until we know what's happening."

Gregor steps to his chair, looking like a tightly wound spring, and chews his lower lip with anxiety.

"Maybe they intend to enslave us?" suggests Ortega as he squints suspiciously at the armored Geek.

Keller looks long and hard at Maiella working along side his navigator. The slender soldier has removed her bulky helmet and goggles, and she is listening patiently to the navigator. The armored woman is completely docile, her body language warm and familiar. Something about her suggests gentility—she doesn't condescend or threaten at all. It is an image that doesn't jibe with their introduction, and Keller struggles to reconcile the vastly different scenes. He opens his mouth to answer, then shuts it, second-guessing himself. "I don't know," he admits finally.

Ortega watches Maiella skeptically, unable to keep from staring at her gold contact terminals. She looks like an eager pupil, with the navigator leaning over her shoulder, giving instructions. Suddenly, another thought crosses his mind. "But what if they are telling the truth... If there are many of them, they could be the protection we've needed to start the colony."

The two men continue their observations silently.

Thompson jogs up beside Argo who is standing over the mangled remains of either a man or a woman. He doesn't move at the Gun's approach.

"They're all dead, Thompson."

Thompson sniffs hard and surveys the scene. "We'll collect the bodies and assemble them here." He takes a step away, but notices Argo isn't following. The big man is still staring at the gore in front of him. "Argo?" he asks.

Finally, Argo faces him. "We found others like us. Our own kind! It's the greatest thing we could ever have found. We'll have fresh DNA to breed out genetic flaws. We'll have access to their star charts and the full range of their exploration, their technology…"

He looks down at the body.

"But we killed them, Thompson. That outweighs *everything*." With his eyes to the floor, Argo walks past Thompson on his grim task.

Thompson studies the pained expression in the remains of the face, the burns, the avulsions, the viscera, and Argo's words echo in his mind, "We killed them Thompson…" It chills him deeply, knotting his stomach.

"Calculations complete, Major," buzzes Maiella in his radio.

"Already?"

"Affirmative. The navigator is very efficient."

"Apparently so," Thompson agrees. "Argo and I are policing the casualties. We'll be presenting them in fifteen minutes for identification." Silence is his only reply. "Maiella?" he calls.

"Understood, out," Maiella states coarsely. Thompson sighs and lifts his helmet off slowly. His hair is longer and lies matted to his head with perspiration. Wiping his forehead with the back of his arm, he sets to work assisting Argo in their bloody task.

FRIEND OR FOE

Keller looks over the covered remains of the slain. Near him stand his bridge officers, another man in a long white coat, and twelve men and women in stained coveralls and toolbelts. Many of them clutch each other, mumbling a few words between the anguished sobs.

Keller lifts the blotchy white-and-red sheets, identifying the bodies, and Ortega records names and titles. Each time Keller announces another name, it smashes the three cadre operators like a truncheon.

At the end of the rows, Keller brings a hand up to his mouth, facing the horrible reality he had feared for so long. But it didn't come at the hands of the reptilian aliens like he thought it would. It came from *his own kind*. The thought is so bizarre it scarcely registers as possible. He looks over at the three newcomers with their drooping shoulders and lowered heads.

Breaking his glance, he turns to the man in the white coat, waving him over. The white-coated man hastens over, and Keller whispers to him.

"Counselor, I want you to observe these three and prepare a psychological profile. Specifically, I want to know if they're sincere or if they mean to deceive us. Bring it to me when you're done."

The counselor nods and shuffles aside. Keller turns to Ortega, asking, "What is the tally?"

Ortega gravely reviews his count, answering, "Seventeen dead." All around him, his crewmates sob with loss.

Thompson steps forward. "We request the duty of disposal."

Gregor pushes off from the person trying to console him. "*Disposal?*" he roars. "These were *people*, you murderous piece of *shit*, not *trash*!"

Keller steps in front of Gregor, wrestling with his own emotions to maintain some semblance of control. He lowers his head and extends his arms, hoping to bar Gregor's way to keep him from starting a fight—a fight Gregor would be certain to lose. He looks up, catching Gregor's fiery glance, and shakes his head gently. Gregor's teeth grind together, but reluctantly, he lets it go.

Keller lowers his arms and turns to face the newcomers. "Major, these people were very close to us…" He looks around at the seventeen red-and-white sheets laid orderly beside each other, sadness gripping his heart firmly. "We need to mourn for them first."

Thompson blinks in nonunderstanding. "*Mourn?*"

The group looks at each other, murmuring in disbelief. Gregor launches from his clustered crewmates.

"You hear that? These three were just gonna take out the *garbage!*" He whirls toward Thompson in a rage, bellowing like a wounded lion. "*You bastards probably knock each other off left and right, but these people you* MURDERED *meant something to us!*

"GREGOR, STAND DOWN!" Keller demands.

Thompson and Argo take it on the chin, but for Maiella, it is a devastating direct hit. Her lip involuntarily juts out, a deluge of desolation and despair washing over her as she disables the safety on her machine pistol. Thompson hears the soft click-click and whirls around.

"Maiella… *Maiella!*"

Snapping out of her trance, she resets the safety, blanks her expression, and stares straight.

Gregor never heard the safety latch, but he sees her taking her hand away from her weapon. His eyes go wide with hatred and panic, believing she was about to draw on him instead of herself. He backpedals, his mouth turned down at the corners, staring daggers through all three of them.

"We don't know this word you use, *mourn*," Thompson explains, powerful waves of emotion threatening to overwhelm

84

him completely, "but I can see it relates to *loss*. We lost half of our operator corps in a split second, so we *know* the meaning." His eyes flare suddenly.

"Apparently, you have the time to indulge such emotions. WE DO NOT. Merely *surviving* requires our full attention!"

Fearing a showdown, the counselor steps between them. "Everyone!" he pleads. "This is a terrible moment for all of us, but we *must* keep perspective!"

He pauses, turning a full circle in the midst of the assembly, looking everyone in the eye. "After all the light years of travel, we thought we were the last survivors of Earth and her colonies. Here, in the depths of space, fate has reunited us. *What are the odds?*"

The counselor scans the faces around him, his eyebrows arched. None speak. Few even look at him. He takes a breath before turning back to Thompson.

"We appreciate your willingness to assist. However, we must care for our dead in our own manner."

"Understood," Thompson replies, embarrassed by his outburst.

He takes a tentative step toward the counselor, one hand gripping the other. "It was not our intent to devalue your comrades... I think we use different words for similar things." He suddenly gets a very distant look about him, and he faces the others in the room.

"As far as we can recall, no human has died by an operator's hands. We are the first to do so, and it is unbearable. We know what we have done, and that is why we must return immediately... so we can be judged for this crime." Thompson turns and whispers a word to his team. At once, the three begin to leave.

Keller calls out to them, "Major, where are you going?" Thompson halts as the other continue.

"We are going to check hull integrity at our point of entry and reinforce it if necessary."

Keller points to the counselor and Ortega. "These two will go with you and assist." Ortega's face contorts with unspoken protest. The counselor simply nods and complies.

Thompson studies Keller skeptically, decides not to argue, and strides down the corridor after his team. Ortega makes his way after them, pausing beside a wall sconce of small arms. The counselor shakes his head disapprovingly, but Ortega ignores the counselor's visual chiding and pulls a thin rifle from its clamp. Ortega stares back with determination as he strides past, loading and readying the weapon. The counselor turns to Keller with his shoulders raised, and the aged captain shakes his head to nevermind and hurry along.

When the operators have marched from sight, the crew breaks into chaotic shouts at their captain. Keller steps into their midst with arms raised, having to yell to get their attention.

Maiella, Argo, and Thompson stride briskly down the corridor, making the counselor and Ortega hustle to keep up. The counselor tugs at Ortega's sleeve, urging him to let some distance form between them and the three soldiers.

"What should we do?" the counselor asks.

"Just keep watch and let me know if you see them do anything odd."

"Odd... You mean *other* than boring through our hull and killing seventeen of us in ninety seconds?"

"*Yes*, other than that."

The counselor goes quiet a moment and speaks with admiration. "I admit, I am fascinated. They seem so... *evolved*. They're tall, fast, more agile than any of us... and so disciplined. Their society must be highly organized, most likely military in origin. Their attack, so swift and efficient... they seemed so inhuman... but in the little I've seen, I can see they *are* human. Did you see how ashamed they were when the captain spoke the names?"

"They *looked* upset," Ortega admits, "but it could be an act."

"Possible," confesses the counselor, "though I don't believe so."

Ortega tightens his grip on his weapon, irritated by the counselor's appreciative prattling. "Time will tell."

"That it will."

The three operators arrive at their entry point, a circular hole carved through the thick hull. Argo hauls out a diagnostic device, sweeping it across the edges of the cut.

"There are some microfractures here I should weld, but nothing serious." The Brick pushes the device along the interior of the cut. "The seal from the virus ship appears strong."

"Can we give you a hand?" Maiella asks.

"No, I can finish this myself in an hour or so."

"Then Maiella and I will scout the ship," Thompson announces. "We need to make sure she can make the trip, and we don't want to bring back any unpleasant surprises."

"Understood. I'll keep my radio on if you require me." Argo pulls a small torch from his belt with his free hand and triggers a brilliant blue jet of flame, his visor automatically dimming to compensate.

Ortega and the counselor round the corner to find Argo welding. The commander levels his weapon at the large operator.

"What are you doing?"

Argo calmly explains without looking, "I'm sealing small cracks caused by our penetration. They aren't threatening, but I don't take chances."

"Where are the others?"

"They're inventorying the ship." With the hand not welding, he points down the corridor. "They went that way."

The counselor puts his hand on Ortega's shoulder. "I'll go," he whispers and jogs off in the direction Argo indicated.

Ortega holds his ground, squinting hard against the bright welding torch and shifting his weight from foot to foot. Being alone with this titan of destruction is not what he had in mind.

Argo senses his apprehension and halts his welding to look at the man. Ortega tenses up at Argo's gaze, aiming the puny rifle at Argo's chest. Shrugging, Argo goes on welding.

"It's unlikely your weapon would pierce my armor, but would you lower it just the same?"

The Spaniard starts to lower his aim, then thinks better of it and pulls the rifle tight into his shoulder. Argo gives him a long, suffering look and goes back to work.

The counselor catches up to Maiella and Thompson, finding them trying to bypass a door lock. Thompson has pulled the panel completely out of the wall and holds it while Maiella rewires it.

"Here, allow me," volunteers the counselor. He presses the panel back into the door frame and enters an unlock code sequence. The door slides open. Maiella and Thompson look at him gratefully then peer into the darkness beyond.

"What's in here?" Thompson asks.

"This corridor leads to one of our twenty cargo bays."

"Twenty?" Maiella repeats in surprise. "What are you transporting?"

"This bay holds Agritech machinery and embryos," the counselor answers.

"Embryos?" exclaims Thompson. "You have genetic technology?" He walks excitedly into the darkness, Maiella closely in tow.

"Well, not as such," the counselor explains. "The embryos are plant and animal." He taps some buttons from the hacked-up door panel, illuminating the corridor, and he sees the two looking back at him in confusion. He reads their expressions, asking, "Don't you have plants or animals? How do you eat?"

Thompson waits for the counselor to catch up and begins walking again. "We synthesize amino proteins, vitamin complexes, and carbohydrates. Our nutrition is complete."

"How do you do that?"

"Some of our oldest machinery handles the task," Maiella replies, "but it requires frequent maintenance"

The counselor nods, contemplating her reply. "Plants and animals do that for us, without machinery."

Thompson nearly misses a step. "They're not machines? What are they?"

"They are living creatures. Their biological functions assemble our nutrients."

"Incredible!" Maiella marvels aloud. "How much maintenance do they require?"

"Their care is largely automated. The machines that care for the animals and plants are very durable and require little maintenance in fact."

Turning to the counselor, Thompson asks, "Are the... plahntz...

and ann-ih-muls producing now?"

"No, they're still frozen. Once we find a planet with adequate soil and atmosphere, we can raise them."

Thompson's mind soars while Maiella digs for more information.

"How many can they support?" she asks.

The counselor shrugs. "Once mature, they can support our entire colony, with a ninety percent surplus."

"Ninety percent *surplus*? At best, we only managed a point-five percent surplus for thirty-eight days." Looking at Thompson, she goes on excitedly.

"An automated, low-maintenance, surplus food supply... With more calories, we could advance genetic research, ore procurement, and free up thousands of hours from synthesis repair... Thompson, we could stop our collection rotations altogether!"

The counselor watches, fascinated, as the operators bounce along like happy children at just the thought of having enough to eat. He cradles his chin, asking, "How many hours of your day are spent working?"

Thompson gives the counselor a 'stupid question' look. "All of them."

The counselor contemplates the answer, attempting a diplomatic response. "Your lives must be very difficult."

As the three approach another door, the counselor walks ahead to open it. The door whisks aside, and a rush of cold air sweeps past them. Lights inside flicker and illuminate a vast space packed with tight rows of gray crates. Thompson gazes in unbridled curiosity, his mouth open in wonder. "What else are you transporting?"

"I have an inventory," the counselor volunteers. "May I show you?"

Thompson nods in assent, and the three depart to another part of the ship. The counselor guides them into a small compartment with very little decoration, just rows and rows of terminals. Choosing the closest terminal, he pulls out some chairs for his guests. Maiella glides down into hers, but Thompson eyeballs his suspiciously, correctly surmising it couldn't accommodate his mass. He leans over Maiella's shoulder instead.

The counselor seats himself and slides in front of the terminal, punching up the basic menus while Maiella pays close attention to the cues and touch commands he uses.

"This is a master list of our cargo holds…" The counselor looks over at them, and they are both riveted to the screen. He can see Maiella eagerly wants to take over. "Do you know computers well?"

Maiella smiles broadly, vainly attempting modesty. "Mm, hmm."

"Please, go ahead!" The counselor slides aside so she can sit directly in front of the terminal. "Just use this panel here, and touch the letter or number by heading, and…"

She is already way ahead of him. She scans the master list and all of its sublists in seconds. "Did you get all of that?" she asks.

"Yes," Thompson answers. "Are explanations included?"

"Affirmative... Oh! There are photos!"

The counselor drifts back, watching the two completely absorbed in their search. He studies their interaction, taking in their body language, seeing how seamlessly they function together; the way they anticipate the other's need or question seems intuitive, and it occurs to him how well they must know each other. Thompson's hand on her shoulder as he leans over her seems so natural, like they are best friends, perhaps always have been.

He notices their efficiency, how Maiella seems to have already mastered the computer system with minimal instruction. They take in the information almost as fast as the computer can display it. Suddenly, Thompson looks over his shoulder.

"Are these the embryos you spoke of?"

The counselor perks up and slides over to the terminal. Pictured there is a fleshy pink blob. "Yes," he replies, "and if you press here, you get a description." With the counselor's key stroke, a thick-bodied creature, supported by four thin limbs, appears. A wide white band wraps the midsection of the stout black animal. Maiella and Thompson lean in with amazement, fascinated by the animal's peculiar shape. "Belted Galloway," she reads from the caption.

Again, the two operators dig into the data, pulling up image after image, soaking up the strange and wonderful images like gleeful children. The longer the counselor watches, the harder he finds it to believe these are the cold killers that stormed in earlier.

Thompson straightens up suddenly. "Argo, how's the repair?"

"Going well," the Brick answers via radio. "I should be finished in about thirty minutes."

"How is your escort?"

Argo halts his welding and looks over at Ortega. The Spaniard snaps back to attention, aiming his weapon again. "Just fine," Argo reports.

"Meet us at this location when repairs are complete. You need to see this."

"What have you got, Gun?"

"Are you still wearing your visor?" Thompson queries.

"Affirmative."

"We're sending you video."

Inside Argo's visor, an image of a collossal freestanding structure appears. It is broad and circular at its base, sloping up to a tall vent. Argo stares intently at the image. "What am I looking at, Gun?"

"Everything needed to start a new life," Thompson responds. "I'll see you in thirty. Thompson out."

NATURE OF THE BEASTS

The counselor strides onto the bridge where Captain Keller is mediating a discussion among his bridge officers and two others in gray coveralls. Keller notices the counselor arrive and, with a hand gesture, halts the debate.

"Counselor," he calls, "please tell us what you've learned."

The counselor thinks carefully as he walks to the circle. "I haven't spent enough time with them yet to be sure."

"Then give us your first impressions." All eyes fix on the counselor as he folds his arms and paces, preparing his words for the impromptu presentation.

"Of the three, there is a clear leader—the tall one is superior rank to the other two—but between the woman and the big man, they may be equal. In conversation, I discovered they spend every waking hour at work, and they had no idea what plants or animals were. All of their food is synthesized, and it is highly labor-intensive to keep those machines operating. It seems mere subsistence is a full-time job for them…"

He trails off, starting a new subject. "They mentioned ore procurement, genetic research, and collection rotations. I'm not sure what collection rotations are."

Sharon, the navigator, unfolds her arms. "Maybe that's why they're here. Maybe they collect ships…"

"Like pirates?" offers Ortega.

Keller considers the possibility and looks to the counselor for a response.

"*Perhaps* like pirates..." the counselor begins, and the group breaks into chatter. He raises his voice to be heard above them. "But their motives are different." The chatter abates as the group waits expectantly on the explanation.

"It seems like they are just barely hanging on, and they spoke about a recent defeat, how they lost half of their operator corps in an instant."

"Yes, I remember that," confirms Keller.

The counselor nods. "The attack on our vessel is most likely an act of desperation. I ask that you reserve your judgment until we know more."

"*Reserve judgment*?" pipes Gregor. "They're *murderers* and they may decide to finish us off. Why we even *discussing* this?"

"I don't believe they mean us any more harm."

Gregor rolls his eyes derisively. "That's easy for you to suppose, Counselor, but did you forget about our dead on deck 4? How could you *possibly* think they won't finish what they started?"

The counselor stares hard at the obstinate Russian. "Because they *stopped*."

The group contemplates the point among themselves, and the counselor gives them time to absorb it.

"Of course we should be *wary*," the counselor continues, "but I don't believe we should be *fearful*. We thought *we* were the last people in existence... so it's reasonable to think they believed *they* were the last as well. Besides, beneath the armor, efficiency, and discipline, they're..."

"Yes?" presses Keller.

The counselor looks everyone in the eye softly. "They're human."

The group of officers exchange glances, pondering the argument, until fear gets a hold of them again.

"I am not asking anyone to drop their guard," the counselor clarifies. "I've only been with them an hour or so. Just reserve your judgment. I see something in them, and if I'm right, these people could be the protection we've needed to start the colony."

"We still haven't found a suitable planet, Counselor," Keller warns.

The counselor returns his captain's stern look. "But we know where one is..."

"NO!" shouts Keller. "We are *not* going back there. *Ever!*"

A heavy pall fills the room. Some look at the floor, some look out the viewscreen into the depths of space, a very distant and longing expression covering them all.

"We've been on this ship a long time, Keller..."

Keller looks hard at the counselor, but doesn't speak. The tension is thick, and no one dares to cut it until the sound of approaching footfalls interrupts the mood. Soon, Maiella is standing at the twisted metal that used to be a blast door. She flinches at everyone's simultaneous gaze and snaps to attention.

"I have been ordered to learn your ship's operation and assume the duties of your"—she swallows hard—"your fallen."

Keller looks queerly at her. "Now?"

"Yes, now," she replies and stands patiently.

"Please, over here." To everyone else's surprise, Sharon gestures Maiella to a chair at her console. Maiella strides over and sits, listening politely as Sharon explains functions and control.

Ortega stands quietly and sidles up beside the counselor. "I went to academy two years to learn navigation. This *chica* is going to learn it in a few months, I suppose?"

The counselor redirects Ortega's attention to Maiella. "Watch."

With a few instructions, Maiella accelerates the pace, intuitively accessing higher functions. Like before, she moves nearly at the speed of the machine, causing the group to gape in awe, their unease elbowed aside by fascination. Subconsciously, they move closer. She pauses, suddenly swiveling in her seat to face Keller, and the group lurches back.

"My team requires a portal unlocked," Maiella states. "Can that be done from here?"

"Yes," Sharon coaches. "Here... where are they? Okay, right here."

"How about I just go?" volunteers the counselor.

Keller sees the opportunity to keep eyes on the newcomers and nods in approval.

"Ship counselor en route to your location," Maiella radios. She returns to her task, and again, fascination fills the group of officers... except for one.

"My Beautiful... My Beautiful..."

With the others captivated by Maiella's ability, Gregor slips away. He looks over his shoulder to make sure no one notices him leaving and climbs the ladders and stairways down to the improvised morgue.

Standing before the door, he extends his hand to the door panel and realizes he is shaking. He balls his fist angrily and punches the button. The door whisks aside, and a rush of arctic air sweeps by him, making his breath condense. He wraps his arms around himself, bracing against the chill.

Stepping into the dimly lit room, he finds seventeen bodies beneath bloodstained sheets, arranged in two parallel rows. Most of the sheets cling wetly, revealing gender, build, and extent of injury.

He remembers them all, but one burns strongest in his mind. Summoning the courage to find her, Gregor's hands rise up to his face and rub briskly, his wedding band very cold against his cheek. Instinctively, he is drawn to one of the still figures toward the back of the room. Apprehension knots his stomach and shortens his breath.

He looks across the red blotches and irregular lumps in the sheet below him. A single lock of corn-silk blonde hair juts from the top and the sight of it makes him hyperventilate.

Furiously, he pounds himself in the chest, trying to beat down the burning in his heart, trying to get his breath back. After multiple strokes, he kneels, steaming in the cold air with grief carved deeply into his features.

He takes hold of the sheet and pulls it back gently. It sticks somewhat, revealing the face of a petite woman in her late twenties,

96

her expression locked in the pain and surprise of her death. Drying blood flecks her porcelain face and mats one side of her hair. Unable to look anymore, he turns away, but all he finds around him are more sheet-covered bodies. Bitter tears stream down his contorting face, and his mouth falls open with despair. Salty drops descend on her, absorbing into the collar of her white uniform.

Gregor wipes a hand across his hot eyes and sniffs deeply. With his other hand, he pulls the sheet down past her chest where large holes have been stamped into her by a high-caliber pistol. His teeth clench. His fists clench. His face flushes with such heat; the chilly air no longer touches him. He looks across her body, how her white medical uniform is tattered with bullet holes and marred with dark splotches. But his eyes stop at her name tag; and when he reads the name, *Iskra Petrova*, the emerging rage smothers in her loss.

"Iskra..." he stammers, scooping her limp body up into his arms. Pressing her hard against him, he rocks her back and forth. "Moy-ah kra-see-vai-yah... moy-ah kra-see-vai-yah..."

He holds her tight for a long time, supporting the back of her head, desperately wishing she would hold him back. She is so cold against his skin. So cold...

Sniffing hard, he lays her down and places her hands over the holes in her chest. Her expression looks less pained than it did before. The small difference matters greatly.

Realizing he is going to be missed by the others soon, he reaches for the edge of the sheet and draws it over her face. When his hand passes in front of him, he sees the blood all over it. He holds both of his hands in front of him and stares at the palms... at her blood, at her life, that was stolen from him.

THE REST OF US

The counselor arrives at the door Thompson and Argo had requested access through, but it is already open. A slight wisp of smoke still rises from the panel beside it, the locking mechanism bearing a semicircular cut. He shakes his head and proceeds through.

The room beyond is dark, and the counselor's footsteps echo through the cavernous expanse. He strides to the breaker panel and activates the lighting. To his surprise, Thompson and Argo are not far away, inspecting a column of metallic cylinders. Once the lights fully come on, the operators deactivate their infrared vision and stride to meet the counselor.

"What's in these cylinders?" queries Thompson.

"The rest of us," answers the counselor, "cryogenically suspended."

"Some of these are room temperature," notices Argo. "Did they fail?"

"No, those are for the duty crew. We have a rotating schedule of two years."

"Looks like you have enough for about eighty rotations," Argo deduces. Scrunching his expression in thought, he observes, "That would mean all of you have had over twenty years on duty. How is it that you have crew so young?"

The counselor smiles. "We have had some additions to the crew in flight."

"You have an incubator? May I see it?"

The counselor laughs. "No, no. They came... naturally."

Argo's interest vaporizes. "*Viviparous reproduction*? Bah! It's dangerous! It puts unnecessary health risks on the carrier and removes them from effective duty. Plus, there is no control over the characteristics of the fetus. *How can you plan a community when so many variables are permitted*?"

The counselor opens his mouth to speak, but cannot fathom where to begin a response. Instead, he chooses discretion, allowing the smile to return. "It's clear we have much to learn from each other."

"What is your mission?" asks Thompson. The counselor throws his head back recalling the information.

"We were employed by Soshiba Varicorp as agricultural colonists." The counselor pauses midthought, seeing in the confused faces of his audience he has already lost them. It drives home how much vocabulary is going to affect communication.

"We worked collectively for an organization that was named Soshiba Varicorp." He pauses to make sure his audience is still with him.

"Okay, go ahead," Argo urges.

"The organization identified a distant star of proper spectral class and confirmed the existence of orbiting planets. One of these planets showed the organic molecules methane and carbon dioxide in the atmosphere, so off we went. One hundred eighty years later, we arrived and began our initial tests of the environment. There were basic forms of life there, but..."

"But what?" Thompson begs, leaning closer.

"The crust of the planet had very high concentrations of radioactive isotopes. Radiation levels were so high, it'll be *thousands* of years before it's habitable. Captain Keller declared the mission a failure and ordered a return home. That's when we heard the first of the reports."

"Yes? Reports about... ?" Argo fishes.

"About an overwhelming alien force sweeping through our defenses. At first, the broadcasts were frequent and numerous; but as the aliens destroyed every life they encountered, there were fewer and fewer people to broadcast. We monitored the reports as they dwindled, and the last ones were the terrified and desperate reports of

Earth's attack. Then there was nothing."

Argo stares with his mouth open. "You witnessed the annihilation?"

The counselor nods morosely. Thompson assimilates the information, but there is an element he did not understand.

"What is this 'Earth' you mentioned?"

The counselor looks at Thompson queerly. "Are you serious? Earth was our planet... our *home*."

Thompson and Argo look at each other profoundly, learning the answer to the great secret no one would answer in their adolescence.

"*You really didn't know?*" the counselor asks, dumbfounded.

Thompson looks seriously at him, shaking his head. He shifts his stance, ignoring the disbelief carved in the counselor's face. "Could there be other colony ships like this one?"

"No," the counselor replies sadly. "Our mission was the only one approved by Congress at the time, and this was the only ship flight-ready during the attack."

"Con-gress?" wonders Argo.

"Our leaders back on Earth... We traveled on, trying to find a planet we could settle, but this ship wasn't designed to explore. Our sensors can't see a tenth as far as Earth's best telescopes, and we don't really know where to go. After a thousand years, we haven't had any luck." The counselor looks thoughtfully at the two men, suddenly curious. "How did your group survive?"

"I don't know," Thompson admits. "We know that we endure, and we must continue to do so."

"Don't you ever wonder about it?"

Thompson ponders the question briefly and responds, "There was never the time."

"So how do you stay hidden?"

"We are careful," Thompson relates. "We allow no transmissions from base with a range greater than two hundred thousand kilometers and adhere to strict behaviors which ensure anonymity."

"What are those?" the counselor probes.

"Attack swiftly, control vessel, eliminate crew, and return. If overwhelmed, self-detonate."

"Self-detonate?"

"Our ships and persons are equipped with high-yield incineration devices," Argo explains. "Our bodies, ships, and equipment will vaporize along with whatever they are close to."

"And you're wearing these devices on you now?"

"Of course," Thompson states flatly.

The counselor feels the urge to back away, but he suppresses it, his curiosity still getting the better of him. "Have any of you had to... '*self-detonate*'?"

Thompson and Argo look hard at each other.

"Yes," the big man says. "The enemy adapted to our methods recently and set an ambush. To evade capture, our operators self-detonated... we lost half of our corps in that instant."

The psychologist inside overwhelms tact, and the counselor can't help but ask, "How did that make you feel?"

"*Feelings are a liability*!" snaps Argo suddenly. He spins on his heel, marching off to another part of the bay.

Thompson watches his friend leave and turns to the stunned counselor. Fretting, he steps closer. "Until that day, none of us had expired from unnatural causes. It was the hardest day of our lives." Thompson turns and makes his way over to Argo who props himself against a stack of cargo with his arm. The counselor looks at the door as if to leave, but reconsiders and walks over to the two men.

"I apologize for my offensive question. My curiosity overcame me. I will leave if you wish."

"No, don't." Argo turns around to face the counselor, clearly embarrassed by his outburst. "I have had difficulty mastering my mood on this matter. It is I who should apologize."

Before the awkward silence can get any longer, Argo asks, "Where is the main colony apparatus?"

"This way," the counselor volunteers and pauses midstep. "There isn't a lot to see. It's packaged for flight."

"Does it still function?" Argo asks.

"Well, we haven't checked in some time, but I'm sure that it..."

"Argo, we'll run a full diagnostic," Thompson interrupts. Facing the counselor, he requests, "Can you take us there?"

"Absolutely. I need to let the captain know you intend to perform maintenance on it first."

Thompson nods in acceptance.

Making his way over to an intercom, the counselor hails, "Captain Keller, this is the counselor."

"Go ahead, Counselor," Keller answers.

"Captain, we are going to perform a diagnostic of the colony reactor and atmosphere processor." There is a heavy pause.

"Very well. The rest of our engineers are currently in cryo, but can be ready in a day or so if needed."

"I don't believe that will be necessary," Argo counters. Into his helmet microphone, he calls, "Maiella?"

Via radio, she comes back, "What's up?"

"Can you warm up the atmosphere processor in cargo bay 12-C? We want to assess its functionality."

"Understood," she radios. "I'll let you know when preliminary start-up is complete. Maiella out." Argo and Thompson look at the counselor expectantly.

"Follow me," he invites, and they stride off together.

Along the way, Argo asks, "What do you know about this thing?"

The counselor shrugs. "Well, it's fully automated, and when fully deployed, it covers over six kilometers square."

"What's the power source?" Thompson inquires.

"Inducted fusion reactor, triple alpha process."

"You fuse helium?" Argo asks amazed. "How?"

"One of our engineers could tell you. I have no idea."

"We use hydrogen liberated from water by electrolysis..."

"Whoa! Whoa," the counselor interrupts before the big man gets going. "You're over my head!"

Argo blinks thoughtfully. "Why not use hydrogen? It's more abundant, easier to procure, and it's higher yield per ton."

"All I know is helium is easier to contain. One of our earliest colony ships ruptured a hydrogen tank and exploded. We recovered most of the ship, but the reactor failed; and without power, everyone aboard perished. To prevent further tragedies, Congress mandated helium-based reactors on all long-term voyages."

Argo's lower lip juts out slightly as he recognizes the benefit. "It *is* ideal for storage—totally inert. No chance of explosion."

"There's another benefit to our fusion reactor..." The counselor pauses to unlock the door in front of them and open it. "We can manufacture basic elements if we need them. Very handy if we need certain materials in flight." Stepping into the dark space, he moves to the breaker panel and illuminates the bay.

The lights flicker for many seconds before finally coming on, and both operators stare slack-jawed at the titanic machine before them. Wonder fills them at just its dimension, extending well beyond their field of view on all sides. There is not a lot of room between the machine and the walls of the bay, but enough to appreciate the scope of its construction. Thompson and Argo step reverently toward it, and Argo extends his hand. Caressing the cool surface, he grins, and Thompson does likewise.

"Once the processor is installed on a planet," the counselor explains, "robots deploy from within to collect raw materials for construction. Ore, minerals, flora, fauna—anything we need is collected and processed into building materials. Then the robots construct domes and living structures for the colonists. The facility is habitable in about a month."

"Incredible," admires Thompson.

From deep within the machine, a low hum radiates.

"Preliminary start-up complete," radios Maiella. "Beginning systems diagnostics. Stand by."

A terminal nearby comes to life, showing Maiella's progress. A line-item list appears slowly at first and becomes more rapid with time. Each line is punctuated with the word "IMPAIRED" in large red letters. Argo strides to the terminal, taking in the extent of the list as it grows longer and longer. He shakes his head and looks over at Thompson. Thompson understands Argo's glance and faces the counselor.

"I think we'll need your engineers after all."

SCRATCHING THE SURFACE

Keller stands silently among his officers as his recently thawed engineers mill about the bridge. They gawk stupefied at the twisted blast doors and various sooty scorches. Once Keller believes they have had enough time, he calls them in. Fourteen new faces gather around him, all bearing the same look of awed disbelief.

"A couple of days ago, we were attacked," the captain explains. "The assailants bored through our hull, shot everyone they saw, and seized the bridge. They were swift, efficient, and savage."

The engineers hang on Keller's words.

"The assailants were human."

Jaws drop and eyes go wide. Keller pauses, letting them digest the weighty news.

"They seem to be a new breed. They are taller, stronger, faster, and incredibly aggressive. They easily interpreted our computer systems and had total control in minutes."

"How did you fight them off?" asks one of the bolder engineers.

"We didn't."

A collective chill rises through the recently unfrozen crew members, building upon solid foundations of anxiety into outright panic.

"*They're still here?*" one asks, petrified.

Keller nods sternly in affirmation. "Yes. They just finished rating our main drive's efficiency and are taking four hours of sleep."

The group sways on its feet, wrestling with disbelief and

bewilderment.

"Wait... they storm in blasting, take the bridge, then stop, go work on the ship, and take a nap?" a shorter engineer questions.

"Correct," Keller responds. Several in the group slump into nearby seats, overloaded with the bizarre information.

"What do they want?" a woman asks.

"It gets confusing from here," Keller admits, rubbing his forehead. "They've laid in a course to their base and have taken a full inventory of this ship. Most interesting to them is our atmosphere processor. They performed a thorough diagnostic, and it has a *lot* of problems. That's why we thawed you— to assist them. Whatever their plans, we need our processor fully functional. It'll take roughly sixteen months to arrive at our destination, so we have some time to determine what we should do about them."

"How many were hurt?" asks another.

Keller grimaces. "Seventeen dead. No wounded." The engineers squint at each other and at Keller. Anger rises in those unable to believe their captain hasn't done more to protect the rest of them.

Keller plainly reads the emotions playing out before him, but continues with his planned speech. "I have prepared a list. They are interred in their cryo-tubes if you wish to pay your respects."

"So why haven't we *killed* the sons-a-bitches? How many are there anyway?" demands the bold one.

Keller purses his lips. "Three."

"*Three?*" the man questions with unrestrained disgust. He strides furiously to a wall sconce, pulling a rifle free. "Fuck them. They die *now*."

Gregor nods and steps over to him, also grabbing a rifle. "I'm with you." The two men slap in battery packs and activate the weapons.

The counselor runs to them both, resting his hands on their rifle barrels, gently pushing them toward the floor.

"Didn't you hear *anything* the captain told you? These three captured our entire ship in minutes. *Three!* Those things you're holding wouldn't even leave a *mark* on that armor of theirs... but don't you understand? They're human! *We're not the last!*"

The men look skeptically at the counselor, unmoving. Seeing their indecision, the counselor continues.

"What Captain Keller hasn't told you yet is that these three didn't know this was a human ship. To survive, they have been scavenging from the invaders. The moment they realized we were human, they broke off the attack, even helped us care for the bodies." The counselor turns to look at the others behind him.

"Somehow, these people have endured the destruction and have been struggling to survive. Their ways may be strange, and their military abilities are terrifying... but as *people*, they're not so different."

Keller interjects, "What have you learned in the last thirty-six hours, Counselor?"

The counselor looks patiently at Gregor and his impetuous associate, waiting for them to replace their weapons in the wall sconce.

"Their organization is regimented, and I believe you were right. They are, most likely, a remnant of a military outpost. Their home is a barren rock in space, sparse on resources, and they have been collecting their needs from the aliens that destroyed our worlds so long ago. So far, they've managed to keep their existence a secret."

"These guys go toe-to-toe with the lizards?" asks one of the engineers.

The counselor nods. "That's why their tactics are so vicious. If they don't get control quickly, the enemy could get out a message that humans still exist." Eyebrows raise with respect and the beginnings of understanding.

"Survival is a full-time job for them where work shifts are twenty hours long, leaving only four hours for sleep. They are exceedingly efficient at task management, and they can be likened to machinery... In fact, I get the distinct impression mechanistic behavior is the ideal in their group, yet... to watch these three interact, I recognize a very strong bond—it's clear they depend on each other heavily to stay alive—and more so, they *really* care about each other."

The counselor looks down to the floor, gripping his chin. "That said, they suppress their emotions, claiming it clouds judgment. Emotions *are* there, however, and they are trying to cope with the guilt from having killed our crewmates…"

"Damn savages," Gregor grumbles. "How can you think they give a shit about us? We could be their *meat* for all you know!"

The counselor looks deep into his eyes. "We don't expect you to forget your wife, Gregor."

Gregor glares silently, angry and wounded. Slumping into a seat, he buries his head in his hands.

Keller looks at his young officer compassionately, but defers to the counselor. "Please, Counselor, go on."

The counselor collects his thoughts and scans the faces around him, making sure he has regained their attention. "Regarding their feelings of guilt, it's not something you'll have to take my word on. You'll see it." He shifts his posture as he moves on.

"Their society seems very skilled, albeit not terribly advanced. All of their gear is reliable and almost indestructible… definitely built to last. Each individual is highly specialized for particular tasks. For example, the three on board call themselves operators, and are further divided into three subgroups called Gun, Geek, and Brick. The big man is clearly the Brick, the tall one the Gun, and the woman the Geek.

"The Geek seems to be a computer specialist and pilot. Though she claimed to be damaged beyond function, she whizzed through our operating systems, mastering them in minutes. Even so, waiting *that* long frustrated her, and I can only speculate how fast she is at full capability.

"The Brick is the technician, skilled at repairing machine and man. He is the engineer, the doctor, and the demolitions expert all in one. He's also the one who peeled those blast doors into their current shape." The group turns at once to the twisted metal, hushed in their fearful awe of such strength.

"The Gun is the combat specialist. He is the strategist, tactician, and leader. He has absolute authority which the other two never question. He is very guarded, yet has allowed a piece of himself to show from time to time. He won't answer direct questions about his society, yet he's revealed they recently had a life-threatening setback: half of their 'Operator Corps' was killed in an ambush, and these operators are the ones who gather resources for the group. With only half as many to provide for the rest, they looked to different areas, hoping for less risky targets; and hence, here they are."

"What else?" asks Keller.

"Physically, they are quite different. The woman is a full two meters tall, and she is the shortest of the three. Strength, reflexes, dexterity, the like I've never seen before… if these three were at the Olympics, they'd take every medal. Either they evolved or they have enhanced their own DNA somehow.

"These operators are the elite of the group, representing the highest level of skill and physical fitness. Above them is a leadership caste, comprised of older, more experienced operators; and they decide all matters for the group. Below the operator caste is a medical/technical caste where most of the original research and development is done. I heard the woman refer to herself as a 'drone' once, which could be a worker caste at the lowest echelon. So far, that is my understanding of the organizational relationships."

One of the engineers steps forward, trying to put it all together. "So what you're telling us is these guys come in blazing, expecting us to be the lizards, or some other species; and when they realized we were humans, they stopped?"

"Yes," the counselor affirms.

"How can you be so sure?"

"We believed we were the last of our kind, so it makes sense they did too."

The man nods thoughtfully. Addressing the group again, the counselor elaborates. "They know, as we do, that being discovered means death. To protect their anonymity, they move through a ship as fast as possible, exterminating anything that could bear witness to their presence. If they can't succeed, they self-detonate."

"*Self-detonate?*" Keller asks, his eyes nearly bursting from their sockets.

"That's right. The ship attached to our hull, and the persons of our guests carry enough explosive to vaporize themselves and most of what they're close to."

"DAMN IT, MAN! THEY'RE WIRED?" Keller rants. "You should have told me IMMEDIATELY!" He gestures toward Gregor, adding, "If one of my officers had acted on his need for revenge, we'd all be *dust!*"

Gregor looks over despondently. "Now we truly *are* their hostages..." For the first time, the group nods in agreement with him.

The counselor shakes his head. "Please! Nothing has changed! True, this ship has many resources and would be an asset to *any* culture; but if they intend to enslave us, why are we allowed to roam free? The woman has already shown she can pilot this ship, and the other two have shown they have the skills to keep it running. They don't *need* us! They could lock us in the cryo-tubes, fly home, and unfreeze us one by one into bondage."

The group considers the counselor's words carefully, weighing the truth of them. They look to each other for cues, searching for help with their verdict in the faces of their comrades. Beside Keller, Sharon lifts her head from her contemplation.

"They did insist on handling burial detail, and they did so solemnly... And I know what you mean about them feeling guilty... they looked like children... like children who knew how disappointed their father would be... like they had failed utterly."

"Even so," Gregor counters, lifting his head from his hands, "we don't know what's waiting for us at their base. What we *do* know is how dangerous these three are. Can you imagine a whole *nest* of them? God forbid we should ever disagree with them—they could just strong-arm us into whatever position they like. You said it yourself, Counselor, they're military... not much for discussion." Gregor looks at the floor, extending his hands in front of him for emphasis. "We are self-sufficient. It's only a matter of time before we find a suitable place to live. So why in hell are we even *thinking* about risking all that?"

Gregor's logic stirs the group, leading to assenting murmurs. The counselor nods, forced to recognize the strength of the argument, but it is Keller who answers.

"I'm glad you mentioned those things, Gregor, because they are important concerns. You must also consider this: our ship is *old.* She has already doubled her expected service life. And if the list of defects they found in our atmosphere processor is any indication, can you imagine how many other issues this ship has we don't even know about?

"But let's assume the ship does hold up, and we do find a planet we could live on, and we plant all of our seed and raise all of our embryos... and we're discovered. What then? Do you really think we'd be left in peace? Who could possibly defend us? We're *technicians*, Gregor. We're *farmers*. There is no way we could ever feel secure..." Keller trails off, losing himself for a moment in thought.

"They're on a different evolutionary path," the counselor resumes. "We have food, air, and water processors, continuously renewable energy. We have the means to provide for ourselves and many more. They don't. They have to scrape their lives out of a barren rock!"

Gregor looks at the counselor skeptically. "If you take their word for it..."

The counselor drops his chin, looking at Gregor through his eyebrows. "Just look at them. Do you doubt it for even a *second*?"

Gregor pops his eyebrows up and looks away, choosing not to answer. The counselor takes it as a confirmation, and addresses the group..

"They need our life-supporting apparatus. We need their strength and protection. If we could successfully join as one, we could truly live again. We could have meaningful lives... and a *home*."

The last word hangs in the minds of all who hear it as they have all longed for it desperately. After a thoughtful silence, Keller clears his throat.

"You both present strong points. It's a risk, but the potential gain is enormous, and we can't ignore that. I'll talk more with them to see what else I can learn, and then we can make a more informed decision. Gregor?"

Gregor faces the captain, eyebrows raised expectantly. "Sir?"

"I want you to go to the soldiers' quarters; and when they wake, ask the leader, the... Gun, to meet with me and my officers."

Gregor squints in annoyance. "Why me, *sir*?"

"Because if you are determined to kill them, I want you to look them in the eye and see if your commitment waivers."

Gregor stands and salutes, barely reigning in his distaste. "Aye, sir."

The counselor opens his mouth to protest, but Keller shushes him with a hand. Gregor turns and abruptly departs. Once Gregor is out of earshot, the counselor steps in front of the captain with a questioning look. Before he can ask, Keller orders, "Go after him, keep an eye on him. Don't let him see you."

The questioning glance turns to relief, and the counselor pads quietly off after Gregor. Turning to his engineers, Keller says, "My friends, the 'Geek' has identified a list of malfunctions on our atmosphere processor as long as my arm. They are ordered by priority. Please get started on them, and the 'Brick' will join you shortly. He's big, so try not to be intimidated when you see him. Any questions?"

"Thousands, sir," replies the tall engineer.

Keller smiles. "Same here. Dismissed!"

Sharon and Ortega divide the engineers into teams and lead the noisily chattering groups out to their assignments. Keller watches them leave. Once he is alone, he sighs deeply and looks out through the viewscreen into the emptiness of space.

UNDERSTANDING LOSS

Gray smoke billows in large whirling vortices. Through the haze, glowing figures— visible in infrared—hunch over with arms in front of them, bracing themselves against the thickened air and confusion.

Pang! Pang! Pang!

The smoke strobes with weapon flashes, and the glowing figures lurch backward. Panicked screams pierce the misted air, and the remaining figures flee, but a giant shadow sweeps by in pursuit.

A slender shadow rushes by in the opposite direction, and the smoke strobes again.

B-r-r-r-r-ak-kak!

A low tone crescendos and rises in pitch, discharging explosively down an adjacent corridor.

Baaahh-rrrroooooooommmmm!

A distant rumble mingles with the tortured shrieks of things dying.

The air clears slightly, permitting longer views down the unlit corridors as they glide by. More glowing figures are visible…

Pang! Pang!

The radiant images snap at the waist and drop.

The journey halts at a large metal door, round and dark gray. A giant shadow shoves past, planting a device on it.

The device erupts savagely, shuddering the deck plates.

Smoke roils, and the giant shadow pushes through to pull apart the door's white-hot remnants. Gliding through the gap, the room beyond is hazy and dark, punctuated by fragments of incandescent shrapnel. At the far edge, a huddle of glowing figures crouches behind a console.

Sailing over the consoles and furniture, the intent to kill is strong and purposeful until a glowing hand thrusts up—a flat palm with four extended fingers and a thumb—a human hand.

"No! Don't!"

Thompson startles himself awake, jerking up from his bunk. His breathing is shallow and rapid, sweat rolling off his face. He scans the room, but bright light from the open door makes it difficult to adjust. Squinting, he holds a hand up against the light and finds Gregor only a meter away. The man holds Thompson's large rifle, aiming it squarely at the operator's face.

Thompson looks first at his own weapon in Gregor's hands then into Gregor's eyes. Neither of the men move.

"If they'd listened to me, you'd be exploding from decompression right now." Gregor's voice is twisted with hate and disgust, his expression a visual definition of loathing. Thompson calmly studies the man, gauging his conviction, finding it intractable.

"Why is that?" the operator asks.

"Because I'd have launched you out of the fucking air lock, that's why!"

As Gregor seethes, Thompson recognizes him. He first saw him on the bridge and later when Captain Keller was identifying the bodies. During the burial ceremony, Thompson was kneeling to lift the body of a blonde-haired woman when Gregor shoved him away violently, shouting at him to get away from her, not to touch her. Later on, he looked over his shoulder and saw Gregor pressed against a stainless cryo-tube, sobbing desperately. He ponders the memories, putting them all together.

"You had a special bond with the light-haired woman..."

"She was my *wife*, you FUCK!"

Thompson doesn't know the words "wife" or "fuck," but the context is plain. Slumping his shoulders, Thompson replies, "What I've taken from you I can never replace."

"*Yeah*? That's the first thing you said right!"

Thompson turns to look at Maiella. She is lying on her side, facing the wall, sleeping angelically.

"I would understand your loss."

"Like hell! What would you know about that? You don't even have feelings, you fucking *zombie*!"

Thompson returns the glare, not needing to understand the words to know their meaning. "We *have* emotions…" His gaze drops to the floor. "We just… manage them."

"Well, you've got the others pissing sunshine, but I see through you, *slaver*. When we get to your base, all your friends are gonna come on board and force us to do your dirty work. *I'm* not going to let that happen."

Thompson looks up patiently. "While I appreciate your protective instinct, reality will be quite different."

"*Oh yeah?*" Gregor smirks condescendingly.

Thompson nods. "The first thing that will happen will be a joyful welcome." He peeks briefly at Maiella. "The next will be our trial, judgment, and exile."

Gregor brings his eyebrows together questioningly, dropping his guard a bit. "*What?*"

Thompson swings his legs over the bunk's side to sit upright at its edge. Placing his hands on his knees, he looks seriously at Gregor.

"Our cadre exists around one principle: human life is *precious*. Everything we do and strive for is to protect and to serve our fellows. Anything less is a harm to the whole." He pauses, looking around at nothing in particular. "We have gone far beyond harm here, and we know the consequence. Everyone knows, even though it has never been enacted." His eyes focus distantly as he recites. "Anyone who harms, or allows to be harmed, another human is a threat and must leave the cadre." He resumes his serious gaze at Gregor. "It's our only law."

Gregor squints at his opponent. "Bullshit," he says, but lowers the rifle anyway.

"I sense that your loss has been greatest, so it is your testimony I will request at our trial."

Gregor stands in silent disbelief, taking a half step back and letting the rifle hang down by his side. Thompson turns once more to contemplate Maiella's gentle slumber. "You didn't come to kill me, for you would have done so. Why are you here?"

"The captain... he wants to speak with you."

Thompson rubs his face. "Tell him I will present myself in seven minutes."

Gregor nods and slowly backtracks. Before he leaves, he props the rifle up on its butt beside the door and steps into the corridor. He does a double-take when he sees the counselor leaning just outside. The two men have a wordless conversation in a split second, and with a single nod, Gregor admits to the counselor there may be more to the operators than he was willing to see.

CADRE ONE

PART TWO

Months pass in a blur of activity. Most of the time is spent restoring the mechanical condition of the aged ship's systems, and there is hardly a spot the operators haven't wedged themselves through or into to verify the entire vessel is secure and functional.

Gradually, the operators come to be accepted by the crew, but the differences in routine and custom are difficult to span. Requests to join in a game or music recital are rebuffed for duties elsewhere. Attempts at conversation rarely go beyond a couple of sentences. And the operators' work habits make every colonist feel lazy by comparison.

There is little to identify with.

Still, the results of their efforts are impossible to ignore. While every system on board benefits from their special attention, it's the little things that are noticed the most: a shine on an old handrail, fresher air in congested areas, the silence of well-lubricated doors as they whisk aside. Even the background noise of the ship has become quieter and more constant (no one noticed how loud it had become over the centuries until the machines were properly calibrated). It is as if the operators have given the colonists a brand-new ship.

When the end of the journey approaches, none of the colonists are prepared, having focused so heavily on their "worker bees," as they called them. Suddenly, they are faced with the imminent reality of the unknown. What will happen now? Apprehension sweeps the ship like a plague. Despite the fact that Maiella, Thompson, and Argo have become trusted faces, the colonists cannot help but fear the untold numbers of people as physically menacing as these three operators.

PRODIGAL RETURN

Maiella expertly guides the enormous colony ship into the familiar solar system. The additional bulk of the ship proves no challenge for her as she intuitively compensates, smoothly decelerating to two hundred thousand kilometers away from her base and home.

"Cadre One," she hails, "this is Team Spectre returning from gathering rotation. Mission successful. Awaiting acknowledgment, over."

A long silence ensues.

"Repeat, Cadre One, this is Team Spectre returning from gathering rotation," Maiella echoes. "Respond, over." Only static comes through the radio. She looks over her shoulder at Keller and Thompson. They both look back at her, confused.

Keller turns to Thompson, but he is just as surprised. In the viewscreen, a formation of alien ships crests the limb of the asteroid, approaching swiftly.

"Oh no…" Maiella gasps. "They found us…"

Thompson's hands automatically unsling his rifle and prime it, his mouth curling to a snarl.

"Do not maneuver," the radio crackles.

Maiella cocks her head, the visual not jibing with the audio. "The blueskins learned our language?" She looks to Thompson for instruction.

Thompson grips his weapon firmly, but there is less alarm in his eyes.

"Hail them again."

Maiella faces the viewscreen and transmits, "Cadre One, this *is* Team Spectre... Don't you recognize us?"

The radio buzzes then replies, "Team Spectre deployed 237 years ago. Do not make further transmission, or you will be incinerated."

A queer chill fills the bridge. Colonist officers exchange questioning glances, each uncertain face amplifying the others' anxiety. Getting Thompson's attention, the counselor asks, "Could this be a joke?"

Thompson resolutely shakes his head no.

Argo stands from his station and moves over to Thompson, whispering, "Have you ever seen ships like that before?"

"Never," Thompson answers, his eyes fixed on the sleek, modern vessels. Behind him, the colonist officers begin to huddle around their captain.

"What have you brought us into, Major?" Keller asks. Thompson does not reply, instead studying the mounting situation and analyzing it for possibilities.

Again, the radio crackles, "Transmit identity for verification."

"Finally," Maiella exhales and keys her radio. "Team Spectre dash Echo Foxtrot Hotel Lima Bravo, Major Gun Thompson dash Mike Delta Zulu X-ray, First Lieutenant Brick Argo dash Tango Mike Delta Charlie, First Lieutenant Geek Maiella dash Alpha Victor Echo X-Ray, over."

"Explain verbal delivery," the radio voice demands.

"Synaptic bridge failure during cryo-sleep compromised function of human digital interface."

"Verifying... Identification will be supplemented by visual reference. Remove all headgear and present yourselves on-screen for verification."

The three operators assemble themselves at the front of the bridge, unlatching their helmets and removing them before the viewscreen.

"Left-face," Thompson calls.

The operators crisply turn in unison.

"About-face."

The three take a half step forward and spin around, taking another half step to end where they started, maintaining their rigid posture.

At last, the radio crackles, "Gun, Brick, and Geek, board shuttle and surrender weapons. You will submit to DNA verification. Out."

In the viewscreen, a small craft departs from one of the sleek black ships. In orderly fashion, the operators restore their helmets and file wordlessly out of the bridge. Keller tries to get Thompson's attention, but the soldier doesn't take notice as he leads his team through the wrecked blast doors.

"I do *not* feel good about this, Captain," Gregor whispers. "Once they're off, we should get the hell outta here."

Keller stares at the black ships poised menacingly for attack. "I think you're right, Gregor. To your stations, everyone!"

The officers scramble to fill their seats and ready the ship to depart. "All back two-thirds," Keller orders. The massive engines ignite, drawing the behemoth ship back, but a searing bolt streaks by from the largest of the surrounding ships.

"Halt your retreat, or be destroyed!" the voice commands.

"All stop!" Keller orders. Desperation and powerlessness mingle inside him, meekly heralding the end of his command.

"Prepare to be boarded," the voice insists, and with a gentle thud, the shuttle arrives.

Keller looks up despondently, scanning the faces of his crew. They are looking to him for orders, needing him to figure a way out for them, but he cannot. He allowed them to fall into an easy trap and left them without protection after all these years. The best he can manage is, "I'm so sorry…"

The officers slump helplessly in their seats, thinking back on the months of time they had to avoid this. They think about how easily they were taken in by the possibilities the operators represented, how their hopes were so effortlessly manipulated. Now they sit, bitterly awaiting the arrival of their captors. Gregor drops his head to his console, barely uttering the word, "Hostages…"

Heavy footfalls approach in unison, and nine fully armed and armored Guns stride past the blast door. Gregor mutters under his breath, "Here comes the gestapo."

The lead Gun stands and surveys the scene. He immediately slings his weapon and slides his faceplate up. Though young, he has a serious appearance that exudes experience and confidence. When he looks around again, the serious look dissolves, his face beaming with amazement.

"I didn't dare believe it 'til I saw it! *Incredible!*"

The other Guns demask and shout out loud. Racing over, they hoist Keller and his officers up out of their seats into bear-hug embraces.

"*You really are human, aren't you?*" the lead Gun exclaims. The operators joyously sweep their armloads up onto their shoulders, bearing them like heroes back toward the shuttle and shouting like elated children. Gregor and Keller exchange a look of bewilderment, but grin with delight as they bounce along. The other officers get caught up in the excitement as well, laughing and hooting with their cheering new friends.

Back at the shuttle, Maiella, Argo, and Thompson smile modestly as the group crams in with them. The lead Gun claps the shuttle pilot on the shoulder, saying, "Take us straight to base, inform General O'Kai of our cargo!"

"Yes, sir!" the pilot replies gladly.

The shuttle tears away from the colony ship, streaking toward the asteroid with phenomenal agility. Argo's eyes gape at the shuttle's speed. He leans close to the pilot so he can be heard above the shouts and cheers.

"How is it we're not being crushed by our acceleration?" the Brick asks.

"About a hundred years ago, we captured a ship that had inertial damping."

"Inertial damping? How does it work?" Argo inquires with deep interest.

"Ah, I'd have to ask a tech about the specifics; but basically, it produces a field that energizes every particle in it, so matter's never in an at rest state."

Gregor overhears the discussion, understanding the phenomenal accomplishment it represents. "Fantastic," he mumbles in awe.

The lead Gun pushes through the crowd to stand before Thompson, Argo, and Maiella. Seeing Thompson's rank, he salutes respectfully. "So you're really Team Spectre, eh?"

The three nod in affirmation.

"We learned so much about you in training, how you always came back with your teams, how you designed the ambush that countered the threat of the stealth ships... You were the models of everything we should strive to be." He stamps his boot solidly. "And here you are again! The greatest find of all!"

"What happened at that ambush?" Maiella asks.

"Huh? Oh right, the stealth ships..." The Gun closes his eyes and presses the back of his hand against his forehead like he is remembering something arcane. "Okay, the teams get in position; and like you predicted, the blueskins appear to investigate their freighter. The decoy virus ship shoots out and attaches to the first ship it sees. Four stealth ships demask right there. So the team leader detonates the freighter. The blast wave destroys the ships that were investigating, cripples the four stealth ships, then rips into a row of *twelve more stealth ships behind them*! Even though the teams were out matched, the team leader decides to take the initiative in all the chaos. He lands a team on the three least damaged ships and gets control of them, but the fighting became really intense where teams would have to jump from ship to ship to keep from getting pinned down and destroyed. Then another ship appears on scene. Our operators believe it's reinforcement for the blueskins, but it isn't... It's General Dryden, Colonel Thorskild, and Major Eris in that fast military ship you had just collected. They fly in like they're going to attack our teams then break off at the last second and land pinpoint shots on the remaining enemy ships."

The shuttle passes the large bay doors of the cadre hanger and clanks gently into the docking clamps at the interior wall.

"It was a bloody fight, and we lost several operators... but we got away clean with three new ships, and we were able to figure out how to detect a stealth ship after studying the machinery on board. That one operation changed everything for us."

The Gun does not notice, but every colonist's face is riveted to his story, awed to be in the presence of people who have enjoyed a military victory over a species they thought were godlike and invulnerable.

"We've arrived," the pilot announces. The shuttle doors slide apart, releasing a throng of cadre operators and MedTechs cheering frantically from the other side. Keller and his officers are guided into their midst where they are welcomed with thunderous shouts and hurrahs.

Gregor grins broadly to his fellows. "Not much of a gestapo, huh?"

"I don't think I'll mind being a hostage here," grins Sharon.

Three MedTechs push through the crowd, seeking out the newcomers, reaching Keller first. "Are you hurt in *any* way? Do you require assistance?"

Keller looks at his crew and the cadre coming together with open hearts and arms, so relieved not to be alone anymore. His own heart swells in his chest at the sight, and he finally answers, "No. I'm better than I've ever been!"

The MedTechs nod at him in acknowledgement and scatter into the crowd to find anyone else who may need them.

Above the crowd, a loudspeaker blares to life, "Attention! Attention! All work details temporarily suspended. Assemble in sublevel 3, hall 9. Repeat, assemble in sublevel 3, hall 9. Over."

"Sublevel 3?" Maiella echoes.

The lead Gun overhears her surprise, explaining, "We've done a lot of digging in the last two hundred years…"

The crowd undulates and moves through the corridor toward the elevators leading down. Keller and his officers ride with the tide, not questioning the direction, allowing the group to lead them. It isn't long, however, before they notice that most of the people around them suffer from a major impediment: some limp unevenly in their gait, some drag a club foot or rely on a prosthetic extension to make a short leg as long as the other. Others hunch from a crooked spine or twitch in their stride with an ambulatory tic. Keller loses himself in his observations, unaware he is staring until a sweet-faced young woman with a prosthetic metal arm smiles at him. He shakes himself out of his absorbed observation, returning the smile warmly though slightly ashamed.

Angry Ghosts

The able-bodied operators have already walked ahead to make the elevators ready for the group. With gentility, they assist the more infirmed into the elevator, treating them as if they were precious things, more delicate and rare than anything else in the universe.

The counselor notices this first, specially attuning himself to observe the interactions of this new group, and he marvels at the compassion and care the operators show toward the handicapped. It saddens him to recall how just the opposite was true on Earth where more often than not, the handicapped were ridiculed, ostracized, and victimized.

The whole group is much too large to fit in at the same time; but the operators make sure the colonists, Maiella, Argo, and Thompson go with the first load. The heavy gate slides closed, and the large elevator descends.

Gregor leans over to the counselor, still taking in his surroundings. "It feels strange to be off the *Europa*. I haven't seen anything new in years… It's really exciting!"

The counselor smiles demurely, understanding the sentiment. As curious as Gregor and the other colonists are about the cadre people, the cadre people seem more curious of them, but there is a good-natured silence as each side wonders what they should say. The polite smiles and foot shuffling go on; then all at the same time, every person in the elevator car begins a question. All mouths stop in the middle of the word they were forming. Colonist and cadre alike give in to the comedy of it, the laughs coming easily and long. Only Maiella, Argo, and Thompson maintain their straight-faced expressions.

With a thump, the elevator reaches its lowest point, and the heavy gate slides aside. Beyond is a short, wide metal corridor ending at large doors, already opened. The group moves out of the elevator, proceeding briskly toward the hall just past the open doors.

Inside, the hall is busy with hundreds of cadre personnel filing in from similar entrances and finding seats. At the front of the hall stands a short stage with a long table stretched across its left half. More cadre personnel stand there, but they appear very fit, with full heads of steel gray hair. Their charcoal uniforms bear large broad panels of assorted colored bars, and their physical shapes are unmistakably those of operators.

One of the gray-haired operators notices the colonists strolling in among the others, and he raises an arm high to hail them, beckoning them forward.

Keller, Gregor, Ortega, the counselor, and Sharon politely guide themselves through the admiring crowd, stepping up onto the stage. The gray-haired operator who beckoned them is a tower of a man and large in build, surpassing Thompson in stature. He wears a pleased smile and introduces himself warmly.

"I am General O'Kai. Welcome to Cadre One!" The general outstretches his large hand to each of them, grasping firmly. "Please allow me to introduce the members of our leadership council: Colonel Shao-Lo..."

A tall, muscular woman with short hair steps forward, greeting her guests warmly.

"Colonel Munro..."

A man of Argo's build steps forward, extending a beefy arm. His other arm is dwarfed in comparison, being much smaller and shorter in length.

"Major Chusan..."

Another tall and muscular man with a heavily burn-scarred face steps forward as he is introduced. He bears a more serious look than the others.

"And Major Ralla."

A leaner woman steps forward with numerous silver electrodes extending just beyond her short cropped hair. She exudes phenomenal confidence, as much as the general himself.

Gregor studies the metallic contacts on her head, making the association. "Are you a… Geek?" he asks.

Ralla smiles politely. "That was my designation when I was an operator. Now I regulate the cadre mainframes and contribute to leadership decisions with the council."

Gregor nods in respectful understanding.

"General," Keller begins, "may I present the senior officers of the colony ship *Europa*: Commander Javier Ortega, Lieutenant

Commander Sharon Jones, Lieutenant Gregor Petrova, the ship's counselor, and myself, Captain Braemar Keller."

The general smiles broadly, gesturing his guests forward. "Please, come sit with us."

The colonists step up onto the stage, and Major Ralla guides them to their seats. There they all sit beside the general who remains standing, supervising the arrival of the cadre personnel.

Major Ralla finds herself beside the counselor, and a question has been in her mind since she met him. "Counselor,… is that your *only* appellation?"

The counselor nods, and seeing her inquisitive expression, he elaborates, "In my role aboard the *Europa*, I frequently have to arbitrate disputes, and I am trusted with highly sensitive information about each crew member. By not carrying a familiar name, it enhances my appearance of impartiality and makes the job easier."

Ralla raises an eyebrow at him. "We don't keep secrets about ourselves, and there are no disputes. Everything is planned." Her smile creeps back. "You could have a name here."

The counselor is caught completely off guard by the major's insight. From what he learned about the cadre from Maiella, Thompson, and Argo, he never expected to find one of them so immediately sensitive to how isolating and burdensome his role has been. He looks graciously on her, giving her a friendly touch on her shoulder.

"Cadre personnel!" O'Kai's voice booms, "Your attention!"

All eyes in the audience rivet on their general.

"I know you are all aware by now that there are new faces here in Cadre One. They came to us aboard a ship ten times larger than anything we have ever collected, and here is their Leadership Council!"

The entire audience shouts a hurrah all at once.

Keller is about to correct the general, but the counselor touches his arm, whispering, "It's how they know us." Keller understands, letting the semantics slide.

O'Kai raises his arms up to reel the crowd back in and continues, "But they didn't know we were here. Someone had to find them and guide them back to us." O'Kai pauses a moment, allowing the crowd to wonder, then answers their communal question. "Team Spectre..."

Shocked gasps go up from the crowd. There weren't many stories passed down through the generations, but the story of Team Spectre was one of them. The exploits of Maiella, Argo, and Thompson were used as parables to the initiates entering the operator corps; and they were described as the epitome of what everyone should strive for, nearly deified. Forty years after their final departure, they were declared lost, and that day became an anniversary to honor the ultimate sacrifice that they and every other fallen operator had made. Now, all watch in reverent awe as these three resurrected operators stride toward the stage at O'Kai's command. Before, the stories made them out as heroes. Now, back from the dead, they are invincible.

Every eye studies them carefully. The old-styled armor, clunky and heavy by modern standards, the oversized weapons, their shorter height, their modest builds—all would suggest inferiority, but not here. Not now. Here they are personifications of capability and supremacy—avatars of hope sent to guarantee the cadre's future.

They stand beside the general and turn in unison to face the crowd, chests out, expressions straight and stern.

"Team Spectre," O'Kai begins, "you three have been known throughout the generations for your superb service records. There was no length you would not go, no task impossible for you to accomplish. We believed you were lost to us, but after 237 years, you *continue* to set the example. Amid the infinite expanse of space, you found our ancient brothers and sisters, guiding them safely home to us. *Well done!*"

The crowd explodes with cacophonous cheers and applause, filling the large hall with excitement. O'Kai smiles out at them, scanning the sea of undulating people, some moved beyond joy to tears. He allows them the moment, even looking at the colonists himself with admiration and fondness. When he turns to regard Argo, Maiella, and Thompson for another round of praise, he sees they are still stern faced and solemn. He steps closer to them so they can hear his lowered voice above the crowd.

"You can allow yourselves to join in. This is a special time where emotion *is* appropriate. There is no shame in it here."

Thompson looks as if he is in pain.

"It's not that, sir. It's something else."

"Well, what is it, Major?"

The hoots and shouts die down as the audience notices the serious candor between Thompson and O'Kai. They pick up on it quickly, the cheering abating abnormally fast, and they lean forward in their seats.

"There's something we need to tell you all," Thompson admits, guilt setting his brow with conviction to confess. O'Kai squints at him queerly, unsure what he could possibly have to say.

"All right, Major," the general allows, "go ahead."

Thompson nods respectfully, checking with Argo and Maiella before proceeding. They nod back at him, dropping their heads. O'Kai steps toward the table of his officers and the colonists, allowing Thompson the full attention of everyone present. Thompson steps to the edge of the low stage, grim and serious. The silence is perfect.

"Friends!" he shouts across the broad hall. "Friends… I call you all my friends though I have never seen any of you before… This moment is incredible… so *good* for us and for our new guests. That we both survived, us and them, with *completely* different tools and skill sets is a testament to the durability of our kind. Now, reunited, we can share those tools and abilities that kept us alive by learning from each other, helping each other… We will *all* be stronger and healthier from this reunion."

The first claps of applause come from the table where Keller, Sharon, Ortega, Gregor, and the counselor heartily endorse his speech. The acclaim spreads swiftly through the room, nearly regaining the original pitch from before, every face so eager for the good news, and overflowing with gratitude to be hearing it. Thompson's face remains hard, however, and he raises his arms to be heard. The shouting dissipates immediately.

"It's the greatest moment of our history… which adds to the pain of our failure."

Questioning glances circulate throughout the hall, including the cadre council members.

"What the hell is he doing?" Ortega asks Keller. Keller shakes his head, staring incredulously.

"During the intercept and capture phase of our rotation, we caused the deaths of seventeen people before we realized the ship we were attacking had human occupants."

Gasps of horror rise from the crowd in all directions.

"For that crime," Thompson continues, "we expect judgment and await our exile from the cadre."

The audience before him is still as the grave, staring at what was once their ideal now reduced to ashes. The subtle hum of the ventilators provides the only audible sound.

Keller's jaw is open with disbelief, and Gregor grabs him by the arm. "Holy shit! He was serious!"

O'Kai shifts his posture, taken completely by surprise. He contemplates the information and looks out into the sea of horrified faces. Turning toward Thompson, Maiella, and Argo, he blinks hard.

"That is... unfortunate. I will form a tribunal to review the incident. Lieutenant Argo, Lieutenant Maiella, and Major Thompson, you will all be restrained in quarters until the review is complete. We expect any information you have on the incident to be surrendered along with all of your gear, armor, and weapons. Understood?"

The three operators stand at attention, chests out, anguish trying to force its way through their stalwart expressions. In unison, they reply, "*Sir, yes, sir!*"

"Major Chusan," the general orders, "escort Team Spectre to quarters and restrain them. Bring their equipment and any information they have on the incident with you to the council chamber. Have Gun Deepak and Gun Keiko assist you as necessary."

"Sir!" Chusan replies, swinging a flat hand to his brow.

O'Kai turns to the crowd, gathering their faltering attention with his powerful voice.

"Normal duty schedule resumes in fifteen minutes! Leadership council convenes in twenty minutes! To your posts!"

The crowd stands as a single unit and shuffles rapidly to the exits. The general faces his second in command.

"Colonel Shao-Lo, arrange quarters for our colonist friends and provide them with any supplies we can spare."

"Sir," she replies.

Taking a knee, O'Kai looks into the faces of the shocked colonists. "As general of the cadre, I am responsible for every action taken by it. I cannot begin to describe how much I deplore the loss of your comrades. When the tribunal begins, we would like your testimony. You may wish to take rest in your quarters first, because the tribunal will not convene for another eight hours."

"Eight hours?" Keller asks in amazement.

"Would you prefer it sooner?" O'Kai asks, misreading Keller's reaction entirely.

"No!" Keller exclaims. "Is eight hours enough? So much happened..." He looks among his own officers for support and finds they seem to share his sentiment.

O'Kai's face is unchanged. "The flight data recorder on their virus ship, along with the A/V recorders on their helmets, will show all the facts of the incident. Then we would like your corroborating evidence. I'll send Major Ralla to collect you. Until then, rest or be free to explore our facility. Colonel Shao-Lo can provide you a guide if you wish." O'Kai stands and strides off purposefully while Keller and his crew stare after him.

"This way to your quarters," Shao-Lo says politely. The colonists stand uneasily and follow the colonel to another floor.

Shao-Lo leads the colonist officers into a large room which appears recently altered. Five lockers beside five bunks stand against three of the room's four sides. There is no decorative interruption of the metal walls, save a small touch panel near the door, which Shao-Lo points toward.

"This panel is for communication, room lighting, and temperature regulation. If you need assistance, touch here, and one of us will attend to your needs." She pauses and fully faces them. "It is very good you are here." The tall woman smiles genuinely and departs. When the doors swish closed, Keller's officers begin loudly talking at once.

"Please! Please one at a time!" Keller insists.

"These guys are gonna get tossed to the wind by their own kind!" rants Gregor.

"I remember when you wouldn't have minded," Sharon reminds him.

"Yeah, well... I got kinda fond of the bastards."

"I know what you mean," Ortega adds. "I think we all have."

"What can we do?" Sharon asks. "The star chamber is forming."

"They *did* ask for our testimony..." the commander notes.

Keller thinks hard then looks at the counselor. "Do you think it'll matter?"

The counselor puts his hand to his chin, returning his captain's serious gaze. "We'll have to *make* it matter."

Keller nods when another thought occurs to him. "Whatever we do, we have to be in *total* agreement. Gregor, are you *absolutely* sure this is what you want?"

Gregor doesn't answer immediately, searching himself thoroughly. "I remember everything... I'll never forget. If it were up to me then"—he raises his hands with both index fingers pointing in a row—"I would've drilled all three, *bam, bam, bam,* and not lost a wink of sleep." He thinks some more, dredging up the aftermath of it all, recalling the agony of having to live without her, believing then that life was never going to be worth living again, blaming the three for ruining hope within him. Yes, blaming them, hating them so intensely it was killing him.

"Remember when you ordered me to their quarters, said I had to look them in the eyes?" Gregor gets a very distant look about him as he relives the moment, acting out the scene. "When I got there, they were sleeping. *God!* I wanted to waste all three of 'em right there. I picked up Thompson's rifle and took a bead on him first, savoring it. As I looked at him, he was sweating rivers: and he was twitching... mumbling something. He sits straight up out of his bunk, and I tuck the stock in tight to my shoulder, just *begging* for him to say something I don't like. But instead, he just looks at me. He isn't afraid. I can see he wouldn't stop me. He looked, just, *tortured.* Like, if I had triggered, he would've thanked me. There was something in his eyes that showed me he hated himself more than I hated him...

and *never once* did he try to make any excuses or try to justify it at all. I thought about that for months afterward. Months. And I'm sorry I wouldn't talk to you about it, Counselor. I know you were trying to help."

The counselor nods modestly in acceptance.

Gregor breaks off, letting his arms droop to his sides. "No, I don't think I've forgiven them yet, but I can't hate them anymore."

Sharon and Ortega nod soberly in agreement, and the five share a moment of silence, feeling its weight.

"They worked their asses off on the ship..." Ortega recollects.

"That's for sure!" Sharon chimes.

Keller smiles, adding his own two bits. "Remember when we invited them to dinner that first time?"

Sharon laughs out loud. "They show up, throw back some cup full of goo, and leave. They weren't even there two minutes!"

"That's their way. They never stopped moving except for a little sleep."

"And they're tough hombres too," Ortega adds. "Remember when Argo and Maiella were working on the intermix manifolds?"

"Oh yeah," Keller remembers ruefully. "They shut the inflow off, but the conduits were so corroded, they exploded from the back pressure. Argo gets up, shrapnel sticking out of his chest and legs, and he hauls Maiella away to safety. He fixes her up then starts pulling the pieces out of himself *by hand, no anesthetic*! I've never seen anyone do surgery on themselves like that, and he barely even groaned."

"I remember they wouldn't let any of us in that room that day," Gregor adds. "A few of the engineers thought they were gonna push past him; but Argo scoops all three of 'em off their feet, carries them outside, and locks the door! They were bitching to me about that the whole morning! Then the conduit explodes, and they realize he probably saved their lives. They shut up fast."

Sharon shivers, thinking about Argo pulling the hot metal from his own body, having to be his own surgeon there amid the sweltering machinery. "We tried to keep him in sick bay, but he wouldn't stay." She swells herself up as much as she can, dropping her voice, jutting her lower lip for her best impression of the big man.

"I have higher priorities."

The group laughs fondly and Sharon lets the laugh turn to a warm smile. "After a while, I felt safer having them around."

"Yeah," Gregor continues, "like, who cares if the lizards find us? These three'd go *right up their ass*!"

The group murmurs their enthusiastic assent. Again, a quiet descends as everyone silently reminisces their favorite memories.

"Yeah," Gregor admits, "I'd miss 'em if they were gone." An agreeing sigh joins his statement.

Keller rubs his chin, looking at his staff with determination. "Then we know what we have to do."

Argo, Maiella, and Thompson sit at the edge of the same bunk, unarmored and hog-tied by short chain quad cuffs. They huddle together, knowing how little time they have left.

"There were never two finer operators," Thompson says at last. "It is to my honor that our lives end together."

"We were fortunate to be under your command," Argo replies. "Your leadership used us well, and we always knew we could count on you to get us home."

"You both warned me to hide my emotions..." Maiella recalls. "I'm glad I didn't. You two are the only ones that could ever put up with me. I'll never have to wonder if you died without knowing how much you meant to me."

All three lean in close, resting their heads on each other. Despite the contortion it requires, they find comfort.

Before long, the tromp of boots becomes louder beyond the door, and the three sit up straight. Maiella sniffs deeply to regain her composure, but something compels her to look back at Thompson longingly. Her body feels light with the exception of her heavy heart sagging inside her chest. There is an emotion that has been growing inside her for some time, but she has no idea how to express it. The cadre has no words for what she feels.

There is only a moment more to get the words out, to tell him what she feels for him. If only her arms were free, she could throw them around him and try to show him what she means; but the restraints are strong, too strong. He can see she wants to tell him something, and he's waiting; but the steps outside are so near, there's no time.

"Thompson! I…"

"Yes?"

The door whisks open, and two Guns in armor stride through, taking positions on either side of the portal while Major Ralla steps to the fore. Argo, Maiella, and Thompson face front, blanking their expressions.

"Gun Thompson, Brick Argo, and Geek Maiella…" Ralla pauses to watch a single tear roll down Maiella's porcelain face. She changes her officious tone, becoming riskily compassionate.

"Are you ready to face judgment?"

In monotone, they reply as one, "*We are.*"

The major kneels and detaches the handcuffs from the leg cuffs then removes the leg cuffs entirely. Standing back up, she looks the three in the eyes. There is no question she knows her duty and will carry it out, yet a conflict lingers. As she looks at them, she knows they are guilty by their own admission and must be sentenced; but they brought home a human ship, complete with her full crew and cargo. She cannot and will not despise them for that.

She places her hand on Thompson's shoulder, and politely orders, "Follow me."

Ralla walks out, and the handcuffed operators follow obediently, the two Guns taking rank behind them. All six march in perfect cadence, their combined footfalls resounding solidly through the alloy corridors.

Thoughts race through Thompson's mind. *Could I have done it differently? Is there a way I can still save Argo and Maiella?*

Before he realizes it, they arrive at the council chamber. The Leadership Council is already assembled. At a table just to the left, Keller, Gregor, Sharon, Ortega, and the counselor look on nervously.

"Major Ralla delivering Team Spectre, as ordered."

"Thank you, Major," O'Kai says glumly.

Ralla steps around the table to join her fellow cadre officers.

"Dismissed," O'Kai states to the Gun escorts. They salute and depart, closing the door behind them. They peer in for one last look Before the doors shut completely they peer in for one last look, sadness etching their scarred faces.

"ATTEN-TION!" Major Chusan declares, and the three operators stamp once, thrusting their chests out. General O'Kai glances heavily at the display console built into the table before him, sighing deeply before speaking.

"We have reviewed all of the flight recorder logs as well as the data recorders built into your helmets, and we have discovered the following: Team Spectre deployed 237 years, four months, eight days ago under the direction of General Dryden. Your destination was uncharted space, a region where at least one vessel had been witnessed at significant distance. In flight, the virus ship suffered a collision with an undetected object, which damaged several on-board systems. Affected systems included life support, navigation, and power cells. Intermittent electrical failures are recorded several times.

"Sixteen months, seven days ago, the wake-up program initialized, yet was only successful in rousing Gun Thompson from cryo-sleep. The program indicated multiple problems with Gun Thompson's physical condition including irregular neural patterns and unthawed left arm. The irregular neural pattern was determined to be the result of repeated partial thawing from power failures. The defective arm was the result of protein buildup clogging the blood replacement outflow tube, which Gun Thompson was able to repair.

"The wake-up program was initialized by a proximity sensor detecting a nearby vessel, specifically the colony ship, *Europa*. There was insufficient power to follow all protocols, so power was diverted to rouse Brick Argo and Geek Maiella. Once awake, Geek Maiella discovered the synaptic bridges had retreated from her human digital interface, again, a result of repeated partial thaws. The irregular neural patterns of all three operators stabilized somewhat as the metabolic boosters took effect, and Team Spectre proceeded with their engagement of the colony ship.

"After perforation of the hull, Team Spectre killed seventeen human crew members before halting their attack on the ship's bridge. Here is the video from Gun Thompson's helmet recorder."

O'Kai taps a key on his console, and a holoscreen opens in the air over the table. Infrared video lends false color to the swirling smoke, and glowing blobs appear though the haze. Violent reports of weapons fire erupt, and the glowing blobs lurch back suddenly. Screams fill the room from the video as the view sweeps through the ship, more blobs being blown apart, dying horribly.

For Thompson, Maiella, and Argo, it is a familiar scene which tears at them; but for Keller and his officers, it is an unexpected transport to the terror of the event. They cringe and gasp at the sounds of familiar voices groaning in agony. Gregor's mouth falls open, quivering when he hears his wife's screams and her rough grunts as the bullets rip through her chest. He shatters completely, turning away, burying himself in his hands and sobbing desperately.

Argo feels his windpipe closing, but he doesn't understand why. The sensation distracts him from his at-attention pose, and he sneaks a peek at his teammates. Thompson is taking it hard and well, but Maiella is coming apart. He nudges Thompson to get his attention then nods at Maiella. Thompson looks to his right and sees her shaking, knees about to buckle. He shuffles over an inch to rub elbows with her. She snaps back and straightens up, getting a grip on her regret.

In moments, the video ends, leaving a smothering silence. Even General O'Kai is affected, and he takes a deep breath before speaking.

"Major Gun Thompson, it is clear you and your teammates suffered some severe problems during your deployment, yet you kept your team alive and returned with more than any operator team has ever provided. We never dared to hope there were others of our kind still in existence. It gives us critical hope that others may exist as well. However, the facts… *are*… clear. It gives me *great* displeasure to invoke our one law: 'Anyone who harms, or allows to be harmed, a fellow human is a threat and must leave the cadre.' Do you have anything to add?"

Thompson looks at Gregor, broken in Sharon's arms. She holds him as tight as she can, herself sobbing at reliving the deaths of close friends. Keller and Ortega are blank, pale, distant. Only the counselor seems to have endured the experience albeit with great sadness.

"Sir, no, sir!" Thompson answers.

O'Kai sighs deeply. "Then unless our new friends have anything to add, I will pass judgment."

The counselor swivels in his chair to face Keller. He gently touches the captain's arm with a questioning glance, and Keller straightens up out of his stupor. He looks into the counselor's face and nods. Facing the general, the counselor leans forward.

"In fact, there is, General. If I may?"

"Proceed, Counselor."

The counselor thinks for a moment to make sure he has his case in order. When satisfied, he stands from his chair to address the council, careful to look all of them in the eye as he speaks.

"When we received the first broadcasts that humanity was under attack, we were afraid, unsure of what was happening. But when we *stopped* receiving those broadcasts, we understood humanity had been annihilated, and we were *terrified*. In the last thousand years, we had only ourselves to rely on, and we kept ourselves alive by leaving most of our people cryogenically suspended, rotating only the thinnest crews to keep the ship together and on course. Those rotating crews were small and also intimate. From ordinary crewmen, they became families..."

The counselor notices many brows furrowing with lack of understanding.

"Family? Okay, I see you don't know the term. A "family" is a close-knit group of people living together who depend on each other heavily for survival. One could call your cadre a family..."

The lights go on for the council members with several "ah's!" and "yes, yes's!" echoing their comprehension.

"When Thompson, Argo, and Maiella came aboard our ship and took some of our family from us, it hurt us deeply. Those people were precious to us, and many of us hated your operators for their deaths.

"The three people you see standing at attention before you were so aggressive, so swift in their assault, and so *lethal* that we were absolutely *phobic* of them, and we longed to be rid of them. We were convinced this new breed of human that had captured our entire vessel in *seconds* was going to end our lives, and everything we had done to survive was wasted. Not a good first impression...

"One fact, however, was incontrovertible: they *are* human. Yes, you all are taller, stronger, faster, maybe even smarter than we are; but you are human nonetheless. It meant we were not the last, and the burden of perpetuating our kind was no longer entirely on our shoulders. There were other humans who had survived, and no matter what new form it took, our species would endure. Like you said, General, it allowed us hope that perhaps *other* pockets of humanity exist; and it eased the urgency we felt to free ourselves of this possible threat. In all of the time we spent traveling the stars, nothing ever changed for us. Now very real change was happening, and though we didn't know for certain if it would be for better or worse, we embraced it.

"During the long voyage here, we got to know Thompson, Argo, and Maiella well. What was immediately obvious was how ashamed they were over the deaths of our people. They were *consumed* by their guilt, even insisting they should be the ones to care for the bodies after the attack. They further explained how they had broken their only law and how it would mean their expulsion from the very family they lived to protect and provide for. We did not believe them at the time, though we can plainly see now that it's true, and your commitment to protecting human life impresses us greatly. Specifically, it removes any concern we had over coming to harm at your hands.

"It does raise another concern, however, that there is no compassion in your family when a mistake is made. From the video you just showed, there was *no* way to identify the glowing silhouettes as human. They could have been *any* bipedal species, and there were no words audible above the weapons fire and explosions..."

The counselor pauses a moment to see how Gregor is doing, wondering if the lieutenant will resent how fervently he is pleading the operators' case. Gregor's sunken eyes look up at him; and though emotionally exhausted, he gives a slight nod, urging the counselor to continue.

"Once Thompson reached the bridge, we see Captain Keller's

hand plainly resolved, and we hear his voice. That is the first evidence we have that indicates the people in the video were human. And that is precisely where the attack *stopped*. Add to that, their life support had failed several times, and irregular neural patterns were detected. They may not have had perfect perception, yet they performed *precisely* as they were trained. How can they be condemned for perfect performance?"

O'Kai slumps slightly and reluctantly straightens.

"That is all true, Counselor, and it pleases me you would try to spare these operators the consequences of their actions. But the fact remains our one law was broken. That law is the principle upon which *all* of our motives are built. If I did not enforce that law, I jeopardize all under my authority. Should I make exception for these three, no matter the circumstances, it suggests I may make exception in the future; and that may cause some to be less careful with the lives of those around them. No. For the good of all, I *must* carry out their judgment."

The counselor thinks for a moment. "This is *your* zone of control. I understand you have the huge responsibility of looking after the entire cadre, and you must do what you feel is best…"

The general nods gratefully and opens his mouth to speak, but the counselor isn't finished.

"But aboard our ship, that is *Captain Keller's* zone of control. What happens aboard his ship is *his* responsibility, and we would not want to think you would force your will on those *outside* of cadre law. To do so would be unacceptable, and we could not remain under those conditions."

O'Kai and his officers open their eyes wide in shock, realizing the counselor just suggested he and everyone from the colony ship might leave. The council members begin to murmur uncomfortably among themselves, but O'Kai silences them with the palm of his hand. He stares hard into the counselor's eyes, searching for any trace of insincerity or lack of conviction. For anyone in the cadre, saying is the same as doing, but these are a strange breed of human... He mustn't allow them to surprise him again.

"You would seriously consider leaving, abandoning the possibility of a stronger, joined community?"

A lesser man would have long since withered under the general's crushing gaze, but the counselor stands resolute.

"Not just consider, General. We would do it. The freedom of self-determination is fundamental to our existence. We could not have it any other way."

O'Kai looks away in disgust, muttering, "The surpluses your lives must have permitted you…" He looks at Thompson, Maiella, and Argo, knowing what he believes needs to be done with them. Reading their expressions, he recognizes their discomfort. He can plainly see the operators *agree* with their judgment. So who is this man to tell him what is best for his people? The insubordination is intolerable to a man who must, out of necessity, make quick decisions. And once made, those decisions must never be questioned…

From the little interaction he has had with the colonists, he is starting to see how incompatible they could be with the smooth flow of authority and action in the cadre; and for a moment, he considers telling them to make good on their threat and be gone…

But he needs them. The generations of genetic inbreeding have only gotten worse, and despite the new technologies they've captured, there is nothing they have acquired which has helped them stay ahead of their copious genetic defects. Fewer and fewer people are incubated that have even the *possibility* of entering the operator corps. This ship full of colonists represents all the DNA they need to permanently breed out the weakened genes and restore vigor to a terribly infirmed population. And having reviewed Argo's inventory of the colony ship, he knows how desperately his people need functioning food and water processors—ones that require much less maintenance than their ancient, faltering amino-protein synthesizers. But can't they see how much they could benefit from the cadre's protection? When each side has so much to gain, how could they leave?

In the end, it doesn't matter. He cannot afford to let them go, and as much as he dislikes it, the counselor is correct—a general of the cadre has no say in the happenings aboard Captain Keller's ship. The corners of his mouth drop as he faces Keller.

"Well, Captain, what would you have done with them?"

Keller stands, a little off guard, and collects himself. "I would have them pardoned and readmitted into the cadre with full rank and privilege."

"Do you understand you are inviting the possibility of future accidents?"

"I do," Keller replies staunchly.

O'Kai squints with disparaging astonishment. "You would put your entire crew at risk to spare these three?"

"Yes, General. We would have it that way."

O'Kai shakes his head at Keller, seriously questioning this man's leadership and ability to care for his people. The lives of everyone in the cadre have never been anything but desperate and precarious. He can only imagine how brief Keller's success would be under such circumstances.

The general faces front and addresses the three on trial. "Major Gun Thompson, Lieutenant Brick Argo, Lieutenant Geek Maiella, this crime is expunged. Though I am pleased we will retain your skills and abilities, this sets a dangerous precedent. Let it be known, this exception can *never* be repeated." Turning to the colonist's table, he continues.

"Captain Keller, I request you and your officers meet with us again in two hours. It is apparent we have different ways of doing things, and if we are to live together, we *must* have a common set of rules."

"Team Spectre, you are dismissed for twenty-four hours' rest and regeneration. After which, you will report to Major Ralla for technical updating and reassignment. Tribunal adjourned!"

O'Kai, Shao-Lo, Munro, Chusan, and Ralla stand in unison, filing out in orderly fashion. Ralla lingers only to remove the accused's restraints, and follows the others out.

Sharon and Ortega stand to join Keller and the counselor. There is a lingering aftermath from witnessing the video after so many months—wounds that were healing have been torn open again. Fighting through the melancholy, Keller rests his hand on the counselor's shoulder approvingly.

"Well done, Counselor. *Well* done."

"Eloquent as always," Sharon adds.

Gregor stands solemnly, still reeling from the experience, and makes his way toward the door. Keller calls after him.

"Gregor, where are you going?"

He stops and turns, looking not at his captain, but into the backs of Argo, Maiella, and Thompson.

"I can't be here right now." He turns without ceremony, resuming his path.

Keller lets him go and looks at the floor, understanding the man's awful conflict. He sighs deeply.

"It's a real victory," Ortega remarks, trying to lighten the mood. "It proves they won't try to dominate us."

Keller nods in agreement. "Yes, it seems that way."

The counselor steps around the table, confused why Thompson, Argo, and Maiella are still standing in place. They have dropped their at-attention stance, but haven't moved, silently staring at the wall ahead of them.

"Thompson! Argo... Maiella? What's wrong?"

"You placed our importance above the cadre," Argo replies. "It is wrong."

Keller walks around the table to stand in front of them. "Aren't you glad you can stay?"

"We didn't want to go," Maiella explains, "but we felt it was necessary."

"You lost seventeen," Thompson states. "We lost nothing. Our personal loss must equal or exceed your own to make matters right again."

Keller dismisses their guilt. "You three have carried your burden long enough, and you more than paid for it with your service aboard the *Europa*."

"We don't understand why you would set aside that loss without demanding the same of us," Argo says.

The counselor smiles. "It's a very human thing called forgiveness. We'll teach you all about it."

Thompson smiles unconvincingly and nudges his teammates.

They turn and stride out. Sharon and Ortega approach Keller, stating, "We're going to go check on Gregor... see how he's doing."

Keller nods his assent, and the two depart, leaving Keller and the counselor alone in the room. Keller walks to the table's edge and sits on it, studying the bare walls. The unhappy aftermath troubles him.

"I imagined this turning out better."

The counselor steps in front of his captain, lowering his head submissively. "Are you displeased with my performance?"

"No! No," Keller counters, "not at all. You were brilliant."

The counselor looks up in confusion. "Then what is it?"

Keller shuffles his feet. "Maybe we should have left well enough alone."

"Sir?"

Keller looks off to the side then looks back. "We just met these people, and did you see how they left this meeting? They welcomed us openly, publicly, completely... now they're suspicious. We backed them into a corner."

"We had good cause."

"Good cause?" Keller guffaws. "Argo, Maiella, and Thompson didn't even *want* to be saved! We should have asked them first... And dragging Gregor through that all over again... *God*, I wish they hadn't shown that video..." He balls his fist and brings it up to his mouth. "We've all lost friends, but Gregor... he just watched his wife's *murder*." His fist opens, and he grips his brow, squeezing tightly. "Everything was so hopeful... and we wrecked it."

The counselor thinks for a moment. "I disagree."

Keller raises his head suspiciously.

"How different are our two cultures?" the counselor asks.

Keller arches an eyebrow. "Like two sides of a coin. Why?"

"With cultures as different as ours, conflict was inevitable. They may not like it, but the cadre is now fully aware we intend to keep our autonomy, and you've retained your authority. We set that boundary early, and that'll save us a *lot* of conflicts down the road."

"And what about interfering in their system of justice? We deeply offended them; *and* we made Argo, Thompson, and Maiella outcasts *in their own society*!"

"That's an even simpler justification. If we hadn't acted, they'd be dead."

"Yes, but at what cost?"

"Cost is irrelevant, Captain. They're alive, and that's all that matters."

Keller nods, reluctantly admitting the counselor is right. He looks to the side again and speaks to the wall ironically. "We were so afraid they were going to dominate *us*... tell *us* what to do. I guess we beat 'em to the punch."

The counselor looks at Keller strangely. "You think we forced ourselves on them?"

"Didn't we? We're the only ones who wanted to save Thompson, Maiella, and Argo! We didn't have any concern for what *they* wanted."

The counselor looks at the floor before replying, "Morality exists independently from human desires."

Keller looks back at him quizzically. "Huh?"

"Captain, have I always agreed with you?"

Keller laughs, "Certainly not!"

"That's right. There were times I barred your way from what you *wanted* to do because it was the *right* thing to do."

Keller gets the gist of it. "Go on."

"Just like when crewman Toro lost his mind and after his attempted sabotage of the main reactor failed, he tried to kill you. You had just beaten him to the ground, and when I walked in, Gregor was passing you a rifle. You were going to kill him."

Keller rubs his knuckles as if they still ache from the fight. "I remember. He had almost killed us all. I was furious, and I wanted to make him an example so it would never happen again."

"I stood between you and Toro, and I refused to let you kill him. Everyone on the bridge was with you. It's what you and they all wanted. But I ignored your orders."

Keller nods ruefully. "Turns out there was a gas leak at his engineering station, hardly noticeable; but it was building up in his system, and it caused a chemical imbalance... After treatment, he was so grateful we helped him, he became a new man. Hardest working, never quit or complained… then the fire… he was the only one who stayed to fight the flames… and he died for us."

"Toro was already working against the same desolation and loss of hope many of the crew were feeling. The fumes at his station for some reason made him focus on that until all he could think about was ending it. In his own warped way, he believed he was *helping* us all by taking away the pain of a hopeless life. If you had killed Toro, someone else would have taken his station, and the same thing might have happened all over. And maybe *no one* would have stayed to fight that fire."

Keller nods thoughtfully at the memory, and even though he hated the counselor for defying him then, he came to be grateful he hadn't killed Toro. It is an obvious parallel to the situation at hand.

"The cadre may disapprove, even hate us for what we did here," the counselor explains, "but it doesn't alter the fact it was the right thing to do. There is no such thing as perfect information, which is why justice can never be carried out summarily—the wheels of that machine are designed to turn slowly."

Keller's head bobs in agreement as the counselor continues.

"Thompson, Argo, and Maiella will prove themselves worthy to the cadre as they did to us. All we did is ensure they get the chance."

Keller's expression lightens considerably, like a great weight has been taken off. Then he grins unexpectedly. "*Man*, you're good at this. You sure you weren't a salesman before you were a psychiatrist?"

The counselor gives a battleship-wide grin as they walk out together. "Who says I quit being a salesman?"

GETTING ACQUAINTED

"*General*," Keller continues with exasperation, "how can you say it doesn't matter how our DNA is combined? *It's part of us!* Why wouldn't we want a say in how our parts are combined? We're making *people* here! People who are going to be our *children!*"

"Yes, Captain," O'Kai grates through clenched teeth, "we *are* making people, but you make your case as if you were donating limbs. Your DNA is a *product. Nothing more!*"

"A *product?*" Gregor leans forward, splitting at his seams. "A fucking *product?* Our DNA, it's… it's who we *are!*"

"It's our intimate self," Sharon restates less forcefully, "our uniqueness… our…our…" She trails off, searching for words stifled by emotion.

"Nothing could be more important or sacred to us," Ortega finishes.

Ralla leans forward, much cooler than anyone besides the counselor. "Captain, you speak of your genes as if they comprised your identity, as if by giving up a sample, you would cease to be who you are. Nothing could be farther from the truth. Do you know how many cells your body sloughs off in a day? We could benefit vastly from a swab of your cheek, and you would still be who you are today."

Keller looks down at the table shaking his head. "No, Major, you're not understanding…" He lifts a hand to his mouth and looks off into space, trying to regroup, trying to make them see.

The counselor notices the lull in discussion and seizes the

146

moment. "General, let's back away from the topic for a moment and take a deep breath. We have reached a point where both of our arguments are valid and important. Please believe that we want to resolve this issue, so let's start again where our real breakdown in communication is occurring."

The pause is a welcome respite to all, and the storm clouds hovering over the table begin to dissipate. Much sighing and rubbing of faces ensues, and after a few deep breaths, everyone is ready to try again.

"General," the counselor continues, "a key difference between our societies is how we think of our own bodies. In your cadre, it appears that everything is shared, and it is a practice born of necessity. We can see how you have struggled to endure, and it is largely due to your extensive sharing of resources, such that there is no ownership of anything. Not even yourselves!"

"Oh-nur-ship?" O'Kai questions.

"Possession of something to the exclusion of everyone else," the counselor explains.

O'Kai furrows his brow at the concept as do his officers. The counselor easily reads the revulsion in their faces to the concept, and he preempts their objection.

"General, we understand why your cadre works the way it does because it *has* to. There is no alternative. To survive, this was your option. I want you to believe that we genuinely respect that."

"All right, Counselor, then can we end this debate?"

"We can, General, if you can make a similar leap of faith that we are this way because we, too, *have* to be."

O'Kai pans his head at his fellows, stymied as to how the counselor could possibly be serious.

"General," the counselor calls O'Kai's attention back to the table. The aged operator squints back at him, wondering what piece of nonsense he is going to utter next.

"Do you believe we have lived the same lives?" the counselor poses.

O'Kai nearly loses his seat, guffawing at the obviousness of the answer. "Clearly, we have not!"

"Fair enough," the counselor concedes. "You became the way you are because of the realities of life around you. Why, then, is it so hard to believe we became the way we are because of the realities of *our* lives?"

The mocking look is gone, skepticism evaporates. "All right, Counselor," O'Kai states, "I'm listening."

The counselor takes a moment to regroup, to make sure he doesn't waste the hard-earned attention he has just won.

"I submit that all our differences are strengths. Each of our two cultures has so much to offer the other, I don't know where to begin! But maybe we should start right here with how we think of our own bodies. In your world, they are community property. But in our world, they are private; and it is paramount we retain the ability to determine what we do with, and what becomes of, our own bodies."

"You're *deliberately* withholding something we need for *no* justifiable purpose!" Chusan explodes.

"No," the counselor counters calmly, "we are simply obeying what our inner voices tell us is right."

"*Slag*," Shao-Lo says in derision. "I think you're trying to use *words* to attain dominance over something you *fear*."

Gregor is almost completely out of his seat before the counselor gets a hand on his shoulder and eases him back down. Gregor stares bullet holes through Shao-Lo, but she is unmoved by his visual attack. Moreover, it proves to her she is right.

"Colonel, it *is* true, your cadre can be frightening to us," the counselor begins, affixing an unflinching gaze at the severe woman, "but is that what we were discussing?"

Shao-Lo blushes slightly at being called out on her non sequitur. "No," she admits reluctantly.

"Okay," the counselor accepts, giving Gregor's shoulder a brief squeeze before continuing. "Now then, we were talking about ourselves, and how we differ in our views, but how those views should not be discounted by *either* side."

Shao-Lo opens her mouth to debate, but O'Kai's stern glare mutes her abruptly. She purses her lips and folds her hands in front of herself. O'Kai scans the rest of his council, ensuring there is no further dissent and defers to the counselor with a nod.

Again, the pause is welcome; and the counselor relaxes his stance, rounding his shoulders slightly. He offers a genuine smile to the cadre officers across the table from him.

"I understand your position. I really do. You have had a *very* difficult existence of scarcity and uncertainty, and the reason you do things this way is because they *work*. Your group is strong and alive. Well, we, too, are strong and alive. What we have done to survive has worked as well. Consider that."

The counselor pauses, letting the message sink in. Shao-Lo, Chusan, Ralla, and even quiet Munro nod their heads in, at least, a tacit acceptance. Wrapping up, he adds, "So long as we don't discount the *needs* of each other, we *can* come together, and we can do so without feeling we have given up something important."

O'Kai's head bobs with agreement. "I believe we understand each other. And on this point, we will agree: in combining the DNA of our two groups, we *will* obtain input for education and occupational determination from the colonist contributors, which will be balanced against the cadre's most critical needs."

Keller nearly bursts with relief. "Thank you, General! I know our people will be much stronger from our joining."

"General, one more thing," the counselor requests.

O'Kai looks at him with a renewed wariness, almost dreading another request from these familiar looking, yet thoroughly alien people. *"Yes?"*

The counselor takes a thoughtful look around the room. "I know we are different. Maybe expecting us to just immediately understand each other is asking too much too soon. That will have to come with time. Instead, can we end this meeting with the accomplishment that despite our differences, we will make effort to accept each other, as we are?"

O'Kai smiles broadly and stands to clasp the counselor's outstretched hand. "I'd like that." On cue, the council officers stand and salute respectfully.

O'Kai retracts his hand, announcing, "Meeting adjourned!"

The council officers huddle around their general as he

immediately begins issuing orders. Keller and his officers huddle up as well. Keller's eyebrows rise then fall with a heavy exhale.

"Jesus!" Gregor exclaims. "Is *everything* gonna be this hard?"

Sharon shrugs, her face echoing the question. Keller stares at the cadre officers. They are so closely engaged, they don't notice him looking.

"I have a feeling we're gonna have to fight with everything we have to keep from getting gobbled up… like a puffer fish in a tank full of sharks."

The counselor puts a hand on Keller's shoulder. "Captain, the cadre is a group that has survived by forcefully taking whatever it needs. Today, its general learned the meaning of the word 'compromise.' Please don't belittle that."

The counselor steps around Keller, making his way to the other side of the broad table. Gregor sidles up close to his captain.

"Sir," he whispers, "why do you let him talk to you like that? If these people see him talking down to you, they may think he's the boss. Personally, I trust you to look out for us more than I trust him."

"I get your point, Gregor…" Keller states glumly, "but I'm no diplomat. I was trained for command of a colony ship, not spanning these cultural chasms."

They all turn at once to watch the counselor, how easily he has broken into the cadre officers' conversation, how receptive they seem to his comments, how comfortable they seem having him near.

"If this was something about the *Europa*," Keller explains, "you're right, I wouldn't have it, but here… I trust him. His detachment gives him an objectivity I could never have."

"With all due respect," Gregor hisses, "as captain of the *Europa* and her crew, can you *afford* to be objective?"

Keller is surprised by Gregor's implication, eyes gaping as he contemplates his subordinate having just lectured him on his duty.

"I realize, Gregor, you are only making sure I keep perspective on my role as captain, so even though it *sounds* like a challenge to my authority, I will not take it as such. The counselor has my full confidence, and that will have to suffice for you as well. *Is that clear?"*

Gregor stiffens nervously.

"Clear as vodka, sir."

Once Keller is sure Gregor understands, he claps him on the arm to show there are no hard feelings.

"Captain!" calls the counselor.

Keller looks across the table to see the cadre officers and the counselor attentively gazing his way.

"What is it?"

"With your permission, I'd like to offer the general a tour of the *Europa*."

Keller scans the faces of his officers. Their wary expressions do not deter him. "Of course!" he replies grandly, "provided the favor is returned."

O'Kai nods immediately. "Perhaps seeing how we live will enhance our understanding."

The counselor smiles fondly as he alone understands what a huge undertaking it will be to deviate the cadre's rigid work schedules.

"Colonel Munro," O'Kai orders, "take these people wherever they would like to go and ensure their safety. Major Ralla, you will go with the counselor and inspect the *Europa*. Brick Argo described several items of interest in his report, and I'll expect your full analysis."

Munro and Ralla snap to attention and salute. "Sir!" they reply in unison.

"But, General," the counselor questions, "won't you join us?"

O'Kai ponders a moment and his mouth curls slightly, somewhat pleased his presence was asked for *specifically*.

Shao-Lo leans forward, saying, "Chusan and I could assume your duties over the next three hours."

O'Kai frowns thoughtfully and accepts with a smile. "All right, Counselor. Let's go."

Colonel Munro throws aside a hulking pressure door with his strong arm. Immediately, the hiss, clank, and screech of heavy industry pours out.

"*This is our primary fabrication facility,*" he shouts above the din. "*Most of our final assembly is completed here.*"

Keller peers past the big man, taking in the total scene of conveyors, sturdy load lifters marching with large metal parts in their grips, arcing sparks, massive automated machines, and, wavering with heat in the background, the foundry. Driving the load lifters are bald humans with metal topped heads and dark lenses over their eyes. Tall numbers are printed on their armored chests.

Two load lifters converge at the head of one of the conveyors, carefully placing the parts they carry; and the group watches intently as the parts are pressed together, heated, welded, and bombarded by a high-intensity beam. Sharon, Ortega, and Gregor step from behind Keller to get their own look at the finished frame rolling off the back of the conveyor. One of the load lifters dutifully retrieves it and marches away while the others arrive with more parts for the conveyor.

"*What are you making?*" Ortega asks loudly.

"*Some of the ships tethered to Cadre One have been supplying us with power from their reactors for centuries,*" Munro shouts. "*In that time, the reactor housings have eroded significantly, and these supports will keep them from caving in.*"

Curiosity draws Gregor toward the room, but Munro's arm drops like a steel gate. "*I'm sorry, Lieutenant. No access without thermal-impact armor.*"

Gregor blinks and looks into Munro's stern but friendly face. He nods in understanding, backing away from Munro's one-man barricade, and the colonel hauls the heavy door shut. With a great clang, the noise of manufacture abates.

"The next bay is our genetic engineering and incubation facility," Munro announces in a much calmer tone. "This is where *we* come from."

He leads them down a sleek metal corridor with several rooms and passages, branching off its gently circular path. Stopping at a floor-to-ceiling round door, he inserts a pass key, removes his gauntlet for a handprint panel, stoops close to an eyepiece, and speaks his name and rank into a microphone. The automated security panel switches each identifying LED to green and refers him to a small touch pad where he enters a private password. At last, the security checks are complete, and the tall door sinks back, rolling aside like a giant cog.

"This way," Munro announces pleasantly and walks briskly inside. Keller, Sharon, and Gregor follow until they catch sight of the door's profile, which even to guess, they figure is a full-meter thick.

"I'd say you're serious about protecting this room, yes?" Ortega asks rhetorically.

Munro turns on his heel. "Of course we are. This is our future." Reaching just to his side, he taps a code sequence into a panel, and the giant wheel-door rolls back into position and the radial maglock at its center rotates into place.

An inner door ahead slides open, beckoning them into darkness. Stepping through, their eyes gradually adjust; and they are aware of a dim, omnipresent red glow throughout the room. Keller stretches his hands out ahead of him until his eyes begin to perceive outlines and shapes. The dimensions come into focus, and he sees a room full of floor-to-ceiling cylinders. As his eyes fully adapt, he sees the middle third of each cylinder is transparent. Sharon steps close to one, gently caressing the plexi-steel, straining to see its contents.

"Embryos…" she notes aloud.

"That's correct," Munro confirms. "Once we have constructed viable gametes, we selectively pair them, and the ones that begin meiosis, we transfer here."

Ortega, Gregor, and Keller follow Sharon's lead, peering in at the tiny blobs suspended in the cylinder's fluid. Thin umbilicals anchor them to the tops of their tanks.

Keller stands back from the tank and, again, notices the red glow. Try as he might, he can't find the source. Munro sees him panning his head about and ends the mystery.

"We discovered the embryos benefit from modest sensory stimulation as they grow, so we provide visible, tactile, and audible input. The red light is an ambient holoprojection. For some reason, embryos raised under this hue are slightly healthier than others."

Sharon presses her hand against the clear tank surface, feeling its warmth and something else. Lowering her ear down to the glass, she hears what she suspected: the gentle *lub-dub* of a human heartbeat.

Looking in Sharon's direction, Munro sees her smiling against one of the tanks. "I'm told the first artificial generations were raised in darkness, with no biorhythmic stimulation. Most of them lacked social instincts, typically isolating themselves from others, and frequently, they developed severe behavioral disorders. With decades of experimentation, we discovered that simulating the interior of a human body provided the embryos with significant cooperative instincts, and they became much more productive personnel."

Gregor grunts cynically as if mocking an advertisement. "Building better people through *eugenics*!"

"Precisely," Munro beams.

"What kind of disorders?" Sharon asks with genuine interest.

"From what I was told, they tended to be obstinate, refusing to work or cooperate in any way. They would harm themselves, and at times"—Munro gets a morose look about him—"they would harm others. Sadly, the early years were filled with many failures as we blundered through the human genome. In trying to keep our own genetic defects at bay, we frequently caused them." He gingerly places his large hand against one of the cylinders, looking into it deeply. "I can't imagine what it must have been like then… to have to discover the results of your failures on living children…" Munro trails off, not permitting himself the indulgence any longer, and he takes his hand off the tank.

"What happened to them?" Ortega asks.

"They were reconstituted, of course."

Keller, Gregor, and Sharon perk up at once.

"Reconstituted?" Keller asks expectantly.

"Yes, reconstituted," Munro repeats. "It is a selective lobotomy to remove the defective neural structures, which are replaced with implanted chipsets. The individual is no longer capable of highly skilled tasks, but they are rugged laborers and can be programmed for a wide variety of basic functions. This way, they can still contribute as useful cadre personnel."

The colonist officers stiffen rigidly, all fascination in them replaced by moral outrage. The four look at each other; and though they want to blast Munro for his Mengela-esque medical practices, they bite their tongues, choosing to swallow their revulsion.

Munro can't help but notice the change in his guests' postures and expressions. He lets some of the air out of his chest, taking a cautious half step toward them.

"Is something wrong?"

Gregor, Sharon, and Ortega won't look at him. Even Keller's instinct is to turn around and walk back to his ship. Such a concept is blatantly contrary to their most fundamental of human rights. Medical dismemberment for the purpose of slave labor...

He thinks back to the meeting a few hours ago with O'Kai and the other cadre officers; and he hears the counselor's voice reminding him to look past the surface, to first accept, and then *try* to understand. As he does so, he remembers how the cadre has no concept of private property—not even of themselves. As he surveys the room with the cylindrical tanks around him, it dawns on him how hard it is just for them to maintain their population and just how much is invested in every embryo.

Philosophical superiority is easy to maintain when survival is not so desperate or so uncertain, he thinks, and it shames him that for even a moment he placed Munro and the cadre beneath him.

Munro still looks inquisitively at him, but Keller doesn't answer. Rather, he calms his mind, taking in the whole of his surroundings. Here, in the soft red glow, the gentle *lub-dub*, and the warm air, he stands in the cadre's womb. This is where they come from. This is their mother. As few as they are, it's no wonder they need everyone, in whatever capacity, to protect her and keep her alive. From the security measures to get in, it also occurs to Keller that few cadre personnel have even seen the inside of this room, so vital it is and precious. And here, Munro has welcomed them in without reservation.

"What you describe, Colonel," Keller replies at last, "shocks us. To have our minds removed and our bodies used against our will is terrifying."

Munro squints, wanting to understand. "Why? Wouldn't you *want* to be a benefit to the others? By your rank, I can see that you have a structure of authority and compliance. Isn't it better to have everyone contributing to the same goals?"

"Of course," Keller concedes, "but our compliance is obtained willingly. To have it forced from us would destroy what we are entirely."

Munro nods reassuringly. "I can't see how, but... We would never attempt any such procedure on you or your crew."

Ortega, Gregor, and Sharon turn to look at the large colonel, trying to gauge his sincerity.

"I have your word?" Keller asks for confirmation.

With complete authenticity, Munro replies, "To us, Captain, saying is the same as doing."

The more they interact with the cadre, the more they understand lying is simply an impossibility for them. But a queer emotion lingers, reminding them how fragile civil liberties are and how easily they disappear in times of insecurity.

Keller relaxes, releasing the air in his chest. "That's a relief. Most of us would see reconstitution as a fate worse than death."

"Worse than *death*?" Munro asks in disbelief. He scrunches his face as if trying to comprehend the incomprehensible. "All we have are our lives. We work to extend them as long as we can, but when we die, we're taken from our siblings to oblivion. There is *nothing* worse than death, Captain!"

The four stand in silence, feeling the gravity of Munro's conviction. Ortega's faith tempts him to debate, but faith has been dreadfully scarce in Keller and Gregor. The two men admire Munro's zeal for life, especially when it is a life of labor, pain, and sacrifice.

"Thus far," Munro announces, "you've seen our primary reactor facility, life support, sensors, maintenance, recycling, engineering, manufacturing, and incubation. That leaves MedLab. This way."

Munro strides briskly out of the soft red glow to the giant-wheel door and taps in the necessary codes, causing it to slide in and roll aside. "Unfortunately, I cannot take you inside the genetic engineering portion—rampant viruses are frequent by-products of our work there. Without prior inoculation, you'd fall ill and die within days."

"Then how do you work there?" Sharon asks.

The group steps past the huge door, and Munro returns it to its place. Striding briskly down the metal corridor, he answers, "Most of the work is done via remote. We design the chromosomes from the safety of our laboratory, and machines perform the actual assembly. When maintenance is required, one of us suits up in protective gear and crawls through the access corridor. That corridor has triple redundancy decontamination features, and anyone going in is inoculated against our most recent set of viral threats. Upon exit, the air in the corridor is evacuated to space, and the individual endures a three-stage chemical and radiological decontamination process."

"Sounds pretty harsh," Ortega notes.

"It is sufficient to maintain our safety."

Ortega leans closer to his captain. "I'll bet Sahara would love to see that place!"

Munro slows his gait and cocks his head. "Suh-hah-ruh?"

"Sahara Taggart," Keller explains. "She's our chief medical officer, currently in cryo-freeze."

Munro smiles broadly. "Ah! Good! That is my designation as well! I look forward to discussing medical technology and practices with her."

"I'm sure you'd captivate her with your conversation..." Gregor mutters sarcastically. Sharon elbows him sharply in the ribs.

Munro arches an eyebrow, aware of the insult, yet choosing to let it pass... but if an operator had shown such disrespect... He balls his strong fist and grits his teeth subconsciously, resuming his normal pace. The others have no idea, believing Gregor's comment passed without notice, and they hurry to keep up with his long strides.

Munro's patience for these odd humans has worn thin, and his steps are swifter, eager to reach MedLab and the end of this tour. Keller and his officers have to trot to keep up, and the polished metal walls pass quickly by.

Ahead, the corridor takes a sharp right then arcs smoothly left as if deflecting around something large.

"Colonel," Ortega calls out. He slows his pace to drag a hand on the convex wall. Munro halts, abruptly turning to face him.

"Yes, Commander?"

Ortega pauses, checking his memory to be sure this feature wasn't explained earlier, asking, "Is there something here you couldn't tunnel through? I don't see any rooms or passages in this direction."

Munro nods, accepting the question. "Beyond this wall stands one of four ground-based UV excimer lasers, our primary defense."

Ortega's eyebrows lift with intrigue, and he searches for an access hatch, but the metal walls are uninterrupted. "How do you get to it?"

"Access is at the silo's base, 150 meters down."

Ortega whistles as he grasps the weapon's scale. "What kind of energy output?"

Munro smiles knowingly. "Sufficient to perforate six meters of titanium with an effective range of four hundred thousand kilometers. Targeting is handled by four satellites in synchronous orbit, and the beam is directed by omni-directional mirror."

"What if the mirror is hit?"

"There are five backup optics per silo; however, when operating in concert, the four silos can deliver sixty shots per minute at full output. It's unlikely anything could get close enough to damage them." Munro turns and resumes his quick pace. Sharon hurries after him; but Gregor, Keller, and Ortega linger, admiring the potent sentry buried in the ground beside them. When Keller turns to ask another question Munro is already way ahead, and the three men run to catch up.

The counselor sits comfortably in Sharon's navigation station aboard the *Europa*. General O'Kai leans over his shoulder in complete engrossment as the counselor pulls up image after image of plants and animals stored as embryos. His jaw drops with amazement.

"And these life-forms… they assemble your nutrients?"

"After a while," the counselor explains. "It takes them a while to mature before they start producing."

"How long?"

"A few months." The counselor looks up at his guest, and he grins when he recognizes the same expression Maiella and Thompson wore when they first saw the colonist's living cargo.

"What do they need?" O'Kai asks directly.

The counselor taps some keys, pulling up a schematic of the circular colony structure. Pointing to each section, he explains, "The biosphere was engineered for maximum efficiency and conservation; so basically, all we need is light, soil, and water."

O'Kai rubs his chin, wondering if such a facility could be deployed at Cadre One. He visually compares the area devoted in the schematic, cross-referencing it mentally with his knowledge of Cadre One's layout. Reluctantly, he realizes he just could not free up enough space.

The counselor watches him, accurately guessing his thoughts. "You're wondering if we could set it up here?"

O'Kai looks down at his guide. "Yes, but we don't have enough room internally. Could this be set up on the surface?"

The counselor shakes his head. "The domes are designed to withstand a wide variety of pressures, but not a vacuum. Nor could they shield the crops against that intense star of yours. Only a planet with an atmosphere will do."

O'Kai thinks about some of the gas giant planets farther out in orbit from their sun. Some of their moons are almost planet size, and a few of them have dense atmospheres… but the tidal forces from such massive planets squeeze and pull the moons relentlessly, causing devastating earthquakes and volcanic eruptions on a regular basis. O'Kai surmises this structure could not endure the shaking.

He stands straight, momentarily stymied, then looks back at the counselor with renewed interest. "Your original mission was to colonize a planet, correct?"

"That's right."

"What about the planet of your original mission?"

The counselor looks away remorsefully. "Uninhabitable. Too many radioactive isotopes in the ground."

"Hmmm," O'Kai thinks. "It was over a thousand years since you were there… could the levels have dropped enough?"

The counselor frowns, shaking his head. "Our geologists said there were sufficient amounts of uranium, strontium, radium, and radon to keep that planet hot for many thousands of years."

O'Kai looks away in frustration and reaches beside the counselor to pull up the *Europa's* flight logs. "In all your light years of travel, did you come across *anything* with a chance at habitability?"

The counselor purses his lips, a bit uncomfortable displeasing someone so physically imposing. "This ship was only intended to travel to a preset destination. She isn't equipped with powerful telescopes or sensitive instrument arrays to discover new systems, just ones strong enough to keep us from flying into something in our path. We've taken the information we *can* collect and have been making educated guesses all this time. It's the best we could do."

O'Kai brings his hand up to his mouth, tapping with one finger pensively. He mentally reviews the equipment at Cadre One they use to track deep-space traffic, wondering if it could be adapted to the colonist's criteria.

"Counselor, how was a world selected for colonization?"

The counselor laughs nervously. "I'm not an authority on that, General. We had an entire division of geophysicists in our company back on Earth who would..."

"*Earth?*" O'Kai shouts excitedly. All other thoughts disappear in his mind. "You know where Earth is?"

"Of course...How is it that you don't?"

O'Kai shakes his head. "In the early days, this facility was much smaller and was not designed for self-sufficiency. The first of us had to use every asset at their command to survive, and building new machines meant building new software. We only had the computers on hand at that time, and we had to clear all the memory we could to store the new operating programs. Any data that was not immediately required for survival was purged... that included information on our ancient home."

The counselor looks up sympathetically, remembering a similar conversation with Thompson months ago, suddenly grasping how it could be these people have no memory of themselves—no history besides the technological advances that have kept them alive. "Thompson didn't recognize the name, Earth, when I mentioned it to him, but you do. Why is that?"

O'Kai nods, explaining, "There is a verbal legacy passed from one general to the next that is kept from everyone else in the cadre. You see, in the beginning, our people longed for their home to great distraction. It affected them in some way which prevented them from laboring at full productivity. When the people were not told they came from some other place, they accepted their lives here and labored to higher potential."

"That's it?"

"That's it."

The counselor's head swims with such astounding pragmatism. "Then why is that information passed from general to general? Why bother?"

O'Kai nods, validating the question. "Our lives are *built* upon our service to higher authority. As general, there is nowhere else to advance, no higher duty to strive toward. Having no higher purpose, we could have fallen victim to the same distraction. We needed to remember Earth, to keep our focus over the many years. But more important, every general knows it is our *duty* to return our people if it is possible. If we forgot about our ancient home, that return would never be possible."

The counselor smiles again at the simple, though stark practicality when another question occurs to him. "Do you know what this facility was intended for before the attack?"

"Genetic research and engineering," O'Kai answers without hesitation. "But that's all I know." O'Kai pauses, no longer able to restrain his curiosities. "You know where Earth is, yet you haven't returned? Why?"

The counselor becomes defensive, turning in his seat to face the general. "We wouldn't dare!"

"Why not?"

The counselor swivels a quarter turn, wondering why the general would ask a question with so obvious an answer. "Our ship has *no* defenses whatsoever… and the blueskins are sure to be there."

"How do you *know*?"

The counselor absorbs the question, weighing it. He looks into the terminal then back at the general, finally admitting, "We don't."

The two men stare at each other, and in the silence, volumes are spoken.

"Major Ralla," O'Kai hails through the communicator perched on his ear.

"Ralla here, sir. Go ahead," comes his radioed reply.

"Delegate your current assignment and report to the bridge of the *Europa*."

"Understood. Ralla out."

Leaning forward again, O'Kai focuses on the viewscreen. "Show me Earth."

THE MISERY OF BEING

A soft tone repeats rhythmically, accompanied by the flicker of room illumination. The communication panel at the head of his bunk lights up, and he swats it with the back of his hand to turn it off. Another four hours of no sleep…

Thompson sits up gruffly, his sunken eyes squinting against the bright light. Only his engrained routine gives him the motivation to get out of bed, and he swings his legs out toward the floor. Rubbing his rough face, he gets to his feet and steps to his hygiene station. A chemically treated towel rests on a rack, and he snatches it, dragging it over himself in the cadre's version of a daily shower. Letting it drop, he picks up a razor, and joylessly scrapes it across the patchy stubble of his beard. The other hand picks up an aging dental appliance and scours his teeth. When done, he considers his gaunt appearance, the drawn cheeks, the bags under the eyes, the pale flesh. He sneers.

Ordinarily, he would do calisthenics but he skips them, moving directly to his locker. Neglected armor hangs inside, muted with layers of soot and unpolished scorches. After pulling on an unwashed undersuit, he snatches the armor pieces from their pegs and slaps them on. In moments, he is fully dressed for duty and he turns to leave, but halts when he catches his reflection in the hygiene station mirror. A shoddy, slouching figure stares back, and he hates himself even more.

With a growl, he storms through the door toward the manufacturing facility. When he arrives, Argo is already there, fully armored. Argo only looks slightly better, his eyes also dark and retreated from sleeplessness. Snapping a salute, he hails Thompson with a raspy voice.

"Good morning, Major. Brick Argo present for duty."

Thompson returns a respectful salute with half the energy. "Good morning, Lieutenant. As you were."

Argo's posture relaxes, and he looks Thompson in the eyes. "Are you getting any sleep?"

"The usual," Thompson answers sardonically. "You?"

"Somewhat. After the trial, I… I can't keep their screams out of my head. I…."

"I know, Argo," Thompson interrupts. "Me, too." A quick scan of the corridor shows someone is missing.

"Where's Maiella?"

"She hasn't reported yet."

Thompson whirls around. "*Again?*" His face twists with angry impatience. "Go get started. I'll get Maiella and join you shortly."

Argo salutes and opens the heavy door, releasing the raging noise of heavy industry. Thompson grits his teeth and stamps down the corridor to Maiella's quarters.

He firmly jabs the buzzer at her door, but there is no reply. Trying the latch, he finds it locked. With exasperation, he barks, "Voice recognize, Major Gun Thompson, lock override, execute!"

The lock disengages, and Thompson thrusts the door aside. He peers into an unusually dark room. "*Maiella!*" he demands.

There is no answer.

He strides into the darkness, seeking out the hygiene station to activate the lighting there, when something fragile crunches beneath his boots. He freezes midstep, anger climbing his spine. He knows why the lights are not on.

He shuts his eyes to suppress his short temper and continues to the hygiene station, flicking on its lights. Turning around, he sees bits of glass and plastic littering the floor, confirming what he already knew. Directly above, the illumination panel has been shattered with a fist-sized hole in the middle of it.

Thompson's eyes drop to Maiella's bunk, and he finds her lying on her back, still wearing her armor from the previous shift. Her eyes are open, staring an infinite path through the ceiling. He looks at her, vexed, but sighs deeply before addressing her. "Are we going to do this *every* morning, Lieutenant?"

Her expression is unchanged, stoic. "Why not?" she asks gloomily.

Anger breaches his containment. "ON YOUR *FEET*, SOLDIER!"

Maiella ends her distant stare and obediently rises from her bunk, standing at an exhausted attention. Thompson looks into her face, which is still sooty from her work in the foundry several hours ago. The grime is even except for a few cleaner tracks running down hollow cheeks.

Thompson glares hard at her, trying to sound convincing despite his own battle with futility. "Our shift began two minutes ago, Lieutenant. We have *work* to do."

"What's the point, Thompson?" she asks softly.

Thompson struggles for an answer. "We're *operators*, Maiella. We are counted on."

Her stoicism finally cracks. "For what? To drag big pieces of metal together and weld them? Drones do our work, Thompson. *Drones!*"

Thompson's face petrifies. "You'd prefer we *were* drones?"

Maiella is taken back by the horrific possibility and drops her face submissively. "No."

He snatches a treated towel from her hygiene station and throws it at her. "Then get yourself *together*. These fits of emotion are *exhausting*, Maiella. And it doesn't matter *what* we do, we *deserve* our assignment, and we *will* perform it without question or hesitation. *Understood?*"

"Yes, *sir!*" she answers sharply, rubbing the towel over her face and hands. The soot from her face and the flecks of blood from her knuckles disappear, leaving a much more presentable soldier behind. She steps around Thompson to retrieve her helmet and gauntlets from the floor then stands before him.

"I'm ready."

Thompson reviews her warily, giving tacit approval. "All right.

Let's move out."

Maiella strides out first. Thompson joins her and pauses at her door. "Disable lock override," he orders plainly, and the door to her quarters glides shut. Squaring their shoulders, the two march down to the manufacturing facility.

Upon arrival, Argo is already hard at work, manually extruding long beams of hot metal. He sees the two and waves them over anxiously. He grunts with the exertion, trying to shout through gritted teeth.

"We have sixteen tons of corridor braces to form, but the metal press is down! If I have to keep pumping them out manually, we'll only make two tons in our shift!"

"*Maiella!*" Thompson yells above the shrieking and clanging machinery, "*Check out the logic controls and software for defects! Argo, get into the access corridor and check for mechanical obstructions or failures! I'll take over here!*"

Maiella and Argo nod seriously and disappear on their missions. Thompson squints at the long, thick lever Argo was pumping; and he swings his arms, limbering up. He grips the handle with both hands, planting one foot on the floor and one foot on a small flange jutting from the enormous, hot machine. Preparing, he retreats to that singularity of mind and heaves with all of his might to swing the lever at nearly the same pace as Argo.

Colonel Shao-Lo stands at attention, her appearance spotless. "Download of the colony ship's star charts is complete, and Major Ralla is heading the team of analysts. The colonist navigator, Sharon, and several of her support staff are assisting the process."

"Good," O'Kai accepts from his office chair. "Go on."

"Cadre energy production has fallen 5 percent, but the deficit can easily be compensated by connecting the colony ship into our power grid. Colonel Munro estimates it could supply another hundred and fifty megawatts if necessary."

"Hmm," O'Kai thinks aloud. "That would let us take the solar collectors off-line to overhaul them. They've needed it for some time.

Have Colonel Munro meet with me to plan the task. Next?"

"Food and water processing aboard the colony ship could supplement another 15 percent of our nutritive requirements, but only so long as the balance of her crew remains in cryo-stasis."

The general leans on his elbows. "Then we'll have to convince Keller to keep them frozen a while longer. Are the colony foodstuffs superior to ours?"

"*Oh, Yes!*" Shao-Lo straightens up, regaining composure. "*Ahem.* Affirmative, General, both in nutritive content and in *other* ways."

O'Kai reads between her words, easily surmising the colonist's diet is much more palatable than tubes of amino proteins and carbohydrates.

"Very well. What else?"

Shao-Lo sucks in her cheeks. She has never had to report failures due to negligence before, but since Team Spectre returned, this is the fourth.

"Operator Team Spectre missed their sixteen-ton quota by eight tons due to a fault in the extrusion press. The fault was discovered to be a seizure from overheating caused by a missed lubrication interval. Team Spectre was able to complete the repair after ten hours, but could not increase production to compensate."

"And who was scheduled to perform the lubrication interval for the extrusion press?" O'Kai queries.

"Team Spectre."

O'Kai slams his iron fist into his desk. "We can't afford these *shortages*!" He sits back in his chair, shaking his head. "What if the colony ship wasn't here to cover our gaps in production, Shao-Lo?"

The colonel stands solemn and silent. O'Kai looks away and slides his chair closer to his desk, folding his hands. "I want your direct assessment, Colonel. Should they be reconstituted?"

Shao-Lo looks up from the floor remorsefully. "Yes, sir. I believe they should."

O'Kai searches for the slightest uncertainty and finds none. "Thank you, Colonel. That will be all."

Shao-Lo snaps a brisk salute and spins on her heel, marching out. Scarcely a moment passes, and the buzzer sounds at his door.

"Come!" the general shouts as he digs into his data terminal. "Did you wish to add something, Colonel?" He looks up, surprised to see the counselor standing before him. "Counselor? How may I assist you?"

The counselor steps forward reservedly. "General, may I have some of your time?"

O'Kai checks his schedule in his terminal. "I have thirteen minutes until I inspect the ore processing facility. What's on your mind?"

The counselor selects a chair opposite the general. "I understand Thompson, Argo, and Maiella have made another mistake, which put your maintenance schedule behind."

O'Kai squints suspiciously. "I'm not sure how you heard about that, but yes, it's true. They missed a critical maintenance interval that led to a breakdown."

"It's going to get worse."

O'Kai continues his wary gaze at the counselor, surprised the man is not making excuses for the three operators. "I didn't think you would say so... but I believe you're right."

The counselor's expression shifts to concern. "What will become of them?"

"I've had two recommendations from my senior staff they be reconstituted. I believe it would be a terrible loss of abilities, but we *cannot* afford any more accidents. We're only just hanging on as it is."

The counselor nods in sad understanding. Reaching into his pocket, he pulls out a slim disk and passes it to the general. "I know I have no authority in your internal affairs. But I have thought a lot about Argo, Maiella, and Thompson; and I've prepared a brief for you. I ask you to please read it before you make a final decision."

O'Kai takes the disk and loads it into his terminal. The counselor didn't expect him to review it now; but he looks on, pleased, as the general reads.

To: General O'Kai, Senior Council Member, Supreme Cadre Authority

From: Counselor, Soshiba Varicorp, Colony Ship Europa, PhD, PsyD, Scientist-Practitioner, Clinical, Experimental, Therapeutic Psychology and Psychobiology

Re: Analysis of underperforming subjects: Major Thompson, Lieutenant Argo, and Lieutenant Maiella

General O'Kai,

Given the structure of your society, I understand your frustrations with Thompson, Argo, and Maiella, especially since your experts can find nothing medically wrong with them. In the cadre, something either works or does not. If it does not work and cannot be repaired, it is scrapped. Here, it appears to you and to your officers that these three operators are beyond your means of recovery and should be reconstituted into drones to recover, at the least, their physical labor potential.

Though you can find no defect, I have discovered one, and these three *can* be salvaged. Despite their unwounded appearance, they *are* seriously wounded, and these wounds will not heal themselves. These injuries are wounds of the mind.

I realize this concept is strange to you, General, and I suspect you are tempted to dismiss this concept as foolish at best or weakness at its worst. However, I believe Maiella, Argo, and Thompson can be restored to their typical performance without cost to cadre resources or productivity. In the following pages, I will describe the nature of their condition, the reasons for it, and the recommended treatment.

Just like a muscle that is injured and fails to function well, the mind can also suffer an injury that causes it to falter. A wound of this sort is often difficult to detect and diagnose; yet in Team Spectre's case, the symptoms are plain: reduced productivity, frequent errors, cessation of nutrition and sleep intervals. These symptoms all point to the same disease: guilt.

Guilt is usually defined as a feeling of remorse or shame for one's wrongdoing, real or imagined. Frequently, guilt can be a powerful motivator for good where the person feeling guilt is compelled to correct the mistake, error, or accident to make things well again. In this case, Maiella, Argo, and Thompson have taken seventeen lives; and those lives cannot be restored. They cannot correct their mistake, and thus, the feeling of guilt remains.

When uncorrectable situations occur, an alternate method for canceling guilt exists, called punishment. Punishment is the cost to the offending person or group for their mistake, error, or accident and can include everything from infliction of bodily pain to loss of freedom to banishment to death and is frequently given in proportion to the mistake, error, or accident. For example, in your cadre law, the punishment for killing a human is exile. This outlet was denied to your operators when Captain Keller and I argued to prevent their exile from happening. Again, the guilt remains in their conscious minds every day.

Let's say that our minds are like a large workbench, and everything we think about and concentrate upon is spread out on the top of it. Now imagine that you have a giant black lump that sits right in the middle of that bench, and everything you want to work on has to be done around that lump. Naturally, the work would suffer, becoming slower, lower quality, and less efficient. Guilt is that black lump tying up all of that space, and your operators are trying to work around it. So clearly, we have to find a way to remove this guilt from their minds.

With any physical injury, there is the danger of complications or supplemental injuries caused by the initial injury. For example, an untreated bullet wound could lead to infections, poisoning, gangrene, or worse. If we imagine a similar situation where guilt is that bullet wound, Maiella,

Argo, and Thompson have been infected with the belief that
they are utterly worthless. Because they hold the same values
as the cadre, they know that they have committed the worst
offense possible; and they can't correct it, nor have they
been punished for it. In their own minds, they believe they
no longer deserve to be a part of the cadre in any capacity.
In fact, they no longer believe they deserve to be *alive*. Their
self-perception, which seems entirely based on their value
to the cadre, has changed radically. They see themselves not
as providers, but as parasites— things that have no place
among the honorable men and women of Cadre One. They
have carried out their own kind of exile where they refuse
the company of others, any kind of comfort, even their own
nutrition intervals. Without knowing why, they are trying to
inflict a punishment on themselves, but nothing they have
done so far seems sufficient to relieve the guilt.

As noted before, the colonists who died cannot be restored
to life, so the mistake cannot be corrected. The only alternative
for us is to devise a sufficient punishment for them that
will—in the minds of Maiella, Argo, and Thompson—equal
their transgression. It should not merely be some impossible
task merely for the sake of hardship; it should be a task of
great importance, great risk, and great reward. It should be
something vital to the future of the cadre and the colonists
alike. It might be a mission with low survivability, because
they could volunteer to sacrifice themselves rather than expose
a fellow operator to death. They will jump at the chance to
truly serve again, and the enormity of their task will make
them feel worthy again.

Because of the harsh nature of the mission requirements,
it is unlikely they will survive; but during that mission, they
will have their sharpest edge. Their guilt will become a potent
motivator demanding they provide *results*. Simply dying will
not be sufficient. If they have success, the cadre will benefit

from their sacrifice; and in meaningful, honorable service, Thompson, Maiella, and Argo can resume their places among their beloved brothers and sisters long gone.

END

O'Kai leans back in his chair. His swift mind cuts through the counselor's lengthy descriptions, seeing plainly the recommendation the three should be exiled after all. He smirks with the irony.

"I can't tell you all of this makes sense to me," he begins, "but you have my attention." O'Kai shifts comfortably in his seat. "It wasn't long ago you were demanding we keep them here, sparing them this 'punishment.' What changed your mind?"

The counselor grimaces. "It isn't that I've changed my mind, General, I simply see Maiella, Argo, and Thompson dying a little more each day; and… I can't help them. And when I heard they may be reconstituted, well… At least this way, they can be remembered for all of their successes, not for their one failure. And who knows?" he adds with vigor. "They might come back."

O'Kai looks into his terminal again, rereading the last few lines of the brief. "Do you have an idea for their mission?"

"I thought you might, General."

O'Kai looks shrewdly at his guest. "You think I should send them to Earth."

The counselor crosses a leg atop the other and raises a hand. "You did say it would have to be a manned mission, that no computer could be programmed with enough contingencies for what it might encounter. We would need operators who can think and act."

O'Kai nods, recognizing his own words.

The counselor drops his hand, raising the other. "Well, here you have a team already trained with all of the mission requirements. Not only are they performing the most basic duties here, they are performing them *badly*. The work Argo, Maiella, and Thompson are doing here doesn't require an operator's abilities and could be handled by almost anyone. If they were taken out of the manufacturing rotation, would they be missed?"

"I see where you're going, Counselor," O'Kai concedes. "I have considered removing Argo, Maiella, and Thompson from their posts; but I don't have a duty schedule with less responsibility than what they are doing now, and no cadre personnel can be permitted to remain idle. The very reason I have them performing some of our lowest priority work is because of their failure rate. I can't trust them with more sensitive tasks because a failure there could jeopardize our survival!"

O'Kai falls silent a moment, reclining in his chair again. "This mission," the general resumes, "would require the strictest tolerances, the swiftest thinking, the most decisive action… and you suggest I entrust it to a team who can't remember the basic lubrication schedule of a *metal press*?" O'Kai points to his terminal. "This brief you wrote raises some interesting possibilities in managing this team's performance, but it is a *long* way from justifying their inclusion in a *critical* mission!"

The counselor lowers his eyes a moment in recognition of the general's point. "I understand your reservations." The counselor uncrosses his legs and leans forward in his seat. "But low-responsibility tasks are part of the problem. There is something I have witnessed in all of you so potent, so perfectly distilled into its purest form: *purpose*. You rise after a brief rest and toil the next twenty hours without fail, without question. Why? Because you have purpose in all of your actions—*everything* you do is designed to ensure your survival. Would you agree?"

O'Kai nods in accordance.

The counselor shifts in his seat. "Maiella, Argo, and Thompson introduced us to that purpose throughout our voyage here. They worked constantly, only taking short rests, repairing and restoring the *Europa*. Since our arrival at Cadre One, I have watched their purpose evaporate. You say any other cadre worker could replace them in their duties? I believe Thompson, Argo, and Maiella are more aware of that than anyone. Here, they are cast out by their brothers and sisters for what they have done and can be replaced by the least able-bodied of their brethren. They are *one hundred percent* expendable and *utterly* without purpose."

"They *do* have purpose," O'Kai argues, "and most recently, their *purpose* was to produce sixteen tons of bracing. How can they not see that?"

The counselor frowns, looking away a moment, then fixes a serious look at O'Kai. "General, do you know what it's like to kill your own kind?"

O'Kai furrows his brow, disbelieving he has been asked such an absurd question. The counselor looks silently on.

"Are you expecting an answer to that?" O'Kai spits.

"I already know you don't. I just want you to say it out loud. Do you know what it's like to kill your own kind?"

"*No*, Counselor," O'Kai states aggressively, "I *don't*."

"They *do*," the counselor volleys back. "They know what it's like to have killed their own kind, and it has wounded their minds so severely they cannot see they still have purpose."

At once, the light goes on in O'Kai's head, recalling the points the counselor made in his brief, drawing them all together. "The guilt you wrote about… is bending their clarity of thought."

"Yes, General," the counselor smiles, "that's precisely it. This mission will be a way Team Spectre can give something back to the group they believe they have harmed, and that will alleviate the guilt they suffer from, clearing their minds."

O'Kai considers the new information, mulling it over, trying to stave off his own opinions and keep his mind open. It is a stretch for him to believe an operator's mind could become so unfocused. He sneaks a sideways glance at the counselor, studying him as if for the first time. Though the discovery process in their conversations has frequently been frustrating, he has come to greatly appreciate the fresh perspectives and options the counselor has presented him. After only a few weeks, he deeply respects the counselor's intuition, trusting him nearly as much as his own council, and he temporarily lays aside the greater share of his skepticism.

"So you believe putting Argo, Thompson, and Maiella into this mission will restore their *purpose* and make them the best operators for the task…"

"Their mistake aside, has any operator team accomplished *half* as much?"

O'Kai nods thoughtfully. "All right, Counselor. I will consider your proposal."

"Thank y—" The counselor is halfway out of his chair, then with a confused look, he sinks back into it.

"Uh, you'll *consider* it?"

"Colonel Munro and Major Ralla will have the most oversight on any mission we plan, so if your recommendation can withstand their scrutiny, we will proceed."

The counselor puckers. "I need to convince both Munro *and* Ralla?"

"That's right."

The counselor grasps the bridge of his nose between his eyes and rises slowly from his seat. "I have some preparing to do."

"Please do, Counselor. This is no ordinary rotation. We need to be thorough."

The counselor nods. "Very true, General." He pushes his seat closer to O'Kai's desk. "Thank you for your time."

"Of course."

The counselor politely excuses himself from the general's office, and O'Kai digs back into his terminal.

HOME...

Having wrapped up his lengthy and detailed case, the counselor sits with dreary patience as Colonel Munro and Major Ralla make their counterpoints, listing the failures and mistakes Team Spectre has committed since their return. Their presentation is well documented, but it doesn't make any difference to the counselor. He knows he is right in his choice.

"In summation," Munro concludes, "Team Spectre has the most impressive service record of any operator team, yet has shown such incompetence of late that they cannot be trusted in such a crucial mission. We are highly impressed with your knowledge of psy-chol-o-gy, particularly the predictive aspects for assessing future potential, but we are unconvinced Team Spectre is a proper choice for this mission."

"Colonel," the counselor counters, "take a look at the *Europa*—those three overhauled and maintained that *whole ship*, and some of her systems are much more complicated than Cadre One's! Their failing is not a matter of ability or coordination, it's mental, and this mission is precisely what they need to become whole again!"

Ralla extends her hand straight at the counselor. "I'm sorry, Counselor. We can't base our decisions on what the *three of them* need. And even if Argo and Thompson *could* be made fit, Maiella could *not*. She's a much-older-generation Geek, and though upgrades are possible, almost all of her synaptic bridges have retreated. Retrofitting her HDI and reestablishing those bridges as an adult

176

carries *very* high risk of brain damage or mortality. If she survived, which is unlikely, she'd have a longer recovery time and would have to learn all over again how to do her job. We can outfit a new Geek operator with a fraction of the risk. Regardless of your opinion on her 'distracted mind,' she *must* be excluded."

The counselor peers at the major, searching her eyes. "Are there any other reasons, any *personal* reasons you feel she should be excluded?"

"*Counselor*"—Ralla smiles patronizingly—"emotionality is not something I'm overly burdened with. My decision is based on efficiency and concern for the well-being of all. No other factors are relevant."

Reluctantly, the counselor concedes, seeing the validity of her argument. In fact, it was he who pushed for personal reasons. Her exclusion raises new questions in his mind, though, as he wonders what will happen to Maiella if she is split from Argo and Thompson. She will be completely isolated from everyone she was ever close to, and he fears her condition will worsen. Even her sanity may fail. If that happens, there is no doubt she will be reconstituted.

His mind drifts momentarily with the horror of seeing her blank and spiritless, robotically performing mundane tasks. Allowing her to fall to such a deadened existence haunts him. But one more look at Ralla and Munro proves it is pointless to argue any further.

"All right, Maiella stays. But we will devise a test that will prove conclusively Argo and Thompson should go, and I'll trust you to provide the new Geek for the team."

Ralla opens her mouth to remind the counselor that question has yet to be resolved, but Munro puts a hand on her arm, gently shushing her.

"What sort of test could we devise that would suffice?"

"It doesn't matter," the counselor replies quickly. "All you have to tell them is it's preliminary to their mission to Earth. Set the test parameters as high as you want, and I know they will meet or exceed them. Run them ragged, be relentless, the harsher the better. And after you've seen their improvement, you'll have the proof you need."

Ralla leans in toward Munro. "It *would* be an interesting

experiment in motivation. And if they do improve, we'll only need to prep one new operator instead of three."

Munro nods in agreement, adding, "Both Argo and Thompson have the widest operational experience of our corps. That will count in a mission with this many variables."

"I ask you to permit me a duty," the counselor begs.

Munro's eyebrows lift. "Oh?"

"If Maiella must be excluded, I'd like to take full responsibility for her. That includes planning her time and schedule, subject to your approval, of course."

Ralla and Munro squint at the counselor with cautious interest. "Your request is not unreasonable," the colonel states, "yet I would hear your reason."

"It takes a damaged cog out of your machine, so to speak; but more importantly, I've gotten to know Maiella well in the time we've been together. Captain Keller told me what reconstitution means, and I couldn't endure seeing that happen to her, not until I've tried everything I can to help her."

"Yes," Munro nods. He leans over to Ralla, explaining, "The colonists have a profoundly *negative* reaction to reconstitution."

Ralla's eyebrows pull together in curious nonunderstanding.

"Very well," Munro permits. "Maiella will be released to your custody, and her duty schedule must be submitted four weeks in advance. Thank you, Counselor." Munro and Ralla stand from their seats across the table.

The counselor stands quickly after them. "One last thing, Colonel?"

Ralla halts with a questioning look until Munro gives her a permissive nod to go ahead. She strides out of the room.

"Yes, Counselor?" Munro asks.

"Breaking the team up will disturb them greatly. I'd like to be the one who informs them."

Munro juts his lower lip out, considering it. He can't see why reassigning an operator team would be disruptive, but he doesn't see any harm in the request either.

"Agreed. You may inform Team Spectre of their dissolution." He is about to leave, but holds a moment. "Anything else?"

"No, Colonel. I thank you and Major Ralla for your time."

Munro nods once and strides purposefully from the room.

Colonel Munro makes his way through the bright metal corridors to General O'Kai's office, and he buzzes for entry. Beyond the door, a commanding voice beckons, "Come!"

The door whisks aside and Munro steps through. O'Kai is seated at his desk, and Ralla rises from her seat, smiling politely at Munro as he enters.

"Colonel," O'Kai begins, "let's have your report."

Munro sits in a chair opposite the general, still mulling over the last two hours of discussion with the counselor.

"He brought some very interesting concepts to the table, particularly the field of *psychology*. It never occurred to me the mind could sustain injury like the body."

O'Kai nods. "Yes, he has many good ideas. But what are your thoughts on the counselor? That's really what I sent you to discover."

Munro thinks for a moment, trying to distill his perceptions, momentarily deferring to Ralla, now seated next to him.

"He has an excellent intellect," Ralla notes, "factual, logical, and rational with a high capacity for creative problem solving and intuitive deduction. Moreover, he seems less attached to his sense of 'self' than the others. Every argument or point he has stressed has been for the benefit of those around him, never for himself, and he gladly accepts additional tasks without hesitation."

"My thoughts exactly," O'Kai adds. "It's refreshing to see at least one colonist has the proper priorities. What else?"

"He seems unburdened by emotions as the others are," Munro describes, "though he places a great deal of concern on the emotions of his comrades, including Argo, Maiella, and Thompson. That aside, I enjoy discussions with him, seeing much that we have in common. His perspectives inspire confidence, and I find myself quite willing to cooperate with him."

O'Kai leans on his elbows, placing one fist inside the other and nodding. Munro's description confirms his own impression to the letter. "So what did you decide?"

"I believe Brick Argo and Gun Thompson could be made fit, but not Geek Maiella."

O'Kai pans his view to Ralla, and from her serious expression, he can see her opinion was decisive in the matter. He looks back at Munro. "Reasoning?"

"Team Spectre was able to repair and maintain the colony ship during its long voyage here. It satisfied me that their recent low performance is not a result of physical damage from extended cryo-freeze but is, in fact, mental; and the counselor's superior knowledge in mental health convinced me they could be returned to duty under certain conditions."

O'Kai chews on the information then looks at Ralla. "Why not Maiella?"

Ralla sits up. "Her mission-essential hardware is damaged. Add to that, it is badly outdated. To upgrade her functionality with current standards carries an **88** percent chance of debilitating brain injury and consumes resources with which a new Geek could be equipped… *without* Maiella's behavioral flaws. The costs strongly outweigh the benefits."

"All right then," O'Kai continues, "what is to be done with her?"

"The counselor has volunteered to take Maiella into his custody," Munro answers. "He will provide her schedule four weeks in advance for my approval."

O'Kai lifts his eyebrows in surprise. "With all of his current duties, he's going to supervise Maiella as well? I think he's going to be working longer hours than we do."

Resetting his brow, he issues his orders. "Major, we are going to need a Geek for this mission. Review your operator corps and make a selection."

"Yes, sir!" Ralla replies.

"Colonel, we'll need a transport vessel, both invisible and fast, that can accommodate an operator team and extra equipment for an extended mission."

"Sir!" Munro replies. "Shall we modify Team Spectre's virus ship?"

O'Kai thinks hard about the suggestion. "No," he says reluctantly. "The virus ships were never designed for atmospheric entry." He trails off, suddenly aware how little expertise they have in aerodynamics.

"Shall I enlist the colonist engineers in the project?" Munro asks.

O'Kai looks up from his deep thought, one hand partially covering his mouth. "Yes," he says at last. "The main colony structure is designed to drop from orbit through the atmosphere, so they must have an idea of the kind of forces involved." He gets a slight smile. "Plus, having a common project may be good for us all… keep us from grinding against each other for a while."

Ralla and Munro return the general's smile knowingly.

"But keep in mind, both of you," O'Kai lectures, "we can only ask them to participate, not demand. And if they do join, there can be only one project leader."

"I understand, sir," Munro responds. "I will consult with the counselor on the best way to obtain their willing compliance."

O'Kai nods, pleased Munro took his meaning appropriately.

"General," Ralla voices, "selecting a Geek operator will be a relatively brief process. How else may I assist?"

O'Kai ponders the scope of the new mission and settles on a particular area. "Following this meeting, you will devise the scope of testing required to assure Brick Argo's and Gun Thompson's fitness for duty. I will review it, then order them both to report to you for testing. If they prove themselves, introduce them to their new teammate and designate a new name. Team Spectre is no more."

Eyeballing Ralla directly, O'Kai leans across his desk. "You are to push them harder and longer than any operator *ever*. Permit them only the minimum of nutrients and sleep. Chase them. Don't let up. If they have a breaking point, it is your *duty* to find it."

Ralla straightens her posture. "I understand perfectly."

O'Kai leans back into his chair and regards his two officers directly. "Are there any other questions?"

As one, Munro and Ralla reply, "Sir, no, sir!"

"Dismissed!"

The counselor steps into his softly lit office aboard the *Europa* where Argo, Thompson, and Maiella are seated anxiously.

"I did everything I could," the counselor explains. "They wouldn't budge. Thompson, you and Argo will be considered, but... Maiella stays."

Argo, Thompson, and Maiella look at each other with chagrinned confusion, not knowing what to do or say. The possibility of being parted just never occurred to them.

Argo and Thompson slump on the edge of the counselor's padded chairs, but Maiella has gone rigid. In all of her rotations and missions, she was without fear, supremely confident in herself and her teammates. As an operator, the possibility of her own death was omnipresent; and she accepted it peacefully, but never once did she consider the possibility she could be left behind. The thought of being left in a cadre of strangers who know her only as an outdated failure leaves her chilled and terrified.

The counselor picks up on her vacant stare immediately.

"Maiella?"

She offers no recognition.

"*Maiella?*" he repeats more forcefully.

Argo and Thompson lift their drooping heads to see why she doesn't respond. The counselor looks at the two operators with a quizzical glance, but they shrug. He cautiously steps over to her, touching her arm gently.

"*Nooooooo!*" she screams and leaps from her chair, bowling the counselor backward over a table. Her shrieks become unintelligible, and she grabs anything not bolted down, hurling it into the walls.

The counselor looks up wide-eyed at the frenzied woman while Argo and Thompson wrestle her down to the floor. She is slippery in her rampage and incredibly strong, making the hefty men work to subdue her. Shouting her name, they beg her to stop, but she doesn't hear. Argo lowers his grip, binding his thick arms around her knees. Thompson lays over her side, wrapping one of her arms around herself like a half straightjacket, and holds tight.

"*Please, don't leave me behind!*"

The counselor climbs to his feet, stepping carefully toward the human heap. Maiella is spent, eyes shut tight, chest gently heaving. Argo and Thompson lay their heads against her.

He kneels, taking her free hand. "You won't be alone, Maiella. You'll be with us, here on the *Europa*."

The woman's damp eyes crack enough so she can look at her two benevolent captors. "We belong together... *how can they split us up?*"

The counselor frets, deciding hard truth is at hand. "Munro and Ralla made their decision based *solely* on what gives this mission its best chance. Argo and Thompson will need a Geek at full-operational ability if they are going to survive." He hates reminding her of her damaged HDI, especially when he sees the torture of it in her face.

Argo and Thompson lift their heads, relaxing their grip on her. The counselor tugs on her hand, urging her to sit up.

"Maiella, look at me."

She pushes herself up from the floor, wiping her eyes, and crosses her legs. She sniffs hard, fixing a watery gaze on the counselor.

"Argo and Thompson are going to be using a new kind of vehicle. Most likely, General O'Kai is going to need the help of our engineers to build it. There will be many new systems installed, and your friends here are going to need someone to test all those systems out, make sure they're safe."

Maiella blinks. "You're saying I should be... the project auditor... and test pilot?"

"You're already familiar with every system we have aboard the *Europa* as well as at Cadre One. That makes you most qualified to troubleshoot and examine every part of any new ship we build. But more importantly, I don't know anyone who would be more concerned about Argo and Thompson's safety, or who would be as thorough."

"I can assure you of *that*," she states directly.

"Good!" the counselor says while rising to his feet. "I'll make the arrangements with Colonel Munro."

The three operators lift themselves from the floor. "How are you going to do that?" Argo asks.

The counselor smiles reassuringly. "Colonel Munro and I have an agreement. Maiella has been transferred to my custody, and I will set her schedule from now on."

Maiella's eyes open wide with amazement; then concern sets in her brow, and she squints while she considers the many implications. A single question comes to mind, and she freezes, almost too afraid to ask what she needs to know. "Will I be…?"

"Reconstituted?" The counselor shakes his head resolutely. "No."

Relief revitalizes her, bringing some color back to her features. In the moments of silence, Argo, Thompson, and Maiella fully digest the counselor's information; and deep within them, there is a foundation again. Though it means being separated, they push that knowledge aside. For now, they feel more like they used to, when they were important and were counted on.

Maiella looks around the chamber, humbled by the destruction her frenzy caused. She leans over, picking up the pieces.

"Please, Maiella, don't worry about it," the counselor consoles. "I'll clean this up."

She stands with several shards of what once was a cranberry-colored crystalline sculpture. Sheepishly, she places them in the counselor's outstretched hand. "I'm very sorry," she apologizes meekly.

The counselor takes the shards and walks them over to a small table. "Emotions are not weakness," he says to no one in particular, "and strength does not come from suppressing them."

The three look queerly into his back, his words a direct contradiction of the dogma pounded into them since their inceptions. He turns to regard them all seriously and focuses on Maiella.

"Look at how strong you became. It took both of your teammates to stop you. But it was unfocused. If you could *harness* that power, you would know *true* strength."

"Brick Argo and Gun Thompson," blares the intercom, "report to Major Ralla's office for assignment!"

Argo takes a last look at the counselor, grunting skeptically before walking out. Thompson turns to follow, but pauses to take in all of the damage around him. He looks at Maiella then looks at the counselor. Without another word, he strides out to catch up with Argo.

SPECIALIST BECKERT

The hammer drill drops from Gregor's hand and clatters heavily on the metallic floor. "*What did they just announce?*" he yells with great surprise.

Keller halts his noisy drilling when he sees Gregor staring intently at him. The aging captain lifts his safety glasses and pulls one of his earplugs out. "*What's that?*" he yells over the other assembly room noises.

"*I think they just announced operator testing, something or...*" Gregor leans over and taps the MedTech beside him who obligingly stops grinding the frame edge. Pulling out his earplugs, the MedTech asks, "*Yes? How may I help?*"

"*Did you hear the announcement?*" Gregor shouts over the din. Keller walks over to listen in.

"*Oh yes,*" the MedTech replies. "*All operators were ordered to report to the arena to judge a new operator candidate.*"

Gregor's and Keller's eyes meet excitedly, and they both run from the room like students late for an exam. The MedTech shouts after them, "*It's okay, it doesn't apply to us!*" But the men disappear without another thought.

The MedTech looks at the framing beside him where two hammer drills lie unused. Sighing, he pulls out a communicator. "*Major Ralla...? You should be expecting Gregor and Keller to arrive shortly, and... we need another two for the assembly line.*" Replacing his earplugs, the MedTech hunches his curved spine and resumes his grinding.

When Gregor and Keller arrive at the arena, they find themselves standing at the back of a very tall and stout group of men and women. All of them wear the dress charcoal grays of the cadre operator, and their attention is riveted directly ahead.

The two colonists stand on their toes, teetering back and forth to peer past the broad shoulders of the operators ahead of them. Totally eclipsed, the colonists find chairs and climb onto them to view the small arena.

There, a young man stands relaxed, clothed only in a loose-fitting pair of nylon shorts. He is lean though deeply striated, and the silver contact terminals on his shaved head gleam. The colonists easily recognize the outline of a cadre Geek, but never have they seen one so free of scars.

Clanks to either side of them announce the presence of Sharon, Ortega, and the counselor as they likewise set down sturdy chairs and stand on them.

"Howdy, Skipper," Sharon quips to her captain. "Couldn't miss this, huh?"

Keller grins his reply and turns to the counselor. "I'm glad you made it, Counselor. We could use your eyes here."

The counselor smirks good-naturedly, "*I* was invited, Captain."

Suddenly, the arena lighting flares. "ATTEN-TION," bellows Major Chusan, and every sinew in the initiate's frame draws taut, his striation deepening. All operators in the arena likewise stamp into a rigid stance, chests out as Chusan brusquely pushes his way to the arena floor. He peers with contempt at the half-naked man as if he were viewing the very embodiment of disappointment.

"What are you called, *trash*?"

"Sir! Specialist Beckert, sir!"

"And what got into that misfiring pack of neurons to think you belong here?" Chusan demands, his burn-scarred face contorting with disgust as he circles behind the young man.

"Sir," barks Beckert, head high and chest out, "I desire entrance to the Operator Corps, sir!"

Chusan stamps in front of Beckert, enraged as if the young man just spat in his face.

"Well, I can tell you straight, you have *wasted our time*, and there is nothing I hate more than a *waste of time*! *There is* NO WAY *a skinny* BONEBAG *like you could ever belong in my corps! You should be* ON YOUR KNEES, BEGGING *me not to* STOMP YOUR FACE IN *for even* SUGGESTING *you are of their quality*!"

Keller, Ortega, Sharon, and Gregor look at each other uncomfortably, having never seen rage like this from an operator, much less their major.

Chusan's face is deep red as he paces in front of Beckert, furiously piling abuse upon this candidate who dares to deem himself worthy. With each of the major's insults, Beckert's jaw sets tighter and tighter; yet his head remains high, his posture perfect.

Colonel Shao-Lo steps from the group of operators and places a hand on Chusan's shoulder, ending the scathing diatribe. The major stands straight and takes a step back while the colonel crosses her thick arms and stares into the specialist's face. She studies deeply, intently, for long seconds, the arena silent around her.

"Chusan," she says at last, "get him out of here and fit him for something soft."

"Yes, SIR!" Chusan answers, striding toward the young man and taking him by the arm.

"Colonel!" Beckert shouts to everyone's surprise.

Shao-Lo whirls on her heel, her eyebrows drawing together with impatience, but indicating Chusan to wait. "What is it, Specialist?"

"Request permission to change your mind, sir!"

Shao-Lo steps toward Beckert, squinting down at him. "I've seen all I need. There is an intensity, a need to serve, that all operators possess. You don't have it."

Beckert's face burns from the stinging rejection, but he will not lower his head. Shao-Lo is about to turn again when the young man announces, "I disagree, *sir*!"

Chusan releases his grip and swings himself between the two, stopping millimeters away from Beckert's face. "What did you say, Specialist? I know it wasn't what I *thought* I heard because we don't breed anything *dumb enough* to question a superior officer!"

Beckert is slightly off guard, but recovers, standing without fear under the major's onslaught. "I said, *I disagree*, SIR!"

Chusan nods and backs away, becoming eerily sedate. In a blur, he brutally smashes his elbow into Beckert's face. The young man stumbles from the ferocity of the impact, and when he gets back to his feet, a cut under his left eye is already seeping a trickle of blood. Undaunted, he straightens his posture and steps back to his prior position, resuming his attention stance directly in front of the major.

Shao-Lo arches an eyebrow with interest.

The colonists gasp in disbelief.

Chusan looks down slightly, wiggling a finger in his ear.

"I'm gonna have to go see a MedTech because I'm SURE I didn't hear that, Specialist." He raises his head, stabbing a hard gray glare into Beckert's eyes. "What... did... you... say?"

Without hesitation, Beckert announces, "I said, *I disagree*, SIR!"

Chusan steals a glance at Shao-Lo and whirls, winding up a devastating kick. With a fearsome yell, Chusan's leg flies toward Beckert's gut and halts just before contact.

The young man does not flinch. He does not even blink.

Chusan retracts his leg slowly, jutting his lower lip. He steps back, eyeing Beckert suspiciously.

"Specialist," Shao-Lo begins, "if you're going to change my mind, you have some work to do. Let's see what you've got."

Beckert takes a fight ready stance. "MOOP!" he shouts and flips backward, landing perfectly in stance. Swift high kicks whir by in rapid succession, followed by sweeps, grips, takedowns, evasions, counterstrikes, and joint locks. He moves with Shaolin grace and agility, supremely balanced and completely focused. The display is diverse, highlighting his skill, flexibility, and comfort in numerous combat situations. When finished, he flips forward into his fight-ready stance and holds.

Shao-Lo gives a nod to Chusan and strides to the edge of the arena.

"Deepak! Keiko!" Chusan shouts, himself moving to the arena's edge.

Gun Deepak and Gun Keiko step from the group, already peeling off their charcoal-uniform coats. Fixing a hard glare at Beckert, they pass the jackets to their fellows and strip off their tight-fitting undershirts. Bare chested, they step menacingly into the ring, flexing their arms and cracking their knuckles.

The colonists look on with anxiety, taking in the numerous scars crossing the two Guns. They look at Beckert, fresh and even without any of those marks, and they wonder how many of those scars come from initiation. Sharon taps the shoulder of a Brick in front of her and asks, "What are they going to do?"

Careful not to disturb the proceedings, the Brick turns his head slightly and whispers, "Beckert must defend himself against Keiko and Deepak."

"How?" Gregor asks, nearly shouting. "Two Guns on one Geek? It isn't a fair fight!"

The Brick turns toward Gregor with a look of grim experience. "It never is."

Gregor looks into the Brick's battered face, the network of healed injuries from numerous collection rotations bearing their powerful testimony.

The big man turns back toward the arena, adding in a muted voice, "The goal for Beckert is not necessarily victory, but to survive as long as he can. He will be judged based on his actions and character against vastly superior opponents."

The colonists watch nervously while Keiko and Deepak take their places at the center of the arena, flanking Beckert. Chusan raises his arm high.

"*Attention!*"

Beckert, Keiko, and Deepak come rigidly to attention.

"*Bow!*" the major orders.

The three flex at the waist respectfully.

"*Combat*, READY!"

The three raise their hands near their face, planting one foot slightly ahead of the other, leaning forward.

"*And...*"

Before Chusan drops his arm, Beckert launches to his left, sinking his heel in Deepak's gut. Deepak hunches from the blow, and Beckert cradles the back of his head, driving it into his knee. Sensing Keiko just behind him, he keeps grip on Deepak and sidesteps, slinging Deepak between them. The two Guns collide, Deepak absorbing the brunt of Keiko's kick. While the two are off balance, Beckert rushes to climb up Keiko's back. Wrapping an arm around her throat, he tries to set a naked choke, but Keiko drops her chin in time to block. She only sways a moment under Beckert's weight before she regains her stance and flips Beckert from her back like a sack.

Beckert sails across the arena floor, tucking and tumbling deftly to his feet. When he stands, he sees Deepak straightening his bleeding, broken nose. The Guns' eyes are predatory, and without hurry, the soldiers stride toward him. Beckert readies himself, bringing his arms up while the Guns circle to either side. He slides to keep his opponents in view, allowing them to get closer. *A little more*, Beckert thinks, drawing them in.

The colonists want to turn away, believing it to be his end but cannot, and their hearts sink when they see Beckert turn to run. The Guns chase, and just when they are sure to tackle him, Beckert fakes and springs back toward them with solid kicks. Deepak evades, taking a glancing shot. Keiko manages to snag the young man's leg. She pulls him in, lifts him at the waist, and slams him fiercely into the metal floor with a clang that echoes throughout the chamber.

Beckert struggles admirably against Keiko's grip, escaping several joint locks and choke holds, fending off many of the rapid fire jabs and elbows Keiko drives into him. Even the colonists can tell, however, that she has the dominant position, yet does not seem to be pressing her advantage. As Deepak strolls around the squirming Beckert, he waves her up with his hand, and it becomes all too clear they are toying with him. Keiko drags her victim into her lap. The young man throws every elbow and knee strike he can, some of them landing, but the brawny woman shrugs them off. She slides one foot beneath her, then the other, lifting Beckert into the air. With a single turn, she tosses Beckert at her partner.

Beckert tucks into a ball, hoping he can line up a good kick, and takes his best shot. Deepak easily dodges and unleashes a devastating wheel kick into Beckert's back. The young man crumples into the floor several meters away, bouncing with a resounding thud. Screaming with pain, he tries to stand, but one of his legs will barely respond. He scuttles away from his attackers, dragging the unusable leg under him. With his good leg, he rises, eyes watering, his back hunched. He watches Deepak and Keiko calmly approaching as he tries to stand straight, but the leg will accept no weight. He hobbles backward, lowers his chin, and raises his arms to fight.

"We have to stop this," Keller blurts, but the Brick shushes him, shaking his head.

"This is the most important. What he does now will decide if he is inducted or not."

"Look at him!" Ortega protests. "I don't have to be a MedTech to see his spine is injured!"

The Brick stoically ignores the comment.

"What if they kill him?" Ortega insists.

The Brick looks at the Spaniard with annoyance. "If you're too delicate to watch, perhaps you should wait outside."

The colonists stand open-mouthed while the Brick returns his attention to the arena.

In the few seconds he has, Beckert closes his eyes, driving back the pain. He relaxes, feeling light again. Through his closed lids, he can sense his opponents, and he continues to shuffle away from them. Gritting his teeth, he tucks at the waist and rotates, flinging himself sideways through the air. He repeats the move when, at last, he feels the crunch of his spine coming back into alignment. Pain rips through him like a lightning bolt, and he crumples. Yet as fast as it came, the pain departs, and he can feel tingling in his weak leg as the strength returns to it. He sways on his hands and knees, putting on a good show, and screams again as if in agony, pretending his leg is still useless. He climbs to the same meek fighting position as before, limping backward.

Deepak and Keiko are close, pounding one fist into the other, scowling at his weakness and fragility. Keiko reaches for him with both hands, and he explodes into her with a punishing kick to the sternum. She launches back her eyes wide with shock. In the same fluid motion, Beckert drops and leg sweeps Deepak onto his back.

Deepak slaps his arms out, breaking his fall. Beckert is on top of him, wrapping a leg around his back and over a shoulder. Deepak scrambles, but Beckert is too fast, locking the leg tight with the crook of his other leg. Deepak rolls, and Beckert rolls with him, not giving up the triangle choke. The young man cinches tighter and tighter, trying to put the Gun out even though Deepak has managed to keep his chin just low enough to block. Beckert strains, punching the Gun's head into the position he wants, hauling on the trapped arm, doing everything he can, focusing so intently he never saw Keiko swooping down on top of him.

She tackles him violently, breaking his leg lock. He is so shocked, she easily snakes her arm around his neck and under his chin. Bracing the choke arm with her other, she arches her back, stretching Beckert's neck, and squeezes hard. The young man's face bulges and goes deep red. He grunts and tries to pull against Keiko's thick arms, but he may as well be tugging against a metal girder. She lay atop him, her weight holding him down, and it is only a few more seconds until he stops struggling. She holds the choke several more seconds to make sure he is completely out and releases him, leaving him sprawled on the floor like a heap of laundry.

Keiko climbs to her feet with some effort, clutching her chest, and waves the MedTechs over. As the MedTechs roll the limp initiate over, Keiko looks down on him. The contempt is gone as she still clutches her chest, panting slightly. Deepak stands beside her, his face emblazoned with the same expression of wary respect.

The MedTechs move swiftly, checking Beckert's eyes and vital signs. One nods to the other and produces a short clear tube with an expanding device on one end. That end disappears down Beckert's throat and reopens his crushed larynx. They attach a device to the protruding end of the tube, and Beckert's chest rises and falls with respiration. Anxious moments tick by, and even Colonel Shao-Lo looks on with concern until the young initiate convulses and sits up suddenly between the MedTechs, nearly head butting them. Blinking with disorientation, he yanks the tube from his mouth and scurries away. Deepak and Keiko hurry over to him, and the young man tries to get to his feet. Just as he is expecting another attack, the Guns reach their open hands toward him. With a pain in his heart greater than the wrenching of his spine, he realizes the test is over and he has been defeated. He cannot look into either Deepak's or Keiko's eyes.

"You did good, Beckert," Keiko whispers as she and Deepak take his arms and lift him up. With bewilderment, he looks into Deepak's face and the pulpy mess of what was his nose. Deepak nods in agreement.

"SPECIALIST BECKERT, FRONT AND CENTER!" roars Chusan's powerful voice.

The Guns release him, and he trots over to Chusan, stamping to attention with a swift salute. "Sir!" he coughs hoarsely.

Colonel Shao-Lo strides out to meet them, and Beckert feels another layer of sweat forming on his brow.

"This was your last test for operator candidacy. Major Chusan and I have scrutinized every score, calculation, and performance review of yours over the last six months. Here, I think we learned more about you than in all of the other tests combined."

Beckert maintains his rigid stance, apprehension filling him as he simply cannot guess what the colonel is going to say next.

"In this final examination, you were placed into a combat situation against superior opponents, and you were ordered to win. We observed you acting aggressively, fearlessly, and decisively, even finding in your injury an opportunity to deceive and surprise your opponents. You held off Gun Deepak and Gun Keiko for one minute, sixteen seconds. You even managed to get a hold of Gun Deepak, nearly submitting him. That's admirable in its own right." Shao-Lo shifts her stance.

"But in your zeal to defeat him, you blinded yourself to Gun Keiko, and she finished you easily. If nothing else, Specialist, this should teach you the value of teamwork. Any one of us may be disadvantaged, but our teammates look out for us, and we look out for them." She pauses, resting her weight equally on her feet.

"An operator should have no fear of death, but neither should they allow it through negligence. The Operator Corps is the *only* defense of our people. It is our *obligation* to survive so we may perform that duty. Do you understand?"

Beckert blinks hard, taking the colonel's solemn words directly to heart, angry at himself for not seeing the truth of them in the arena. He wanted victory at all costs, and it blinded him. "Yes, sir!" he replies gravelly.

Shao-Lo nods. "There have been times when an operator has given his life for others, but it was always after every other option had been exhausted. Even if victory seems in your grasp, you must choose to survive. Do you understand?"

"Sir, yes, sir!" Beckert answers.

Shao-Lo scrutinizes the young man carefully and asks directly, "Do you understand that an operator is *expected* to accomplish what is logically impossible on a daily basis?"

"Yes, sir, I do!" the young man declares, and a light burns from his eyes as he recognizes the preliminaries to the oath of induction.

"Do you understand that an operator is *expected* to protect and provide for every human life without any concern for difficulty or burden to themselves?"

"Yes, sir, I do!"

"Do you understand that this service is continuous and can never be set aside?"

"Yes, sir, I do!"

"Do you understand the extent of an operator's responsibility?"

"Yes, sir, I do!"

"Prove it," Shao-Lo says, folding her arms in expectation.

"The survival of humanity is *my* responsibility. Mine *personally*. My actions determine the fate of our people. If I fail in my duty, I permit the destruction of all I know and value. And I alone will be the cause of it."

Shao-Lo nods without comment, feeling Beckert has exactly captured it, though something makes her pause before moving on. "Do you believe it?"

Beckert brings his eyebrows together. "Sir?"

"With a corps of operators and a leadership council overseeing the cadre, how could any *one* operator believe the fate of our people rests purely on their shoulders?"

"Easily, sir. Every operator has a task to perform. Only when we work in perfect concert do we have a chance to survive. If any one of us fails in our duty, the system fails. Therefore, our survival truly rests on each of us, *entirely*."

Shao-Lo nods again with satisfaction. "How many of the enemy would you kill to ensure our survival?"

"*All of them*, sir."

The colonel pauses, mentally weighing the candidate before her. "What do you think, Major?"

"I'm satisfied, Colonel," Chusan replies.

Shao-Lo whirls to face the corps of operators behind her. "Do you believe Specialist Beckert has demonstrated his worthiness?"

The numerous voices merge into a singular baritone, "SIR, YES, SIR!"

Shao-Lo spins again to face the bare-chested initiate, recognizing in the corners of his mouth how hard he is trying to restrain his elation. Allowing a slight smile herself, she adds, "Major Chusan, would you do us the honor?"

"Sir!" Chusan shouts, stepping in front of Beckert and affixing a diamond-hard stare. "Specialist Beckert, do you swear to defend and provide for the cadre even to the cost of your own life, to obey every order swiftly and effectively, to exemplify the standards of the operator's code, and to make the survival of humanity your personal responsibility?"

Beckert returns the gaze and, in absolute sincerity, announces, "With all that I am, I SWEAR IT!"

Chusan holds his left arm straight out to one side, and Major Ralla steps from the crowd, holding a folded charcoal uniform. She drapes it carefully over Chusan's extended limb, winking at Beckert before returning to the crowd. Chusan swings his arm forward, presenting the uniform to Beckert. "Welcome to the corps, *Sergeant*."

For the first time ever, Beckert sees a smile cross Chusan's granite face. Beaming with pride, the new Geek takes his charcoal uniform, holding it to his chest like a cherished gift while the corps thunderously cheers, "*Sergeant Beckert*, HURRAH! HURRAH! HURRAH!"

A gentle pressure lands on his shoulder, and when he looks, the MedTechs are urging him down into a stretcher.

"What? No, I'm fine," he protests, but Chusan leans in.

"Go with them and let them take care of you. I know you're in pain."

"Yes, sir!" Beckert responds and compliantly lays himself down, still clutching his dress grays. The MedTechs hoist the stretcher and parade the cadre's newest Geek past his cheering comrades. The group pushes in close so they can all give him a solid punch in the arm on the way by.

Chusan points at Deepak and Keiko who are just buttoning up their jackets. "You two, report to MedLab."

The Guns salute and stride out after the MedTechs.

Shao-Lo leans into Chusan, adding, "Resume the duty schedule. I'll be in engineering if you need me."

"Sir!" Chusan answers, swinging a flat hand up to his brow. Facing his corps, he calls out in his characteristically harsh tone, "ATTENTION!"

All eyes face front.

"RESUME DUTY SCHEDULE! CORPS, DISMISSED!"

The operators salute as a single unit and file out in orderly fashion, leaving Keller, Ortega, Sharon, and Gregor standing on their chairs, still reeling with amazement.

LIEUTENANT COLONEL ANDERS

The counselor pauses from his frantic typing to gaze at the walls of his new cadre office. His usual crisp appearance has slipped, his white shirt is wrinkled with a curling collar, and his dark hair juts at odd angles.

On his desk, three monitors face him, all of which have different information displayed; and beside them, a stack of data disks await his attention. From the left monitor, he draws on his notes from interviews he has completed with each individual. In the right monitor, he reviews the subject's work history and service record and combines all of that data with his own perceptions into a detailed report in the center monitor.

As his eyes wander the walls, it is neither the Spartan décor nor the metal walls that make him pause. It is the fact he *actually volunteered* to psychologically profile the cadre for General O'Kai. While once deeming himself intelligent, he now scans the room for some sign of just what the *hell* he was thinking. Sighing deeply, he gets back to work when the door chime sounds.

"It's open!" he calls out.

There is no reply. He stops typing and looks toward the door. "Come in!"

The door slides aside, and a young cadre woman hobbles in carrying another armload of data disks. "I've f-f-finished admin-min-istering the tests, C-Counselor. W-where w-w-would you like them?"

Gesturing to the edge of his desk, he answers, "Just put them here with the others."

She sets them down carefully and steps back. "Is there anything else, s-s-sir?"

The counselor smiles gratefully at her, "No, Arjay, that's all I need for now, thank you."

Arjay stands as straight as she can and snaps a salute.

"Oh no, you don't have to salute me!" The counselor protests, but confusion sets on the woman's face.

"But you're my s-s-superior... Why would I not?"

He looks into her face and considers explaining the difference between being a cadre subordinate and being someone's assistant when he remembers the stack of data disks still waiting to be reviewed. "Never mind, that'll be fine, thank you."

She smiles pleasantly and steps from his office. He grins and shakes his head once, diving back into his work.

"*Counselor,*" the intercom blares, "*your presence is requested by Lieutenant Colonel Anders.*"

The counselor perks up midkeystroke.

"Colonel Anders?"

Peering down at his center screen, he saves his work and closes it out, much more interested in meeting a new cadre officer. When his monitors wink off, however, he catches his reflection in the shiny screens. Squinting at himself, he scrutinizes his wild hair and wrinkled shirt. Grimacing, he smoothes his hair down with both hands and tucks his shirt in tight to stretch out the creases. Rising from his seat, he snatches his white coat from the back of his chair and hurries from his office.

When he steps out into the bright corridor, he immediately realizes he doesn't know where to go, so he scans the corridors and asks the first person he sees: an armed and armored Gun with two healing black eyes and white tape across the bridge of his nose.

"Excuse me," the counselor begs, "I need to find Colonel Anders's office. Can you direct me?"

"Of course," the large man affirms. "I'll take you there." Into his helmet microphone, the Gun states, "Major Chusan, this is Gun Deepak. I am escorting the counselor to Colonel Anders' chamber and will resume patrol in seven minutes."

"Confirmed, Gun Deepak," comes his radioed reply.

"Out," the tall soldier concludes and looks expectantly at the counselor. "Please follow me." Deepak shifts the rifle on his shoulder and marches briskly in a new direction. The counselor hurries after him, trotting to keep pace with the Gun's long strides.

The corridors turn and branch then straighten out into a long, narrowing hallway barely big enough for a Brick to fit through. With each step, the counselor feels himself becoming more buoyant.

"Is it me," the counselor asks, "or are we getting lighter?"

"You're correct. Cadre One is a large ring tunneled into this asteroid," Deepak explains. "The gravity enhancement is strongest at its rim. We are moving toward the center where only the asteroid's natural gravity has effect, roughly one quarter normal."

"Why is the Colonel's office way out here?"

"Colonel Anders and others like him have mobility issues. The lower gravity makes it more comfortable for them."

Soon, the door at the end of the corridor is visible, and the counselor has to concentrate on his gait not to bounce himself into the close ceiling.

"Have you completed my profile?" Deepak asks.

"No, not yet, though I don't think there'll be any surprises. I can't imagine anyone better suited for your tasks than you."

The counselor was speaking earnestly, but Deepak grins proudly. Stepping ahead, he taps a button at the door.

"Colonel Anders, the counselor is here to see you."

The door shifts with a hiss and slides aside smoothly, permitting the counselor his first look inside.

"I must return to patrol," Deepak states, catching the counselor a bit off guard. "Call for me if I may assist."

"Thank you, Deepak," the counselor replies absently as he peers into the red-illuminated chamber beyond.

A labored voice, originating from the nose and back of the throat beckons. "Come in, Counselor."

At first, all he can see are piles of interconnected computers and machines. Cautiously stepping inside, the counselor ducks the suspended monitors and cables.

"Here," the voice guides, and he looks over a bank of terminals to find its source. Propped up in a recliner is a withered man, head slumped to one side. What sprout from his torso more resemble gnarled roots than limbs. Multiple tubes and cables feed into his skull, neck, chest, and abdomen; and on his crown rests the familiar HDI of a cadre Geek. Arrayed around his recliner are numerous panels and holowindows showing staggering amounts of data and graphics.

The counselor takes in the entire scene, politely studying his host. Even with all the tubes, disfigurement, and hardware, there is something familiar about him.

"Ah, Counselor," the colonel smiles contortedly and inhales deeply. "I'm glad... you could come."

"How could I refuse a colonel's invitation?"

Anders receives the flattery warmly and, with what mobility he can muster, gestures the counselor toward a chair. "Is your office... adequate?"

"Perfectly so. And thank you for making time to see me." The counselor pauses to look around at all the electronic activity around him. "I can see that you're very busy."

"Yes... you too." He again inhales deeply. "Your ideas on the mind... fascinating... and useful."

Anders clears the largest display panel in front of him so they both can view it. On it, images of Thompson, Argo, and Maiella appear, filling the wide screen. The pictures shrink and slide left into a vertical column while statistics and descriptions appear to their right. Anders continues, drawing deep breaths at every pause.

"Gun Thompson, and Brick Argo... perfect test record since reassignment. Exceeded endurance expectations... no errors. Reviewed favorably... by Major Ralla. Geek Maiella... exemplary performance... after reassignment. Approved for partial restoration of HDI... surgery successful."

Anders falls silent, contemplating the huge turn in productivity from the three. His clear eyes peer out at the counselor from behind his visor. "We are few... To have them restored... is a tremendous gift. You are to thank."

The counselor looks at his feet modestly. "I'm glad I could help."

When he looks up, he sees he is still being intently studied. Curling his face into a question, he asks, "Is something wrong?"

"O'Kai said you were... different from the others..." He draws a particularly deep breath, and there is a long pause before he adds, "Now I understand."

The counselor nods, accepting the colonel's observation.

"We do not... understand the colonists. Their motives... elude us. Yet our groups... must combine... You are able... to bridge gaps... in communication. We will depend... heavily on you."

"I'm available anytime you need me." Looking closer at his host, the counselor finally begins to understand what seems so familiar. "May I ask you something?"

"Yes."

"Are you *related* to Major Ralla?"

Anders smiles fondly. "Much of my genetic code... pertaining to intellect, cognitive ability... passed on to her. She received some of... my other qualities... as well."

"I see," the counselor notes, stroking his chin, but the resemblance to Major Ralla raises another question in him. "I've worked closely with the cadre leadership council and never heard your name until today. Are you on the council?"

"No," Anders answers directly.

"As a Colonel, how could that be?"

Anders blinks. "In leadership... speed of word and action... are paramount. I have neither. I advise... with authority. They decide... and act."

The counselor leans back in his chair passing his eyes over the chamber again. The screens have never ceased their copious streams of information, and the counselor becomes self-conscious. "Have I distracted you from your work?"

"No... these monitors display... my output. You have not... interrupted."

The counselor looks into the monitors with renewed interest, trying to fathom how one person could concentrate on so many tasks at once. As his eyes move from one display to the next, he sees streams of data and code, coupled to images of circuit paths that rotate and change in three dimensions.

"Are these from the new ship being built?"

"Yes," Anders replies and inhales deeply. "Many systems require... massive revisions... and increased efficiency." He continues to inhale. "Your colonist engineers... have been great assistance... especially with aerodynamics."

The counselor narrows his focus to one particular view of the ship's exterior—a teardrop sliced in half the long way like the virus ships, but much wider with three bulges on the flat side. Pointing at the lumps, he asks, "Is this where the operators sit?"

"Yes. Each occupant... enclosed in crash pod... for free fall after ejection." He inhales deeply. "We wish to simulate... meteoric event."

"If the blueskins investigate the crash site, won't they find debris?"

Anders nods slightly. "Operators will detonate... thermal explosives. Will vaporize all... but the smallest particles. Should give the team... a head start."

Anders lolls his head to his shoulder, looking at his guest as directly as he can. "Making Geek Maiella... project auditor... very risky. How did you know... she could do it?"

The counselor smiles with confidence. "What I saw her accomplish on the *Europa*, I knew she could do anything. And making her responsible for the safety of her teammates?" He shakes his head. "There was no way she would let herself fail. They mean more to her than anything."

The counselor looks back at the colonel, and Anders's amiable expression is gone. Instantly, the counselor realizes what he has said. Maiella is, in the cadre's view, unnaturally attached to her team, yet another disappointment to heap on the pile. He curses himself, being so loose lipped; but at the very least, she is safely in his custody. She won't be harmed. He pushes through his anger with himself, forcing himself to meet the colonel's gaze again.

"We are fortunate..." Anders begins, "to have someone... with excellent understanding... of the mind. We do not like the reason... but value that she is functional again. Proves we must stay open... to possibilities we would not have considered... in the future."

Relief fills the counselor as he realizes the colonel is admitting his mistake in advocating Maiella's lobotomy. Moving on, he asks, "Argo and Thompson have been sequestered for weeks now. How much longer will they be in special training?"

"Ralla and her staff… simulating as many contingencies... as they can conceive. When she feels... they are ready… she will release them. After that… they will integrate... with new teammate... Geek Beckert."

"Beckert?" the counselor echoes as he mentally recalls the induction at the arena. The name also conjures a recollection of one of the cadre's more interesting personalities. In the psychological profile interview, Beckert seemed bright, optimistic, and unusually curious. He had a thirst for not just knowledge, but understanding. There was no doubt he would make an outstanding Geek even to Thompson's and Argo's standards, but he gets a twinge of sadness at the thought of someone so young being sent on a mission with so little hope of return.

Beckert's inquisitive mind made him an ideal student, and the counselor wishes he had more time to spend with an open-minded operator... one who could learn and understand the colonists' ways would go far toward helping ease tensions between the two groups. The feeling may be a bit selfish, he realizes, but being the *only* liaison between the two groups has been a crushing burden. Having someone to share that burden would have been welcome.

"Yes, I remember Beckert," the counselor recalls. "He's an excellent choice. Fearless, stalwart, intuitive..." He trails off, remembering the awful beating he took at the hands of his fellows and the crowd around him just watching. Yet Beckert survived, and the swells of pride in his swollen face proved his spirit was completely uninjured. He was tough and *definitely* operator material, no question.

"You left out... sensitive."

The counselor looks at Anders who is managing a slight smile. He is shocked a cadre officer would even acknowledge such a thing in an operator.

"I agree," the counselor replies, "but how do you mean?"

Anders's deep inhale dislodges some phlegm, and he coughs for a moment, slowing the flow of data on all monitors. Once his fit passes, the look of pain fades and the data resumes its pace.

"I read your brief... to General O'Kai. Saw Team Spectre improve. Made me curious... what else you... had insight into." The colonel readjusts himself on his recliner. "I read your archive... from the *Europa*. More than a thousand years... you served as ship counselor. Saw deaths... and new lives."

The counselor nods in recognition.

"Of it all... I'm intrigued by your assertion… 'emotions are extensions of instinct... can guide toward correct action... when data is missing.'"

The colonel's eyes roll up to the low ceiling as he continues quoting the counselor's archive.

"'When facing difficult decisions... the way we feel… can supply clues toward the best choice.'" Anders looks off into the far end of the room. "Intriguing concepts. Possibly why... Team Spectre survived so long."

The counselor cocks his head, a little surprised at what he is hearing. "Are you revising the operator's code of behavior?"

"No," Anders counters decisively. "Allowing for... greater creativity… and intuition. Extending perception to all sources... including the irrational."

The counselor buries his disappointment, but not fast enough for Anders to miss. The withered man looks back hard, yet sympathetic.

"We still cannot permit... attachments among the operator corps. They cause hesitation... at crucial moments... conflicts in decisions. An operator must remain… stoic, ready to act on any order... no matter the consequence."

Lowering his head, the counselor yields to the colonel's mandate. "I understand."

A soft tone at the door sounds. "Colonel, it is time."

Anders looks toward the door, opening it without lifting a finger, and three MedTechs file in. Turning his face to the counselor, he adds, "Please excuse me, Counselor. I am glad you came... I needed to thank you... personally… for all you have done... and what you are still... doing every day."

The counselor smiles warmly back, appreciating the rare show of gratitude. He stands from his seat so he can get out of the MedTechs' way.

"You're very welcome."

The three take positions around Anders, gently cradling him, lifting him slightly, then delicately set him down on his back. The counselor steps backward toward the door, watching as the numerous monitors around the colonel halt their flows of code, save data, and power down, leaving the room a little darker and quieter than before. Anders is only visible in the gaps between the MedTechs, and he sees what care they take not to jostle or mishandle him as if he were the greatest of irreplaceable treasures. They open his shirt, revealing a long seam in his torso, extending from his throat down through his lower abdomen. One of them leans close to him, speaking into his ear, and he nods. In a fluid motion, one of the MedTechs opens the seam its full-length while another swoops in with a suction nozzle. Anders gasps with discomfort, grunting and writhing under the onslaught while they work to clear the intruding fluids.

Suddenly, the counselor feels embarrassment for having lingered too long and turns to give the colonel his privacy. The sight brings bitter memories of Earth's hospitals where such a man would have led a desolate life, devoid of dignity, little more than an embarrassment to his family. Here at least, despite his handicaps, he is venerated and cherished.

Stealing one last glance, he sees they are already zipping him up, and he wears an exhausted but much more relaxed face. It is a difficult thing to reconcile: how ruthless and aggressive these people can be, yet how compassionate as well. He stores that last look and exits the chamber quietly.

ALL AS ONE?

Thompson clicks on his armor the same way he has done hundreds of times before. With all of Major Ralla's "training," he has practically been living in it, though today is different. Today, he is going to strap into the cadre's newest ship, not just its simulator. Ordinarily, he would be exhilarated at the thought of commanding the latest in cadre/colonist technology; but as he clamps his chest plate into place, he truly understands that he is not coming back.

The possibility of any kind of return was not designed into this new craft. It is a one-way transport, designed to obliterate itself on impact with its destination. And this is an entire *planet* of his enemy. He cannot kill them all. He will probably not even make a dent. The best he can hope for is to survive long enough to provide some useful intelligence, something the cadre could use to gain some kind of edge in a future assault. He hauls his reinforced boots over his feet and suddenly sits up straight.

He is never going to see Maiella again.

The thought troubles him so deeply that no amount of concentration will dismiss it. He pauses to think about her, images flashing by of her sitting at a ship's console, controlling the entire vessel easily or streaking down a corridor, both pistols blazing. He remembers her smooth style, her infallible skill, and her grinning confidence on every mission. That is when he nails it: he is afraid to go without her.

Thompson squashes the emotion quickly once he recognizes it. He reaches out for his helmet, but something lingers. Is that really what is bothering him? He sets his helmet next to him as he thinks more about her. Again and again, he sees her smiling face, always confident, never worried, that is, until they boarded the *Europa*...

He ruminates over his memories of her: play wrestling in slippery oil, rapidly defeating the computer security on a captured ship, seeing her asleep after a difficult day. He scarcely notices how calming it is just thinking about her.

An ache begins in the center of his chest. Confused, he thumps his fist into it until it goes away. Whatever else it is that is bothering him will have to wait, he reasons, and he stuffs thoughts of her deep down.

Returning to business, he hurriedly finishes gearing up, checks his rifle thoroughly, and strides to the door. He pauses, looking back into his chamber; and after clicking the light off, he turns and marches down the corridor.

His long strides carry him through the familiar corridors, and soon he comes to the memorial.

"IN HONORABLE SERVICE, THEY GAVE THEIR ALL" the heading announces.

It has expanded a great deal since he has last seen it. Hundreds of faces are laser etched into the smooth metallic wall with lifelike detail. Across the top and larger than the others are the Generals. Thompson scans them from the beginning, stopping on Dryden, gazing long at his old General's weathered features. He seems so much older than he remembered...

Beneath are the Colonels, Majors, Captains, etc. down to each and every Operator who fell in the line of duty. His eyes quickly seek out Enyo, and the sight of her triggers a distant spark of emotion. She was the last one he saw before leaving on the mission, and her final order to him rings clearly.

"I brought 'em back safe, Colonel," he says to her image, as though it could offer him the approval he sought.

His eyes drift through the ranks and he finds Major Zaius, his old instructor. Settee and Drusus are close by as well, looking exactly as he remembered them. But where is Lukas? That fresh-faced Geek covered in ore dust… nowhere in the ranks of Operators. Thompson's eyes rise higher and higher until he finds a grizzled yet commanding face, HDI contacts gleaming on a bald cranium. A wide grin crosses the Gun's face.

"General Lukas… good for you."

Thompson's eyes wander the wall, marking how with time the operators begin to look more and more alike, until he comes to a gap. A Major and, directly beneath, two junior officers have been scoured from the wall. His gauntleted hand reaches out to the space, and he looks up to the heading above the Memorial again. IN HONORABLE SERVICE…

Bowing his head, he marches away.

It is only a few more paces before he is standing at Argo's door. He buzzes for entry, and it promptly slides open. On the far side, Argo stands armed and armored, saluting crisply. "Major," the big man states respectfully.

Thompson returns the salute and nods. "Present arms."

Argo swiftly unslings his large weapon, spinning it a half turn, and halting it at a forty-five-degree angle in front of his chest.

Thompson hefts the large weapon, arching his back to support it, yet still handling it comfortably. He turns it over, checking every angle, action, and display until he is satisfied of its condition. Passing the cannon back, Thompson looks Argo in the eyes. The two men stare wordlessly at each other, and in that silence, volumes are spoken: their shared experience, their brotherhood, their disgrace, their joy to serve again, and their acceptance of life's end.

Argo hauls his weapon's strap to his shoulder, and Thompson reaches out to him.

"Are you ready?" the Gun asks.

Argo's eyes are steel. "Yes, *sir*."

Nodding solemnly, Thompson orders, "Let's go," and the two soldiers march down the corridor.

"Where's Beckert?" Argo asks.

"He is in the bay, wrapping up the final checks with Maiella."

For the remainder of their path, the men stride without speaking, soaking in the last looks at their treasured haven, their home. They see no one else, and their footfalls echo abnormally loud in the empty halls.

Ahead, the men recognize the broad corridor leading to the primary hangar bay. The long path seems to have passed by too abruptly, giving them both an uncomfortable twinge. Lowering their heads, they press forward to the large, heavy doors ahead.

At their approach, the bay doors grind apart. Bright illumination pours through the widening crack, forcing the soldiers to squint. As their eyes adjust, they see a large gathering of colonist and cadre alike clustered around a perfectly black shape at the center of the bay. Both of them are familiar with the design of this new craft, but this is the first they have laid eyes on it. It has the same two-dimensional appearance as the virus ships though is easily twice as large. The front is bulbous and round, which tapers back to a narrow tail. The underside of the craft is flat, save three modest bulges arrayed across the ship's beam, with four articulated struts which suspend it from the deck.

Argo and Thompson keep pace as they stride into the bright bay. All eyes fall on them, and many of the colonists hoot and shout as if they were celebrities.

Narrowing their focus, the two operators march directly toward the ship, and the small group of people clustered there.

O'Kai, Munro, Ralla, the counselor, Keller, Ortega, and Sharon all turn their attention to the heavily outfitted soldiers at once. Thompson and Argo stamp to a halt, saluting with perfect synchronicity.

"Gun Thompson and Brick Argo reporting as ordered, sir!" Thompson announces.

O'Kai salutes back. "At ease. Are you fully equipped and prepared?"

"Yes, sir, we are."

Maiella steps out from behind one of the underside bulges on the craft. Beckert emerges behind her, fully armored and equipped.

O'Kai turns to her. "Is all in order?"

"Affirmative, General," she replies and hands over a tablet she had tucked under her arm. O'Kai scans it and hands it back to her.

"Proceed," he mandates.

Maiella steps past him to stand at attention before Thompson and Argo, saluting rigidly. Thompson takes in her appearance, pleased to see her after the months spent apart. Her hair is cropped evenly below the height of her contact terminals, and her charcoal uniform is immaculate. She hands the tablet over to him, stating in an exaggerated voice, "All systems green bars, Major. Vessel fueled, primed, and ready for departure. I relinquish command to you."

Saluting, Thompson takes hold of the tablet, but Maiella doesn't release it immediately. When he looks up at her face, she is looking back intensely.

"I have verified every system aboard personally. For a complete log of these tests, consult file XT497 located in the Config Protocol Subroutine." She looks at Argo to make sure he was listening as well and releases the tablet.

Thompson quickly scans the tablet, already sure everything is in order. Handing it back, he confirms, "File XT497, Config Protocol Subroutine. Got it."

Turning to her side, Maiella gestures. "May I present Geek Beckert?"

Thompson steps forward, scrutinizing the young operator and the fit of his armor.

"Pre-sent arms!" Maiella commands.

Beckert swiftly draws his machine pistols from the small of his back, spinning them masterfully around his finger so the grips extend toward Thompson. The Gun snatches both pistols, flipping one to Argo, and the soldiers manipulate all of the switches and actions. Once the inspection is finished, they toss the pistols back at Beckert who grabs them from the air effortlessly, twirling them into the clips on his back.

"Geek Beckert has been fully briefed on all hardware and software required for this mission," Maiella explains. "He includes the latest computational ability in his HDI, updated with our full catalog. In combat, he has proven himself worthy of his rank, certified with highest accuracy and lowest response times of his class."

Thompson listens to Maiella's descriptions, taking her at her word; yet he cannot dispel his skepticism—something in his eyes, maybe. As if channeling his doubt, Maiella adds, "I was harder on him than you ever were on me. He has my full confidence."

Thompson takes a sharp breath, his skepticism annihilated by her conviction. "Thank you, Lieutenant."

Argo steps closer to the young operator. "Have you flown this vessel, Sergeant?"

"Yes, sir!" Beckert answers eagerly. "I've logged sixty hours of actual flight time with 240 hours in the simulator."

"How does it handle?" Thompson asks with interest.

Beckert looks around Argo to answer directly. "It's not as agile as the virus ships, but it has a much higher speed, roughly 3.2 C."

"And you're familiar with *every* system on board?" Argo probes.

"Yes, sir," Beckert replies, getting a woeful look about him. "Lieutenant Maiella was... *thorough*."

"Have you made all of your preparations for this rotation, Sergeant?" Thompson inquires.

Beckert stands tall and straight. "I have."

Thompson nods and reaches a hand toward him, which Beckert clasps. "Welcome to the team."

Argo does likewise, but when Beckert clasps his hand, the big man gives it an extra squeeze. "We'll be expecting a *flawless* performance."

Beckert does his best to maintain composure under Argo's crushing grip. "Ah yes, Lieutenant, I can assure you of that!"

Argo releases him, and the Geek sighs imperceptibly, flexing his hand to work the blood back into it.

"Major Thompson," O'Kai declares while stepping closer to them, "it would be inappropriate to retain the moniker Team Spectre so long as all of its constituents are still viable." He pauses to look Thompson, Argo, and Maiella in the eye. "Your new team name shall be Forestall as that is the exact purpose of your mission. To forestall the enemy and give us some edge to exploit in evicting them from our original world."

He reaches out to Beckert, shaking his hand vigorously and laying a compassionate hand on his opposite shoulder. When Argo and

Thompson extend their hands in farewell, O'Kai stares at them coldly. Rejected, the two shamed men draw back their hands.

The counselor steps forward, protest already forming in his open mouth when Keller grabs him back.

"Counselor!" he grumbles sternly. "*Don't!*"

The counselor turns on his superior to argue, but Keller's warning look overrules any point he was about to make. He turns around and looks at O'Kai, then from the general, his eyes wander to O'Kai's supporting officers and across the many faces of the cadre. Their common feature is an icy gaze directed at Thompson and Argo.

They are glad to see them go.

Warily, the counselor fades back into his group, taking in the powerful mood. As hard as he fought to save Argo's, Maiella's, and Thompson's lives, in the end he had no idea how badly the cadre *needed* to exile these three. Every MedTech, operator, engineer, and officer had so perfectly concealed their disgust, managing to work together with them, that the counselor believed they had accepted the three back into the fold. What a great irony, he thinks, that he was working on Thompson's, Maiella's, and Argo's behalf so they could go. Now that he sees the naked revulsion, he fully grasps why Keller reigned him back: the cadre's one law was broken, and the guilty *must* pay.

Fearfully, he looks at Maiella, an island among her own kind, reviled, and—once Thompson and Argo are gone—completely alone. He searches her face of stone and can see the longing to go beneath the surface. She knows what the future holds for her here.

"Major Thompson!" O'Kai barks. "You know what is expected of you. I suggest you get to it."

Thompson and Argo stiffen, snapping clean salutes. Thompson turns on his heel to Beckert. "Board the vessel and begin preflight."

"Yes, sir!" Beckert replies enthusiastically, and he jogs to the ship, climbing in from below. Thompson steals a glance at Argo, and the big man gives him a nodding go-ahead.

"General," Thompson states modestly, "Brick Argo and I know

our exile is just. I regret Maiella cannot join us though we understand why." He pauses and looks his general in the eyes. "If there is *any* way we can send Beckert home safe, we will."

O'Kai weighs Thompson's words, his harsh glare softening slightly. "That would be appreciated."

Thompson and Argo face Maiella. She has maintained her rigid at-attention pose. "Farewell, sirs."

The two men step close to her, each gripping one of her shoulders. She reaches out to them as well, and the three desperately fight back the emotions surging through them. Resting their heads together, the warmth from Maiella's flushed face radiates, and they feel her trembling slightly. Reluctantly, they pull apart, a single staccato sniff escaping from Maiella. Argo points at himself, then at Thompson.

"You'll be with us."

She blinks hard, her heart filling with lead. With the best smile she can muster, she looks into Thompson's face. She knows there is no way she can go. There is no point entertaining any notion of it, but she desperately wants to hear them give some assurance they will return, that there is at least some chance she won't be alone.

Thompson looks into her, feeling her begging him for anything that would allow her hope. His eyes fall to the deck, rising slowly. "Be strong."

Maiella inhales sharply, straightening her posture. "I will."

Thompson inhales deeply himself and turns to Argo, announcing, "It's time." Argo nods stoically.

The Gun is about to join him when he takes a last look at Maiella, soaking her in the way a dying man would soak in a last sunset. Her spotless uniform, her gold contact terminals, her rigid stance, her wrinkled chin from her involuntarily frown—all leave an indelible mark in his memory.

Cueing Argo, Thompson spins on his heel so both of them face O'Kai. Argo synchronizes perfectly. "General," the Gun begins stridently, "Team Forestall requesting permission to depart Cadre One!"

"Granted," O'Kai states deliberately. The two operators snap rigid salutes, which the general returns respectfully.

The Brick and Gun turn in unison, striding determinedly toward the craft. While Argo loads himself in, Thompson walks the ship's perimeter, inspecting each edge and surface.

Ortega takes in the dour scene with disgust, a verse issuing from his hanging mouth: "Thy prophets have seen vain and false things for thee: and they have not discovered thine iniquity, to turn away thy captivity; but have seen for thee false burdens and causes of banishment."[1]

Sharon, Keller, and the counselor look in astonishment at the Spaniard who is still watching Thompson and Argo. Ortega turns his view to O'Kai and finds the general staring back. Ortega locks gazes with him in an unspoken test of wills until the loud hiss of the ship's hatch sealing distracts both men. Multiple systems engage, filling the bay with a low-frequency hum.

O'Kai shouts above the din, "NORMAL DUTY ROUTINE RESUMES IN TEN MINUTES! DIS-MISSED!"

The cadre attendees salute in a unified action, bellowing, "yes, sir!" They file from the room with automated purpose, leaving the colonists huddled and confused by what they believed should have been an emotional bon voyage.

O'Kai sends his officers ahead, holding his place a moment longer. He marches straight for Ortega, head lowered, halting a very short distance from him. With menace, he peers down at the Spaniard. "False burdens and causes of banishment... ?" he paraphrases vehemently.

Without flinching, Ortega answers, "That's right."

Beneath his steel exterior, O'Kai boils. The insult of having his orders openly rebuked in front of his cadre nearly breaks his level emotionality. Squinting at Ortega, he leans in and asks in a low, harsh voice, "And how is it that you survived, Commander? Did *you* carve your living space from irradiated stone? Did you find a way to provide for your people when they had *nothing*? Can *you* protect them from our enemy?"

Ortega can only stare back, but it is answer enough for O'Kai.

"Then *never again* presume our ways are inferior to yours."

---

[1] Lamentations 2:14

About-facing, the towering general marches off after his officers.

His face ablaze, Ortega whirls around to his captain. Before he can even speak, Keller cuts him off.

"Let it go," he orders sternly.

Ortega looks at Sharon, Gregor, and the counselor for back up; but they are silent.

"We know how you feel, Javier," Keller adds, "but let it go."

Ortega turns to watch O'Kai stride out of sight, and he shakes his head. Keller claps him on the back, saying, "C'mon. Let's go give them their proper send-off. We have a party to host."

To emphasize the point, the low hum from the ship rises in pitch as more systems reach operating temperature. Ortega acquiesces and faces the humming ship.

"Just a moment, Captain. There's something I need to do for them."

Keller nods his head in approval and strides toward the milling group of colonists. Throwing his arms up, he hollers above the noisy ship.

"Everyone, your attention! Let's move up to the *Europa*. I know this was a little more somber than we hoped, but we all worked hard on this project, and you deserve a *party*! We're meeting in rec rooms 5, 6, and 7. Bring your appetites..." He gets a sly grin. "And the bar is open ALL NIGHT!"

The crowd whoops with tension release, their cheers momentarily eclipsing the ship's cycling engines. Sharon and Gregor gently shepherd the hooting group toward the waiting shuttles in the bay.

Ortega stands before the smoothly roaring ship, placing a hand over his heart. The other hand he extends to the ship, making contact. Bowing his head, he prays.

Inside the craft, Beckert is strapped in and linked via multiple cables. As he is watching his system monitors, he catches sight of Ortega leaning against the hull. "Major," he calls with an intrigued glance, "have a look at this."

Thompson stops buckling in and leans over to Beckert's displays. "What's he doing?" the Geek asks.

Jutting his lip, the Gun raises his eyebrows. "No idea."

Beckert pays it no more mind and resumes his tasks, but Thompson continues to watch. After another moment, Ortega looks up and, with the hand that was over his heart, draws a cross in the air. His lips move in inaudible speech, and he withdraws to the waiting shuttle.

"Life support fully green," Argo alerts. "Cryo-recliners fully green. Technicals fully green."

Thompson slides back into his recliner, clicking the harnesses. The humming pitch rises suddenly.

"Main engines coming online," Beckert states. "Reactant intermix optimal. Navigation updated and calibrated, course laid in."

Thompson activates his own screens, streaming data from both of his teammates. Every system displayed is operating perfectly. "Green bars, ready for stars," Thompson states with comfortable familiarity. "Take us out, Geek."

Beckert scans the bay to be sure everyone has exited or boarded a shuttle. "Cadre One, this is Team Forestall. Confirm bay is evacuated, over?"

"Team Forestall, evacuation confirmed. Pressure equalizing. Proceed toward external bay doors."

"Understood, Cadre One," Beckert replies, and the craft sways gently as he guides it forward on its articulated legs.

Thompson studies the inside of the craft, getting used to the setup and arrangement. It is not so different from the virus ship, just a bit roomier. His eyes trace the seams in the bulkheads, and he recognizes the edges of the egg-shaped compartment.

The swaying of the craft alerts him to a new feature he had not suspected. As the vessel rocks, his recliner compensates by cradling him in all directions, keeping him level. His eyebrows rise with interest as he explores the sensation.

"Geek, why aren't our recliners secured?"

Beckert looks over his shoulder. "These pods are like big crash helmets. If we hit at an angle or on a slope, we'll be isolated from any kind of sudden spin…" A kid like grin stretches from ear to ear. "We'll be less likely to be liquefied on impact."

Argo glares from his side of the craft. "Comforting."

The swaying abates, and Beckert radios, "Cadre One, we are holding at external bay doors, awaiting clearance, over."

"Team Forestall, stand by," comes his response. Thompson spends the time reviewing his screens, assuring himself all is operating smoothly when his mind wanders and the heavy feeling he had in his quarters returns. There is the familiar anticipation of a new mission, not to mention the thrill of being the first cadre operator *ever* to experience their ancestral world, Earth. Even so, it is outweighed by powerful feelings of loss: loss of companions, loss of home, and more poignantly, the imminent loss of life. His mind reviews a visual catalog of people and things he will never see again, and the most difficult of them all to accept is Maiella. Then he remembers.

"Beckert, pull up file X-ray, Tango, Four, Niner 7 in the Config Protocol Subroutine."

"But, Major," Beckert protests over his shoulder, "there *is* no Config Protocol Subroutine."

"Trust me, Sergeant, it'll be there."

Beckert finds it to his great surprise. "Uh, all right, sir, I have it."

"Send it to my and Argo's display."

Beckert complies, and in a flash, a window opens in Thompson's and Argo's screens. From it, Maiella's face smiles warmly at them. She takes a step back, and they can see she is wearing her charcoal grays. It seems she recorded the video shortly before their send-off.

"Hello, Gentlemen!" she grins mischievously. "You probably knew I couldn't let you go without getting some last words in." She pauses, a dark cloud arriving over her. Shaking her head, she shoves the gloom aside, forcing her smile back. "I had to tell you both how proud I was to serve with you. I'd like to have told you in person, but with the whole cadre there, well... I'm sure you understand."

The gloom returns, and she looks to one side. "Uh..." she starts, then clears her throat, and faces forward again. "I know what we did was horrible. And we could never in thousands of lifetimes make up for it. It should be me in there with you, not Beckert..." She looks at her feet for several seconds.

"Maybe if I had triple-checked the NavCharts, or if I had plotted

our course more carefully, we never would have flown through the..."
Both of her hands grip her skull.

"And my HDI wouldn't have been damaged, and..." She drops
her hands, looking away.

After a lengthy sigh, she faces her audience again. "I let you both
down. It hurts to know that... and because of that, I can't be there to
look out for you." Her head droops with melancholy. "That hurts the
most."

Raising her head, she has new vigor. "That's why I was so hard
on Beckert. If *I* can't be there for you, I had to make sure whoever *is*
there was good enough."

Her eyebrows rise, and she loses herself in thought for a second.
"Yeah, he's inexperienced, but he's the best Geek I've ever seen, and
I know he'll be able to handle his end."

She leans closer to the screen, smiling. "He's *really* good..."
Looking away, her smile straightens; and with frank candor, she adds,
"Better than me." Her eyes peer out through the screen. "I pushed him
to a degree you wouldn't believe. I put everything I know into him, so
at least a part of me will be with you.

Thompson looks over from his screen at Beckert, and the young
Geek is oblivious, concentrating on his tasks. Thompson smiles
fondly at him, stirred by Maiella's endorsement and comforted at the
thought of some part of her traveling with them. When he looks back
at his screen, Maiella's face is wracked with sadness.

"I don't know how to say good-bye!" she sobs at last. Fearfully,
she looks over her shoulder, concerned someone may have heard the
outburst. Pulling herself together, she places one hand in the other.
"And I don't know how to let go..."

Her eyes glance over her shoulder again, making sure no one
is around. When she turns back, her face wears a look of detached
indifference. "The cadre would just as soon I walk out of an air lock.
I even considered it, but now? I don't care about that anymore. And
yes, the colonists are good to me..." She breaks off midsentence,
struggling for the words. "...because of what we did, I'll never be one
of them."

Agitated, and frustrated at how difficult it is to express what she is thinking and feeling, she suddenly looks up, going for broke.

"You both *know* me. I don't know why that means so much to me, but it does. And I don't know how to let that go!"

Anger flares in her.

"Forget what the cadre thinks! Do your job, get all the data, blast those blueskins to oblivion, just bring yourselves *back. All* of you." The wave recedes, washing her face of all emotion, leaving her hauntingly desolate. "You're all I have..."

Sobering suddenly, she squares her shoulders with the screen. "Bring yourselves home. I'll be waiting to welcome you." Her face brightens as she imagines that happy homecoming. Taking a step back, she salutes with a big grin. "Don't do anything I wouldn't do. I'll see you soon."

The video ends, and the two operators soak in the emotional aftermath. Argo lets out a long sigh while Thompson closes and deletes the file.

"Team Forestall," the radio blurts, "bay equalized, you are cleared for departure."

"Understood, Cadre One," Beckert answers.

Broad bay doors separate, and the cabin swaying resumes as Beckert walks the craft out onto the crater floor. Each step carries them farther from the gravitational enhancement.

"Prepare for ascent," the Geek announces.

Hunkering down on its struts, the craft leaps explosively upward. Beckert triggers a key, and the undercarriage falls away as a complete assembly. Small plates slide closed over the attachment points, and Beckert ignites the thrusting engines. The craft soars high above the crater rim, gravity's effect dissipating dramatically.

Off to starboard, the *Europa* glints large and impressive; and it triggers a bewildering range of thoughts, strangely pertaining to duty and loyalty.

"Major," Beckert shouts above the thruster's roaring crackle, "incoming message from Captain Keller!"

"Put it through," Thompson orders, and on all three of their displays, Keller's lined face appears. Behind him are a crowd of colonists, packed together in the cramped shuttle enjoying their drinks and cheering one another with noisy clinks.

"Thompson, Argo, and Beckert... it's hard to say everything we're thinking right now. We hate to see you go. But we are grateful you found us. If you hadn't, we'd still be wandering the cosmos, hope dying a little more until... well. And we know you still carry guilt for the deaths of our people. We have said it before, and we want to say it again to make sure you know that *we forgive you*."

Keller pauses thoughtfully.

"I realize you operators aren't much for parties, but what the hell. Gregor has something he wanted to say."

Keller steps aside and Sharon, Javier, Gregor, and the counselor unfurl a quickly painted banner.

Fuck those lizards up!

From offscreen, Keller's voice shouts, "*Jesus*, Gregor! *No*, the *other* thing!" He walks into view and collects the contraband, trying not to laugh.

Gregor grins and pulls out another furled banner. The others help stretch out the new one, painted in fine calligraphy.

We'll tell our children about you.

Keller smiles and takes a long swig from his glass. "Hey, anybody got somethin' to say to these guys?"

All eyes turn toward the screen; and cheers erupt in thunderous outpourings of elation and gratitude, arms raised in the air, swishing drinks, and clapping. Keller lets the shouting go on for a while, then steps in front of the screen. He is about to speak when several random hoots start the cheering all over. Keller gets a super-sized grin, grabbing his temples and laughing along until, at last, it is quiet enough for him to be heard.

"This is all for you and in your honors." Keller's smile straightens, and he leans forward with sincerity. "Everything you have done, and especially what you are doing for us now, gives us hope... As the captain of this crew, I can't tell you how much of a gift that is. God willing, we may even see you again. *Europa*, out."

Thompson nods heavily. Pushing all other thoughts aside, his focus turns to the mission.

"Geek."

"Sir?"

"Execute."

Beckert's goggles flash with complex code, and the ship surges into the void with a flash.

Index

ABOUT THE AUTHOR

 Allen was born in Newport, Rhode Island in 1973. After earning a B.A. in Political Science, he abandoned his plans for law school to work in sales.

Through the ups and downs, his journal was a constant companion, and in it he developed the thoughts and impressions which shaped his novels. *There must be more to life than scraping by*, he believes, *and there must be something left of the world worth passing on*. More than themes in his books, these beliefs guide him in his day to day life.

When modern life becomes too crowding, he escapes to the natural parts of the country. Franconia Notch, New Hampshire and White Lake, New Hampshire are favorite camp sites. His visit to Yellowstone National Park was life-changing, however, as he had no idea a place so beautiful and magnificent could still exist in a consumer-based society. Upon his return, he became an active advocate for conservation, recycling, and green technologies.

He shares a home in Salem, Massachusetts with his cat, Tom, and his dog, Hamlet.